G000152284

THE
REPATRIATION
OF
HENRY CHIN

A NOVEL BY
ISAAC HO

los angeles

The Repatriation of Henry Chin
Copyright © 2011 Isaac Ho
All Rights Reserved.

No part of this book may be reproduced in any form or by any means, electronic, mechanical, digital, photocopying or recording, except for the inclusion in a review, without permission in writing from the the publisher.

Published in the USA by
Digital Fabulists
11684 Ventura Blvd #205
Studio City, CA 91604
www.digitalfabulists.com

DF-FIC-1005

ISBN 0-615-54838-5
ISBN-13: 978-0615548388

Cover photograph by Martin Walls

Printed in the United States of America

THE
REPATRIATION
OF
HENRY CHIN

PROLOGUE

"This wasn't what I had in mind. This wasn't the way I planned to govern." The President's voice was tense, agitated. He wanted to yell and lose his temper but he knew he couldn't. Temper tantrums were a luxury he could no longer indulge, not even in private. He looked out the window of his limousine at the American flag waving over the Capitol.

"This deal will get us through tomorrow," consoled his aging Chief of Staff.

"And then what? What will they ask us for tomorrow? It's checkmate in five moves," the President retorted.

"We need to maintain the illusion we're in charge. Panic would be worse. Beijing is willing to negotiate. That hasn't always been the case." The Chief of Staff shifted in his seat.

"I don't know if I even have the authority to make this deal."

"You're the President. Under Article 2, Section 2 of the Constitution you are empowered to negotiate treaties—"

"With the advice and consent of the Senate. I know my Constitutional law," the President barked.

"Then what is the issue?"

The President adjusted his suit coat. "The issue is that we have not involved the Senate. And we're sneaking around the Capitol like we're joyriding in my dad's car and don't want to get caught!"

The Chief of Staff rose to meet the President's gaze. "Well if that's all you're worried about—"

"I can't give away what I don't have!" The President immediately shrunk back in his seat at the sound of his own voice and cleared his throat. "We'd have to find a way to overturn U.S. v. Wong Kim Ark and a pesky little thing called the Fourteenth Amendment."

"Which would all be moot if you don't make this deal. Do you think Beijing is concerned about our Constitution?" The Chief of Staff took out a pack of cigarettes and lit one.

"I wish you wouldn't do that."

"It's either in here or at my nephew's cottage in wine country. Consider this my revenge for your health care bill." After one drag, the Chief of Staff crushed out the cigarette. "Besides, by the time it gets to the Supreme Court, it won't be an issue. It'll be done and the country survives another day."

"But we won't survive as a whole country. It's bad enough we've had Chinese Americans under house arrest but we're throwing them... U.S. citizens to the wolves."

"Mr. President, think of this as an act for their own good. If you don't put Chinese Americans in protective custody, they will bear the brunt of blame for our deteriorating relationship with China. Better that they be locked up than killed by an angry mob."

"Protective custody? It's a poor euphemism for incarceration. This isn't a good solution."

"It is today." The Chief of Staff could no longer hide his impatience. "I know what's bothering you. You can't let your own personal moral code govern your decision, not when the fate of our country is at stake. Don't think of it as Buchenwald. Think of it as Tule Lake. You've got a pretty good grasp of the English language. Give it a fancy name."

"This isn't right," the President reiterated.

"Save your soul or save the country. Pick one."

The President continued to gaze out the window. The Chief of Staff leaned in. "You saw the news. $135 billion of our assets frozen today. What if Beijing wanted to seize all $2.7 trillion we owe? If this satisfies them, then you have to do it."

"But what about tomorrow? They'll ask for something else tomorrow," countered the President.

"You have to do something. This isn't nothing. This is something."

"Until tomorrow. We're here."

The Presidential limousine came to a halt just outside the gates of the Chinese embassy. After pausing a moment to allow the gates to open, the limousine pulled under the portico and came to a stop.

One lone Chinese aide greeted the President as he stepped out of the limousine. The President shook his hand.

"I am the President of the United States. I am here to speak with Ambassador Li."

"Yes, the Ambassador is expecting you. However, he is expecting only you." The Chief of Staff immediately understood.

"What do you mean?" asked the President.

"He means that my presence is not required," said the Chief of Staff.

The aide stepped up to quell the tension. "Your man may stay here and wait. The meeting shouldn't take too long. The Ambassador has a very busy schedule today."

"We're pleased the Ambassador could squeeze in the leader of the free world." The Chief of Staff's voice dripped with sarcasm.

"I am happy to comply with the Ambassador's wishes," added the President.

"If you will come this way." The aide led the President up the steps and into the embassy.

In the embassy's anteroom, the President was met by the Chinese Ambassador and his staff. The President looked around and was surprised by the opulence of the interior decoration. Wood paneled walls and antique mahogany furniture with delicate vases and sprawling watercolor landscapes were beautifully on display. In the air was a hint of sandalwood, a familiar scent that permeated the homes of his old Chinese classmates when he was a boy.

The Chinese Ambassador extended his hand and the President shook it. The Chinese Ambassador began speaking in Chinese, which his aide translated into English.

"The Ambassador apologizes but his schedule has changed. He has only a few minutes to spare today. Would you like to postpone the meeting until next week?"

"The Ambassador is well aware that time is of the essence."

"Yes, but the Ambassador has concerns about some of your positions."

"Such as?"

The aide looked at the Ambassador. "Mr. President, there is not enough time to go through the particulars now. I would have barely enough time to voice my concerns before we had to end the meeting."

"Mr. Ambassador, I am a very quick study."

"Of that I have no doubt," the aide translated. "But your process is tedious. Before you can give us an answer you must stage a press conference, a talk show appearance, an official statement, a prime time speech and an ad hoc conference with your Congress before you can reply back to us? You must see it from our point of view. Unless you have the actual authority to take unilateral action, these meetings are nothing more than merely theater. We have no patience for theater."

The President considered his next words carefully. "I understand, Mr. Ambassador. I assure you, I have the authority to take action."

The Chinese Ambassador sized up the President. Then he signaled for one of his aides to approach. The aide held out a large proclamation on parchment. The document was written in Chinese with both the Chinese National Emblem and the U.S. Presidential Seal embossed on it. As the President looked it over, the Chinese Ambassador handed him a pen.

"We took the liberty of codifying our terms in advance," the aide translated.

"I'm sorry, I can't read Chinese."

The Chinese Ambassador nodded to his staff. They pulled open the double doors leading to a sitting room. The Chinese Ambassador put his arm around the President.

"I can explain everything to you." The Chinese Ambassador led the President into the sitting room. "This is how it will happen..."

Later, at the White House, the President sat in his chair while a make up artist applied some face powder to remove some of the sweat sheen off his face. The President closed his eyes and tried to slow down his heart rate with some deep breathing exercises.

A junior aide arrived with a sheaf of papers. "Mr. President? The speech is complete and has been loaded into the teleprompter. They're waiting for you in the Oval."

"The Oval?" The President bolted up in his chair. "I'm not making this speech from the Oval."

"You're live in less than five minutes. The live feed is set up. There's no way to change it in time."

The President jumped out of his chair and pushed the junior aide aside.

"I didn't want to make this speech from here," the President bellowed as he burst into the Oval Office. The room fell silent.

"Mr. President, could I speak with you in here please?" said the calming voice of the Chief of Staff as he gestured toward a side door into his office.

Inside the Chief of Staff's office the President unleashed his anger. "Not in the Oval. Not this kind of speech. From the press room or the Rose Garden but not in this country's highest seat of power!"

"Fine." The President was shocked at how quickly he won this argument with his Chief of Staff. Sometimes deciding what to have for breakfast took half an hour. "We'll postpone the speech long enough for these guys to reset all the equipment... where would you like? In the press room?"

"What's wrong?" asked the President.

"Nothing." The Chief of Staff hit his intercom button. "We're moving the speech to the press room. Now!"

As the President took his place at the press room podium, he gazed out at the cameras set up where reporters normally sit. His copy of the speech was neatly folded in his inside jacket pocket just in case the teleprompters failed. Look at the cameras, not at the people, the President silently reminded himself.

"Fifteen seconds Mr. President," the stage manager commanded. The President took a quick sip of water and inhaled deeply through his nostrils. The spotlights came on. Five, four, three...

"Good evening my fellow Americans. Today the Beijing government ordered one hundred thirty five billion dollars in U.S. assets frozen after we were unable to extend the forbearance on our debts. The impact on U.S. jobs was immediate and despite suspending all trading activity, the New York Stock Exchange saw its biggest drop since the Bailout of 2008." Now comes the pivot, the President thought to himself.

"Backlash against Chinese Americans was equally as swift with hate crimes reported in nearly every major American city. I have decided to take immediate and decisive action. Scapegoating Chinese Americans is inexcusable, it's unacceptable and it must stop. The Repatriation Act, which I'm signing today, extends civil rights protections in an unprecedented manner. For their own protection, the federal government will relocate Chinese Americans to Repatriation Centers isolating them from further hostility and violence."

The President paused as he said that last sentence out loud. There was more to the speech; talking points about the country's economic future and the promise of global stability but it was all a blur to him. He suddenly realized the full impact of that last sentence and why his Chief of Staff didn't put up a fight or even a fuss; not because he was incarcerating innocent Americans whose crime was being born to parents who share their ethnicity with a current adversary, not because he was offering hope of economic recovery when there was none in sight, and not because when the terms of the secret treaty with Beijing became public, it would require his resignation. It was none of the above.

In terms of shaping and steering the destiny of the United States and the rest of the world, the President realized what his Chief of Staff knew all along: that his actions today made the Office of the President of the United States irrelevant.

§

CHAPTER ONE

Henry Chin looked down at the contents of his shopping cart. The pork shoulder roast was on sale. At full price, Henry wouldn't be able to afford it. A three pound roast was unusually large and unavailable during the hours Henry was normally allowed to shop. A roast this size would yield several days worth of leftovers. With different sauces and sides each leftover could taste like a brand new meal.

The pork roast seemed incongruous for a man like Henry. He was a slight man, in his early forties with wire rimmed glasses and a clean-shaven face. Henry had let his hair grow long and flop down over his face to better obscure his Chinese ethnicity.

Without thinking, Henry grabbed a small paper sack of flour. Eggs and milk were not available today but flour can sit in the pantry until eggs and milk became available. Too often it's the other way around.

Henry picked up some frozen orange juice and some carrots then ran through his mind the spices he needed: pepper, paprika, garlic powder... brown sugar. Henry was surprised he remembered this time. One more aisle and then he could go home.

As Henry searched for a small carton of brown sugar he noticed a man standing at the end of the aisle. He kept his distance but Henry could feel him staring at him. It was an instinct that Henry trusted and that had served him well.

Henry held the carton of brown sugar in his hand for a moment. It was a deliberate pause to let his onlooker know he was about to make his exit. It was also a pause to give him an opportunity to avoid an unnecessary confrontation, if that was their goal. Henry dropped the brown sugar into his cart and turned toward the registers. His onlooker did not disappear.

The man standing at the end of the aisle was wearing a dark khaki shirt masquerading as a uniform. He was in his mid forties but didn't have the stereotypical mid life paunch rent-a-cops so often have in the movies. He stood his ground as Henry wheeled his cart toward him.

As Henry rolled his cart, the man in khakis blocked his exit from the aisle. "I have my I.D.," Henry volunteered.

"Yeah, I'll need to see that, slowly."

Great, thought Henry, a zealous rent-a-cop. Henry knew the drill. With his left hand still holding the cart, he brought up his right hand, palm up before pulling his wallet out of his front right pants pocket. Once he had his wallet out, he brought his left hand over and pulled out his Department of Homeland Security issued I.D. card.

It was a simple card. White and laminated. A color photo with text in that strange computer OCR type. A twenty eight digit I.D. number and a magnetic stripe on the back. Twenty eight digits seemed a bit excessive considering you'd only need eleven digits to represent every living person in the world. No more than thirteen digits were needed if you wanted to I.D. every human being whoever lived.

"I'll have to take this."

"It's the new one. I just got it three weeks ago."

"New rules."

"If you take that, I can't buy anything. How am I supposed to eat?"

"It's the rules," the guard insisted. "Besides, if you're really hungry, tell them you're Chinese. You'll get to eat for free at the ration centers."

It took all of Henry's willpower not to roll his eyes. The food ration centers were a joke. They were open a few hours once a week and they distributed rice and vegetables that the supermarkets were ready to throw away. Uncle Sam's compensation for the lost freedom.

Henry took a step forward. "Hold it," the rent-a-cop ordered.

"What now?"

"You can't leave until the police come and process you."

Henry ran through all the options in his mind. It was bad enough that he could only buy food on odd numbered weekend days. Henry didn't have one of those new digital antennas for picking up radio and television over the air. Information was scarce to come by and the restrictions changed with alarming frequency.

The rent-a-cop must have sensed what Henry flashed through his mind for just the briefest of moments. As Henry sighed, the guard took a step back and had his baton out and down at his side. On its face, the I.D. card looked fine. All you have to do is flash it at the greeter to gain entry. But if the police ran it through their scanner they'll find it was stolen from a Korean man about three weeks ago.

This was the first time Henry used the I.D. card. With his wide face and dark complexion, Henry was often mistaken for Korean. Since the economic turmoil with China began, every Chinese living in America was, for all intents and purposes, under house arrest. Without breaking a few rules, a Chinese person would probably starve to death on the allotted rations. Henry had to provide more and provide it under the scrutiny of a microscope.

Except he screwed up and he knew it. He should have come at a time when it was more crowded. He should have worn nicer clothes like a sport jacket or dress shoes. Hell, he should have combed his hair and cleaned his glasses. Presentable people tend to draw less suspicion.

Henry didn't have to look but he knew there were at least two more rent-a-cops behind him at the far end of the aisle. It was only a matter of time before the nature of his purloined card would be discovered. Henry slowly lifted his hands, exposing his palms... only his palms weren't empty. In his hand was the sack of flour.

"Drop that," the rent-a-cop ordered.

"No problem," replied Henry.

With all his might, Henry slammed the sack of flour down onto the floor, splitting it open, sending a white cloud of fine powder into the air.

Okay, thought Henry to himself as he backed down the aisle. That bought me about five seconds. Now what?

As the cloud engulfed him, Henry grabbed a box of book matches off the shelf. Instinctively, he tore the cellophane off and in one motion, struck the match and threw it into the heart of the cloud. Henry covered his head with his hands as he hit the ground.

The lit match ignited the flour and a ball of fire filled the air. Shoppers all around him screamed.

Chaos, confusion, thought Henry. I've got another thirty seconds.

Keeping low, Henry ran toward the back of the store. The flame ball was going to burn itself out in a few more seconds. Henry couldn't count on that brief flash to ignite anything else. Henry knew better than to count on luck. This was it. He could hear the cries of confusion. Then Henry saw his chance.

All the rent-a-cops in the market abandoned their stations and ran toward the fire. Their lack of training was going to pay off for Henry if he could remain patient. He spotted an abandoned shopping cart, calmly took hold of it and casually pushed it toward the back of the store. Once he determined that all the rent-a-cops had run toward the fireball, Henry quietly slipped out the back.

Henry knew he botched this. This wasn't the way he was trained to operate. The entire trick is to get in and get out before anyone even knows you're there. Approaching sirens echoed throughout the back alley. His instincts were telling him to pick a direction and run as fast and as far as he can but his training told him something else.

Henry looked out from the loading dock. He saw old cars, a chain link fence, a construction site across the railroad tracks... and a porta potty.

Henry turned back into the store and quickly found the custodian's closet. Henry spotted a jug of bleach and grabbed it.

He quickly jogged across the back parking lot and scaled the fence into the construction site. Henry pressed himself up against the side of the porta potty. He reached over for the handle but couldn't open it. It was padlocked shut. Henry could sense that he was running out of time. Henry looked up and spied the vent stack. I'm committed now. I've got to make this work, Henry thought to himself.

Henry quickly stacked two cinder blocks and climbed up to grab the vent stack with one hand while holding onto the jug of bleach with the other. With all his strength, Henry managed to pull himself up on top of the porta potty.

Gotta do this fast, Henry thought. I'm a sitting duck up here. Henry unscrewed the vent cap and slowly poured the bleach down the vent stack. This had better work.

Once the jug was empty, Henry took a quick look around before he jumped down off the porta potty. Now it was time to listen to his instincts. Henry spotted a row of houses in the distance and began to run as fast as he could.

It was the length of a football field Henry had to cross but the uneven dirt made the run treacherous. One misplaced step, one twisted ankle and it was all over. Plus, he was kicking up all this dust, a dead giveaway to anyone who bothered to look. Henry didn't like depending on other people to screw up for his plans to work. As much as he wanted to believe it to be true, not every government employee was incompetent. Henry could only hope there was enough confusion to create an opportunity.

Henry reached the wooden fence of the first house and flipped himself over it. He came to rest with his back against the wall, desperately trying to catch his breath. His eyes scanned the backyard. Children's toys were scattered about. He looked up at the house. The windows were closed and the lights were off.

Henry's analysis was interrupted by the sound of a truck coming to a stop. Henry peered into the front yard. In the street, a SWAT team set up a makeshift checkpoint. Unfortunately, for Henry, he was on the wrong side of the checkpoint.

Inside the house, a dog barked. Henry slipped over to the back door and peered inside. Through the window he could see a beautiful yellow labrador. This was the kind of dog you couldn't help but fall in love with. Young, couldn't be more than two years old. Energetic, probably chewed up at least half the furniture in the house. Friendly, a belly rub instantly made you his best friend.

Then it came.

From the construction site came the explosion that Henry was waiting for. The combination of bleach with the large quantity of stale urine in the porta potty created a highly unstable compound. Unstable enough to ignite a fireball into the sky chased by a black column of smoke.

Okay, thought Henry, that should be enough of a distraction. Henry took another look into the front yard. The SWAT team wasn't distracted. These guys were trained properly. They went about their business setting up the checkpoint.

This can't be it, this can't end in some stranger's backyard. Think. Think! The yellow labrador barked again and scratched at the door clamoring for a new playmate.

"Shhh!" It was a pointless gesture, trying to get a yellow lab to hush but we're socialized to believe it makes a difference. Henry knew the next step. Once the checkpoint was finished, it would be the base of operations for conducting a door to door search. The construction site was not an option. Going from backyard to backyard had too many things that could go wrong. Henry had to slip past that checkpoint.

Henry found a tennis ball and picked it up and began to squeeze it. Sometimes a physical activity, no matter how small, was enough to lower the mental barriers to creativity. Writers often say they have their best epiphanies when they take a walk or when they are in the shower.

The tennis ball felt nasty in Henry's hand, no doubt from the countless games of fetch with the yellow lab... then Henry had his epiphany. He broke the small window on the back door with his elbow. Careful not to cut himself, Henry reached inside, unlocked the door and opened it while bracing himself for about 150 lbs of puppy love and affection to tackle him to the ground.

Henry instinctively reached for the yellow lab's belly and began scratching instantly becoming his best friend. Henry held out the tennis ball and the yellow lab immediately sat at attention, still as a statue.

"You want it? You want it?" Henry teased. "Go get it!" Henry flung the tennis ball into the street with all his might.

Like an Olympic track star, the yellow lab bolted over the fence after the tennis ball. Henry counted to five and then made his move. He leapt over the fence and angled himself away from the line of sight between the SWAT team and the yellow lab. Somewhere in Henry's brain, he believed that if he averted his gaze and didn't look at the SWAT team, then they wouldn't look at him.

Brisk, not fast. Brisk, not fast. There was an art to moving at a pace and rhythm where you blend in with the background noise. Twenty more feet, fifteen, ten... Henry was almost past their eye line. Ten more steps and he would be behind them. Three, two, one.

But this was not a time to relax. Keep walking, brisk not fast. There was still the risk he was in the corner of someone's eye. Breathe, breathe, breathe.

Henry almost screamed when the shot rang out. Don't look, don't look, mind your own business, don't look. Fight the curiosity. Don't look.

Henry could hear a long string of obscenities being shouted. It was the unmistakable sound of a superior officer dressing down a subordinate. Henry could hear his own heartbeat pound in his ears. And then he heard the bark of the playful yellow lab. Henry indulged himself with a sigh of relief. Don't look. Head up, back straight, eyes forward... keep walking.

Henry pushed open his basement window and crawled through. By now, the sun was beginning to set. The flashing lights of the SWAT team easily lit up the neighborhood. The door to door search was in progress.

Henry quickly kicked off his shoes and stripped off his pants. From the laundry basket he grabbed a pair of sweatpants and pulled them on. One more thing to do and he'll be presentable. Henry grabbed his electronic ankle bracelet off the washing machine and gingerly began to snap it in place.

Just then, the doorbell rang. The ankle bracelet was just as difficult to put on as it was to take off, especially if you don't have the key. Gentle nudge left, push right with just the right amount of pressure. Exhale... click.

Henry opened the front door and was greeted by Private Hanson who shone a flashlight in Henry's face.

"Sorry to bother you Mr. Chin. I need to check your ankle bracelet."

"Now? Is anything wrong?"

"I can't say. Your ankle Mr. Chin." Henry extended his foot toward Officer Hanson. This kid was barely out of high school. Officer Hanson scanned Henry's ankle bracelet and then looked up.

"I'll need to see Elizabeth's too."

Henry turned his head upward and bellowed out "Elizabeth!"

Elizabeth descended the stairs. She had just turned eighteen and was little more than a mallrat in pajamas. Her facial features easily betrayed her mixed parentage. She wouldn't be considered Chinese by a Chinese person and a White person wouldn't know what she was.

"I need to see your ankle." Elizabeth held out her foot for inspection. Officer Hanson scanned her ankle bracelet and then gave her a nod.

"Thank you. It goes without saying, stay indoors. If you have any medical emergency, call for an escort."

"It goes without saying." Discipline, Henry thought to himself. That mockery was bordering on contempt. Henry flashed a smile at Officer Hanson. "You have a good night and take care of yourself."

"Thank you Mr. Chin. Goodnight Elizabeth." Before Henry could shut the door, Officer Hanson held up his hand. Even though he was talking to Henry, he was looking at Elizabeth.

"I shouldn't tell you this but we have new orders. They're ordering us to move you... everyone tomorrow."

"What? Tomorrow? Where?" asked Elizabeth.

"It was in the President's announcement today. Bad things are happening. You'll only have time to pack essentials before we move you to some place safer."

"I appreciate the head's up," Henry said. Officer Hanson gave a small nod and backed away as Henry shut the door. Henry checked the window to make sure he was gone.

"Daddy, where were you?" demanded Elizabeth. "You said two hours. It's been six."

"Something went wrong." Henry opened his jacket and fished out two cans of beef chili. "At least I got us some dinner."

Elizabeth picked up one of the cans and turned her nose up at it. "This is nasty."

"Eat it," Henry barked. "You have to build up your strength. The next few days are going to be tough. Do you have sturdy shoes?"

# # #

Immigration and Customs Enforcement was the newest government agency but despite that, their briefing hall was a throwback to 1960s architecture: tile floors and wooden folding book rests. This was temporary until their new office building in West Los Angeles was completed. Until then, they were stuck working out of this old university administration building.

Ten years earlier, Don Morgan would have worn a bow tie like his grandfather wore. Though he was far removed from his grandfather's life, he understood that his great grandfather was a slave, freed shortly after the Civil War. A bow tie was what a gentleman wore and he instilled this upon his son who passed it down to his son and finally to Don. Don loved to wear bow ties. It made him look older which is helpful when you grow up with chubby cheeks. Don was turning sixty three this year. He didn't need help anymore to look older. Now, he just wears his collar open, tieless.

He looked out over the seated ICE Agents. These men were young. These men should wear bow ties, he thought to himself. They all wore dark blue or charcoal gray suits with white shirts. No stripes were allowed. A dark solid colored tie was mandatory. They were recognizably G-Men in any age.

"Come to order please." Silence fell in the hall as Don continued. "The Repatriation Centers are operational and the relocation of Chinese Americans will begin shortly. However we have more immediate and pressing tasks. Lights."

The room darkened as a PowerPoint slide of the United States came up. Urban areas in New York, San Francisco and Los Angeles were colored red. Seattle and

Atlanta had some red but not as much. Don continued, "Local law enforcement has reported an uptick in violent incidents possibly initiated by Chinese Americans. Intelligence agencies believe this may be the beginning of a coordinated resistance effort, possibly even the formation of a Chinese fifth column. FBI has put together a photo array of possible members of this nascent resistant movement. They have asked for our help to locate these persons of interest, or anyone we suspect might be conspiring to commit acts of violence during the repatriation roundup. We are instructed to take them into custody for questioning. The checklist is accessible via your smartphone VPN."

Almost immediately, the agents activated their smartphones and looked over the protocol. Hands went up in the air.

"Director Morgan, the checklist doesn't define suspicious behavior," asked one ICE agent.

"How about that?" replied Don sarcastically.

"Nor does it require Miranda," said another.

"We want to allow you the broadest discretion possible. As you can see, Los Angeles is an area of particularly high concern. That will be our focus."

"Director Morgan, is this legal?" Don looked around the room. As Director of the Southern California district, he actually had very few powers of discretion himself.

"It is now. You have your orders. Dismissed." Don signaled for the lights to come back up as the PowerPoint slide faded out. All Don wanted to do was go back to his office and finish his cup of coffee before quitting time, but he wouldn't get his peace and quiet just yet.

"Director Morgan! Do you have a moment?" Don recognized that voice right away. It was the voice that always had a hand out attached.

The voice belonged to Nick Babcock. He was young and eager. Eager was today's spunky, but being eager without some earnestness was annoying to Don. It was one of many reasons why Don didn't like Babcock. Babcock was always asking for things as if he were entitled. Don knew his personnel record backwards and forwards. Babcock came from privilege and he acted accordingly, though he didn't have the tenacity at anything to back that up.

"Director Morgan, I want a chance to show what I can do. I was third in command of the task force that sniffed out illegals in Georgia. It was our twenty-eighth largest raid in history."

Don had no time for this shit. He fired back, "Babcock, where's your investigative report on the penetration of illegal immigrants in urban farmers' markets?" Babcock was momentarily taken aback. "No? Until it's on my desk, SHUT UP!" That silenced the few remaining agents in the room.

As Don turned to leave, Babcock spoke up. "I've paid my dues."

That was the wrong thing to say to me, Don thought to himself. "Lieutenant Colonel Mark Babcock of the United States Marine Corps paid his dues. He served with distinction, honor and valor in Vietnam, and he was twice decorated with the Silver Star. Your father has very long coattails. Someday, you might too." Don could tell Babcock wanted to say something. Any sass or lip and this could be Don's excuse to bounce Babcock from the agency. African Americans had to live with the perpetual stigma of affirmative action. Legacy admissions should be as equally a stigma on Whites.

"Do you have something to say, Mr. Babcock?"

"No Director Morgan."

"Then I have a cup of coffee to finish. We're done." Don hated that he had to treat Babcock like this nearly every time they interacted. Mostly because he took no pleasure in dressing him down and because it was exhausting to do so.

§

CHAPTER TWO

Henry removed the photographs off the wall one at a time. Dust caked on the top of the frame. It never occurred to Henry all these years to clean these pictures. It might have helped with his chronic allergies if he did.

Holding the pictures in his hands, Henry looked at them... really looked at them for the first time in almost ten years. One particular picture might have been the last photo of their family together. Elizabeth had just graduated from elementary school. She was wearing white knee socks and her hair was permed. He remembered explaining to her that Chinese girls never looked good with permed hair but that was the style then and her mother went along with it. Thank goodness she outgrew it. Thank goodness her generation never went through the 'big hair' phase that seemed to plague every other generation. Thank goodness she wore her hair long and straight now and that it didn't suffer permanent damage.

Henry squinted at Veronique's image. As difficult as their marriage was, he still missed her deeply. His marriage to Veronique surprised no one more than him. She was born in France in some vineyard chateau. She had a very easy social ability about her. She came to the United States as a student and ended up marrying Henry. That's how she got her citizenship. However, the assumption by anyone who didn't know them was that it must have happened the other way.

For as long as he could remember, Henry wanted desperately to fit in. Unfortunately for him, he grew up in the shadow of World War II, the Korean conflict and Vietnam. In all his childhood playground games, he always got chosen to play the enemy soldier. His role was always the outsider.

Despite his ethnicity, Henry had plenty of American cultural bona fides. He knew the rosters of the New York Yankees and the San Francisco 49ers because he grew up watching these teams play and idolized the players. Henry knew white southern slang from his time serving in the U.S. Army and could easily recall a dozen extremely vulgar insults about your mother. He was a fan of obscure television shows and cheap action movies. Veronique was none of these things.

Veronique's English was spoken through a laughably thick French accent. To most of the people they knew, her accent made her sound cultured and refined. Henry couldn't help but sound like a kid from the streets. Despite being French, Veronique couldn't tell the difference between a merlot and a cabernet. Henry could pick out the Irish lager from a sampling of German ales.

Veronique came from old money, though she never cared about it. She almost seemed to deliberately eschew all the trappings of high culture. She never talked about her family with Henry. Vacation trips avoided Europe at all costs. Henry always suspected that Veronique married him to piss off her father. He always enjoyed that thought because he felt that if that were true, Veronique got more that she bargained for.

Veronique's secrecy about her past was a source of conflict between Henry and Elizabeth. Ever since Veronique's death, Elizabeth believed she was the forgotten heir to a European kingdom. That once her true identity was known she would take her rightful place on a throne in a palace with dozens of servants to minister her. Teenage girl fantasies as far as Henry was concerned.

"You don't have much more time, Mr. Chin," said Officer Hanson. Henry tossed the photographs into a cardboard box marked basura.

Henry walked over to the foot of the staircase. "Elizabeth, are you done packing yet?"

"Don't rush me!" Elizabeth bellowed back.

Henry rolled his eyes at Officer Hanson. "When you have one of your own, you'll understand."

Just then there was a knock at the door. "Henry!" The voice came from Clyde Wilson, a wiry, middle-aged African American man. Instinctively, Officer Hanson drew his sidearm.

"At ease," Henry commanded sharply. Henry winced at the force of his own words.

"Henry, you've got something that belongs to me," demanded Clyde. "I want it before they take you away."

"And here I thought you came to say goodbye."

"You knew this day was coming. Why did you wait to the last minute? You wanted to screw me out of what is rightfully mine?"

Officer Hanson stepped forward. "I'm sorry sir, you'll have to leave. Now."

"Not without my stuff." Clyde held his ground. Despite being unarmed, Clyde's posture was formidable next to the police rookie.

"Stand down. I'll get him what he came for." Henry turned away toward the closet and carried out a large, camping backpack with lanterns, carabiners and rope hanging off the side.

"What if I didn't come today? I'd be screwed," Clyde accused.

"You knew where it was. You couldn't get off your own lazy nigger ass to come get it?"

"Fuckin' Chinaman!" Before Officer Hanson could react, Clyde was on top of Henry.

"Break it up you two! Break it up!" Officer Hanson pulled Clyde off Henry. Henry wiped some of the blood off his cut lip. "You got what you came for. Now leave."

Clyde picked up the backpack and headed toward the front door. "I hope you rot in hell, all your people!"

As Clyde left, Elizabeth stared down from the top of the staircase. "Was that Uncle Clyde?"

From outside came the sound of a car horn. "Mr. Chin, it's time," instructed Officer Hanson.

"I have three suitcases," said Elizabeth.

"Sweetheart, three suitcases? That's too much! You'll have to leave something behind."

"You only have one. You can carry one of mine." Henry watched helplessly as Elizabeth began dragging her suitcases down the staircase one at a time. "You can take the big one."

Officer Hanson chuckled to himself. "When I have my own, right Mr. Chin?"

Henry breathed a sigh of relief at Officer Hanson's joke. Henry's bag was conspicuously small. Just a carry-on case that could barely hold a change of clothes. Henry had packed light... much lighter than anyone else who faced the same situation.

The commuter shuttle bus pulled up to the end of the driveway. Officer Hanson signaled Henry and Elizabeth to board it. Elizabeth wheeled her two suitcases behind her but couldn't seem to keep them upright. Henry turned to take one last look at his house.

It seemed like the American dream, a two story, three bedroom house with a garage at the end of a cul de sac. When he bought it, he was a young man with a new family and a career. The G.I. Bill had paid for his education to become a pharmacist and Alhambra, California was where he planned to quietly live out a dull, boring, uneventful life. His life turned out to be anything but.

The changes in his life were incremental. There wasn't any one big event that you could point to and say, 'I should have left then.' A minor inconvenience here and there seemed childish to complain about. The price of gasoline was up, the cost of groceries were up. So when Henry had to make three separate trips home to retrieve information to cast his vote in the last election, it didn't seem like much.

All the time he lived in this suburban Chinese enclave of Los Angeles he never had to produce an I.D. to vote. During the last Presidential election, that changed.

Edwina Fischer was apologetic. She was close to eighty years old and a volunteer for the election canvassing committee. Henry knew her from when she came to the pharmacy and filled her prescription for Coumadin every month. Despite their casual acquaintance for nearly ten years, she said she needed him to produce more than a drivers license in order to vote. Henry had to drive back home and retrieve his utility bill with his name on it to prove he lived where he said he lived. However, Edwina's supervisor said that a utility bill was not enough. Henry also had to prove his citizenship so he went home and retrieved his passport. Just to be safe, he also grabbed what few other vital documents he had.

But none were satisfactory.

Edwina's supervisor informed Henry that a passport, a Social Security card or even his Veterans Affairs card were not enough to prove his citizenship. A fake birth certificate could easily pave the way for all those documents.

Unfortunately for Henry, his original birth certificate was buried in ashes some dozens of feet below street level, lost during the Northridge quake.

Edwina's supervisor magnanimously cut Henry a break and issued him a provisional ballot, which would be accepted upon Henry producing a valid birth certificate at City Hall. At best, it would take the better part of six weeks for California's Department of Vital Records to issue a new birth certificate. Henry's vote would make no difference.

Henry looked around the polling place. "How come you don't require birth certificates from everyone?"

The supervisor replied matter-of-factly, "Just from those we suspect aren't citizens."

"Why do you suspect me?"

The supervisor stared at Henry with that classic bureaucratic 'don't waste my time' look. "C'mon, don't be stupid."

That was the time Henry should have complained. That was the time Henry should have said something. That was the time Henry should have begun talking to his neighbors and organizing some kind of protest. Even though Alhambra was a Chinese enclave, it shared its Congressional District with Burbank, Pasadena and Glendale, three predominately white communities which split the Chinese population into three insignificant pieces.

The last time this area had an Asian American representative was 1962. The way the district lines were redrawn since then ensured that Chinese Americans would have as little influence as possible. It was a strange thought to Henry that this area was more politically progressive back in 1962 than it was today.

Henry never shared his political insights. He didn't want to make waves. Instead, Henry merely applied for a new birth certificate.

"Dad, I need some help." Henry snapped his head around. Although he was lost in thought for barely a few seconds, Henry's reverie seemed to last for much longer. Henry grabbed Elizabeth's luggage and loaded it onto the bus.

The commuter bus was a modified vehicle. The windows were reinforced with steel bars and steel mesh. Henry and Elizabeth found the last two seats where they could sit side by side. Henry looked around at the other passengers. All were elderly Chinese couples. They must have come from the nursing home, Henry thought to himself.

"Nei zi m zi keoi dei daai ngo dei heui bin dou?" an elderly woman whispered to Henry. Henry waved her off, shaking his head.

"I don't speak Chinese," Henry said apologetically. But, in fact, Henry did. She had asked him if he knew where they were being taken. Henry didn't know but he didn't want to start a conversation with her. He didn't want to get involved—

There was that same old thinking rearing its ugly head again. Don't get involved, stay low, don't make waves. His instincts told him that even a harmless old Chinese woman could pose problems. Maybe he wasn't the only one who thought this way. Maybe this is why they have so many problems now.

"Dad, why do I have to go?"

"The government didn't give us any choice."

"But I'm half White. Most people think I'm Mexican. You look Korean, sort of. Why can't we just lie?"

Why can't we just lie? thought Henry. Why didn't the Chinese railroad workers just grow back their hair? Why didn't women just demand equal pay? Why didn't slaves just walk off the plantation? Elizabeth didn't concern herself with the gray area of history. If it wasn't on TMZ, it wasn't in her world.

"There's no such thing as hiding in plain sight," Henry told her.

"You never answer my questions with a simple yes or no!"

"You asked me why. 'Why' questions can't be answered with a simple yes or no."

Many hapas did ask why, especially if they were exactly one half Chinese and one half something else. But then again, this was the country that said, by law, that if you had one drop of Negro blood in you, you were considered Negro. He had spent most of his life shielding Elizabeth's from America's shameful racist past. The schools didn't teach her about slavery or segregation, or the Japanese Internment or the premeditated genocide of Native Americans. These were difficult topics to talk about... not exactly polite dinner conversation.

Henry didn't know what to tell her but found himself talking anyway. Tell a story, the first thing that comes to your mind. It will lead you to the answer. "Remember when you were in second grade and you shoplifted pencils from Anderson's Drug Store? You hid them, you were afraid to use them in case someone recognized them. You were so nervous about getting caught that you threw up for two days before you confessed." Then Henry found the point he was searching for. "Always looking over your shoulder... that's not any way to live."

Henry hated himself for what he just said. What the government was doing was wrong and he was making excuses justifying their behavior.

Elizabeth stared him down. What should he expect from an eighteen year old girl? He was her father, there was nothing he could say that would make her happy anyway.

The shuttle bus cruised along the surface streets. Henry thought this was unusual. In Los Angeles, there was hardly any errand that didn't require some time on a freeway. They were headed north along Los Robles headed toward Pasadena.

Henry didn't drive into Pasadena much. His job at Rite Aid was so close to his house that sometimes he would ride his bicycle to work. He always considered himself a blue collar kind of guy and Pasadena seemed too top shelf a place for the hoi polloi. Good Chinese food was about the only thing Henry couldn't cook and in Alhambra and nearby Monterey Park, there was no shortage of good and inexpensive choices.

Elizabeth was a different story. As soon as she was old enough to drive, she and her high school friends would hang out in Old Town watching the weekend crowds go in and out of the clubs. Too young to get in herself, she'd smoke the stray cigarette and flirt with the bouncers. Henry knew the odds would eventually turn in her favor that she would get in but as long as she was with her friends he felt some comfort.

As a passenger, Henry was able to gaze out at the scenery, what little wasn't blocked by the thick trees.

"I hope this isn't going to be a long ride," complained Elizabeth. "I think I'm going to throw up."

Henry knew she wasn't kidding. Ever since she was a young child, Elizabeth couldn't ride in the back seat of the car. Until she was old enough to sit up front, every car Henry owned had the slight hint of stale vomit. She always had to sit up front.

"It's not," Henry said unconsciously before he bit his lip. Unfortunately, there did come the inevitable follow up question.

"How do you know?"

"Henry hated lying to his daughter. "We didn't get on the freeway. Do you want some Dramamine?" Henry held his breath hoping his daughter would leave it at that.

But Henry did know where they were going.

"Dad, you're a pharmacist, don't you have anything stronger?"

"Not without a prescription, sweetheart."

"Like that really matters now." Elizabeth turned away and stared blankly out the window, her arms crossed and her body curled up as tightly as she could hold herself. The trees gave way as they turned onto Colorado and passed by the Civic Auditorium before turning north onto Fair Oaks. Now came the traffic.

Commuter shuttles started merging slowly onto Fair Oaks. Traffic police cordoned off streets so the shuttles would have as free a flow as possible. Small bands of protesters and counter protesters dotted the streets. This was the reason why their destination was kept a secret for as long as possible.

There had already been violent clashes in the streets over the economic situation. Many people who lost their jobs blamed the Chinese and took their anger out on whatever Chinese they could find. This wasn't surprising to Henry. Los Angeles had a rich history of scapegoating Asians. From the burning of Korean grocery stores resulting in 54 deaths after police officers were acquitted of beating Rodney King to as far back as 1871, when 84 Chinese were lynched in a riot in Calle de Los Negros that would come to be known as the Chinese Massacre in Nigger Alley.

The reason for this current round up was to protect the Chinese from any further violence. However, Henry knew that mankind, as a whole, had a shoddy record when it came to round ups.

The protesters were anemic. On one side of the street were signs that read "Equal Protection Means Equal Protection!" and "I Love 14!" On the other side of the street were "America for Americans!" and "The Chinese Must Go!" Not exactly an original sentiment, Henry thought. The signs all looked hastily made with bad handwriting and misspellings.

What Henry thought was interesting was that all of the protesters were White. Any person of Asian descent who wasn't Chinese kept out of sight as much as possible. No one wanted to be mistaken for Chinese if they could possibly avoid it. T-shirts with Korean and Japanese flags were very popular.

The old stereotype had its roots in truth: White people had a hard time telling apart one Asian face from another. That's why the Department of Homeland Security issued their own I.D. card.

The shuttle buses were pelted with fruit as they crawled along to their destination. The road turned into a large parking lot and one by one the shuttle buses found a parking spot. Henry and Elizabeth disembarked with their luggage. Henry gave a quick hand to the elderly couple but soon, they were all ushered into a long queue into the staging area.

Any football fan would immediately recognize where they were. The single tiered concrete saucer, the iconic sign and symbol were unmistakable. The only things out of place were the Army soldiers stationed at the top of the bleachers. Their rifles were drawn and aimed downward into the parking lot.

Elizabeth noticed this and pointed it out to Henry. "Why are they aiming their guns at us?"

"For our protection," Henry droned.

"Our protection? They're aiming their guns at us," she emphasized.

"It's history repeating itself," Henry replied. Henry snorted as they walked past a sign that read, "Welcome to the Rose Bowl."

§

CHAPTER THREE

Near the entrance gate of the Rose Bowl was where Homeland Security set up their check-in stations. ICE had their clerks set up behind a long row of folding tables, two clerks per table. Behind them were large garbage cans, which Henry quickly realized were for the disposal of contraband and paperwork.

One thing Henry always thought the United States was bad at was iconography. Being such a young country relative to the rest of the world, the U.S. had no sense of history. Blunders like our former President calling a military action in the Middle East a 'Crusade' were unforgivable. History repeating itself indeed. The tables, the clerks, the queues... did anyone study World War II and the Holocaust? Did anyone in the current administration happen to see Schindler's List?

Henry stood in line behind Elizabeth. The sun had peeked out from behind the clouds and now was blazing down on them. Henry took out a yellow bandana and wiped his brow. Elizabeth sat on her suitcases. Dust kicked up as they slowly moved closer to the clerks. Weaving in and out of the lines were ICE agents. To Henry, they were easily recognizable. Dark suit, white shirts, sunglasses with that plastic coil hanging out of their ear. The ICE agents were comparing Chinese people in line with photo arrays that were coming up on their smartphones.

One agent got Henry's attention. At the pharmacy, Henry learned how to spot shoplifters by watching their eyes. Most shoplifters were nervous and would check too many times to see where the employees were. Anyone who made eye contact with you more than once was very concerned about knowing where you were. Even though this ICE Agent wore sunglasses, Henry could tell he seemed very interested in him. Henry didn't want to tip his hand and let him know he was very interested in him as well.

Finally it was Elizabeth's and Henry's turn. Elizabeth immediately ran afoul by having three suitcases. Elizabeth's logic was that since they were allowed two apiece and since Henry had only one, she was entitled to three.

When that logic didn't play, Henry tried to explain that one of her suitcases was indeed his. They opened it up for inspection and it was very clear that the clothes inside did not belong to Henry. There was a fifty fifty chance they would let her keep it.

While they inspected Henry's suitcase, he pulled out a Ziploc bag full of Flintstone chewable vitamins. "Do you have a prescription for those?" queried the clerk.

Henry held out the bag for him to inspect. "That's Fred Flintstone. That's Barney Rubble. I have a vitamin deficiency." Henry tried to chuckle but the clerk remained humorless. Henry took out a small bottle of hand sanitizer and squirted out a dollop.

"Where can I get a bottle of water?" The clerk nodded toward some nearby vending machines.

The clerk finished going through Henry's suitcase. "You don't have a lot of stuff."

"I used to backpack across Europe when I was young. I know how to pack light."

"Teach that to some of your fellow repatriots." Henry winced. The government has a euphemism for us now: repatriots. Ugh.

"I'm going to get a bottle of water."

"Make it fast," said the clerk who had already moved on to the next person in line.

Henry sneaked a look over his shoulder as he walked slowly over to the vending machines. That ICE Agent was still on his tail. Dammit, Henry thought. He had tried so hard to blend in with everyone else, he wondered if that's what caught the ICE Agent's attention. Henry decided to risk one good look at the guy.

He looked up. The ICE Agent wasn't looking at him. Henry realized what had caught his attention. It was Elizabeth. It made sense, she was a very pretty girl and unusual with her mixed race looks. The ICE Agent was probably having impure thoughts about her.

Henry studied his face. The agent's face was a New England caricature: square jaw, blonde hair. Henry saw something distinctively twitchy about him. He wasn't a young man at peace with himself. He wasn't centered. Whatever this ICE Agent was looking for in his life, he hadn't found it yet. Henry hoped that whatever this young man chose to chase after with his life, it wouldn't be him.

Pretending that he was still cleaning his hands, Henry popped open his hand sanitizer bottle. However, instead of squirting the dollop into his hands, he squirted it into the Ziploc bag of vitamins. In fact, Henry nearly emptied the entire bottle. Leaving the Ziploc bag open, he crumpled it into a ball in his fist. Henry removed his eyeglasses as he wiped the sweat off his forehead again. However, this time, Henry took his eyeglasses and angled it toward the sun, looking at them as if he were inspecting them for smudges.

But what Henry was doing was trying to capture the right angle of sunlight with his glasses and aim the focused light down at the Ziploc bag. The sun was highest in the sky at this time and probably wouldn't get any stronger. Henry didn't have time to practice this beforehand but he was hoping this was going to take no more than a few seconds. But under these circumstances, a few seconds could seem like hours.

Then he smelled it: the odor of burning plastic. As the Ziploc bag caught fire, he quickly shifted it in his hand so he wouldn't burn himself. He non-chalantly tossed the Ziploc into one of the garbage cans and then deliberately kicked it over on its side.

Large colored flames of orange, blue and green shot out from the garbage can.

"Fire! Fire!" Henry yelled. In the confusion, Henry grabbed Elizabeth and pulled her behind a concrete pillar.

"What's going on?" she asked.

"Follow me," Henry commanded. Henry pulled Elizabeth around a corner only to run into a small squad of Army privates. In full voice Henry bellowed, "Fire back there! Fire! Corporal! Take your squad through there and begin S and R! Move!" Without a moment of hesitation, the Corporal dispatched his men toward the growing billow of smoke.

"What the...?" Before Elizabeth could finish her sentence, Henry pulled her along to a cinder block restroom kiosk. Henry took a moment to listen to the surrounding noise. He heard more movement of soldiers in the distance, rhythmic footsteps and the unmistakable clang of battle-rattle. Henry and Elizabeth slipped around to the far side of the restrooms. There they were stopped by a chain link fence with thick underbrush growing all around it.

With all the sarcasm her eighteen years could muster, Elizabeth threw her arms akimbo and said, "Now what?"

Without missing a beat, Henry put his fingers in his mouth and let out three, very high pitched staccato whistles. Emerging from the underbrush was Clyde.

"We don't have much time," Henry said.

"No shit," Clyde replied.

Clyde whipped out a set of bolt cutters and quickly snipped a hole in the chain link fence large enough for Henry and Elizabeth to step through.

"Give me your foot," Henry ordered Elizabeth. Henry grabbed the bolt cutters and snipped the electronic monitor off her ankle. But something else got Henry's attention: Elizabeth's designer high heeled sandals.

"I told you to wear sturdy shoes."

"You didn't tell me why!" Elizabeth retorted.

"We don't have time for this," barked Clyde. He grabbed the bolt cutters and snipped off Henry's electronic monitor.

"C'mon!" Clyde led them across the practice putting green but Elizabeth fell behind because of her sandals. "Just beyond those trees!" pointed Clyde. Henry kept pace with Clyde. "Go! I got her!" With permission to run ahead, Henry took off.

Clyde scooped up Elizabeth and threw her over his shoulder in a fireman's carry. By the time Henry got to the trees, Clyde nearly caught up with him.

As they broke through this narrow line of trees, they came upon a service road where a white cargo van was parked. Henry opened the back doors as Clyde dropped Elizabeth inside. Clyde circled over to the drivers seat as Henry climbed on board and pulled the rear doors shut. Henry and Elizabeth huddled up as Clyde started the engine and put the van in gear.

The cargo van was windowless. On the first turn, Henry grabbed the side to steady Elizabeth.

"There's a tarp back there," Clyde said. Henry nodded even though Clyde couldn't see it. Henry grabbed the blue plastic tarp and lifted it up.

"Get under it," Henry commanded Elizabeth.

"Ew!"

"You'll live." Elizabeth curled into a ball as Henry pulled the tarp over the both of them.

"Guys, quiet." Clyde slowed the van down, doing a nearly perfect California roll. Just as the van felt like it was coming to a complete stop, Clyde turned the steering wheel left and drove the van away at normal speed.

"Okay, you can breathe," Clyde exhaled.

"How close were we?" asked Henry.

"You don't want to know," said Clyde.

"Uncle Clyde?" Elizabeth peeked out from under the tarp.

"At your service."

"I have to call Eliana." From her pocket, Elizabeth pulled out a cell phone she had concealed. "I have to let her know I'm okay."

Immediately, Henry grabbed the cell phone out of her hand and snapped it in two. Henry then tore open the battery compartment.

"My phone!" Henry pried out the SIM chip and snapped that in half with his fingernail.

Henry climbed forward toward the drivers seat. "Roll down your window." As soon as his window was down, Henry flung Elizabeth's cell phone out of the van one piece at a time.

"You didn't have to do that," complained Elizabeth.

"Your phone has GPS. They can trace us."

"Dad! My life is on that phone!"

Henry knew the next words out of his mouth were crucial. "Sweetheart, the life you knew doesn't exist anymore. Nothing will ever be the same again."

"What about my things?" Henry looked over at Clyde.

"They weren't going to let you take them, wherever they were going to send you," said Clyde.

"But the President said he was moving us to protect us," protested Elizabeth.

Henry sighed deeply. "Inmates in a prison are well protected too." Henry watched to see if the enormity of their situation was sinking in. Elizabeth leaned back against the side of the van and grabbed her knees.

"Uncle Clyde, can you turn on the air conditioning? I'm going to get car sick."

"Lizzy, I can't turn on the A/C. If I do, we'll never make it up the mountain."

"Where are we going?"

Clyde steered the cargo van northbound on Route 210. The exit he was looking for was the turn off for the Angeles Crest Highway. The traffic looked normal. No additional commotion or sirens. Clyde threw the van into low gear and drove it up Route 2 into the Angeles National Forest.

With all its twists and sudden elevation changes, this highway was a motorcyclist's dream. Unfortunately, it was also Elizabeth's worst nightmare. Elizabeth crawled up front and sat shotgun. She put on one of Clyde's old baseball caps to hide her hair and complexion. Elizabeth pushed herself back as far as she could in the seat but it did nothing to quell her nausea.

"Stick your feet out in front of you and lift. Make your stomach as tight as you can," Henry offered.

"Don't hold your breath. Breathe through your nose," Clyde finished.

"You two practice this comedy routine?" Elizabeth looked away but unfortunately out the window. Unable to see the road and use it as a reference point, Elizabeth became disoriented. She quickly rolled down her window and puked.

Henry wondered about his daughter's motion sickness. He had heard tales of Native Americans who couldn't adjust to urban life: working inside, under a ceiling surrounded by walls would be a living hell for a person who was raised outdoors. Could the opposite be true? Could a person who spent a lifetime growing up inside a house, playing video games, and watching TV become disoriented at the sight of the horizon?

Maybe there was something to it. Ever since Henry married Veronique, the majority of his life was spent indoors. He calculated that once he had a family, more of his days were spent indoors than outdoors. That hadn't always been true. As a child, the exact opposite was true.

Henry considered that Veronique could have been the reason. Proper European girls were delicate and needed to stay out of the sun. No picnics, no hiking, no summer camp for Elizabeth. Horseback riding lessons would have been an option if Elizabeth showed even the least bit of interest.

Henry looked out at the jagged snow-capped mountains rising high up along either side of the road. There was a time he would have lived his life as a mountain man. With no wife and no daughter, it would have been an easy choice to make back then. It was still an easy choice to make today. Only the answer was completely different.

After about an hour, Clyde leaned back. "We're about ten miles from Newcomb's Ranch."

"Yeah, if there's a BOLO out for us, that's the first place up there they'll look," concurred Henry. Newcomb's Ranch was the only restaurant along this stretch of highway. On a Sunday afternoon, you could stop here for a meal and a beer. The parking lot was almost always full of motorcycles. The other watering hole was Hidden Springs Café but that was lost in the Station Fire and never rebuilt. Newcomb's Ranch also had the only flushing toilet for miles. Henry thought it best not to mention this little fact to Elizabeth.

"Chilao is the next campground," said Clyde.

"Good idea. Do you want me to wake Elizabeth?"

"No Henry. Let the poor thing sleep as long as she can. Being awake right now is nothing but a nightmare." They were lucky. They didn't pass a single car on the way up. Not one motorcycle or, best of all, the one lone CHP officer who patroled this entire stretch of mountain highway.

The Chilao area was subdivided into several campgrounds. Little Pines campground was closed, also a victim of the Station Fire. "Manzanita must be open," wished Henry.

"It better be," said Clyde. And it was. The campground was deserted. There was no sign that anyone had been up there since the weekend. These campgrounds were gaining popularity with college kids who wanted to get away and binge drink for the weekend. Unfortunately, it scared away a lot of families. Clyde swung the van around to the far side of the loop and pulled into a campsite.

Henry pushed open the cargo van doors as Clyde came back around. "Catch," said Henry as he tossed Clyde his backpack.

"What did you think of my acting debut?" smiled Clyde.

"You're lucky you have a day job. Keep it." Henry lugged the backpack over to the picnic table. He was about to open it when they heard Elizabeth alight from the front seat, stumble to a tree and puke one more time.

"I put two days worth of freeze-dried in your pack," said Clyde.

"That's it?"

"Best I could do. Anything that even smells like survival gear, the Feds are keeping a really close eye on. I'll try to rustle up whatever I can for our rendezvous at Colby Canyon."

"I'm sorry. Whatever you can scrounge up would be very helpful," said Henry.

"Just like old times?" asked Clyde.

"I hope not," said Henry. "Old times we were getting shot at." Elizabeth let out one last violent dry heave. She steadied herself against the tree.

Clyde leaned in and whispered to Henry, "Her sandals are going to tear up her feet."

Henry looked down at Clyde's feet. "What size sneaker do you wear?"

Elizabeth sat on top of the picnic table. She pulled a white sweat sock over the white sweat sock she was already wearing. "Try it now," said Henry. Elizabeth tugged on Clyde's sneaker. It was still loose.

"Pull the laces as tight as they'll go," suggested Clyde.

Henry patted Clyde on the back. "You'd better get out of here before the park rangers make their evening rounds."

"You're right. Take care of yourself." Clyde turned around and gave Henry a giant bear hug.

Elizabeth turned away in disgust. "Ew."

"Your father is the hardest working man I know." Clyde and Henry fist bumped. "Colby Canyon."

"Colby Canyon," Henry repeated.

"What's in Colby Canyon?" asks Elizabeth.

"That's where we're going to resupply in a couple of days," said Henry.

"And then what?"

Clyde chuckled a moment before he broke out in a barrel chested rendition of O, Canada!

"Canada?" asked Elizabeth, dumbstruck.

"More Asians in Canada than in Mexico. Easier for us to blend in. Down here, they'll think we'll all run to Mexico."

"I can speak some Spanish. Everyone in high school thought I was a Chola."

Princess Chola, Henry thought to himself. "They speak English in Canada, you know."

"I'd better get out of here."

"Hey Clyde, it's illegal to drive barefoot in California."

"Hey Henry, you're a lawyer now?"

The two men threw each other a crisp salute before Clyde climbed back into the cargo van and drove off. Henry stood, almost frozen, listening for the last echoes of Clyde's cargo van as they faded away into nothingness.

"C'mon." Henry gave Elizabeth a gentle pat as he strapped on his backpack. He grabbed Elizabeth's sandals and headed over to the large bear dumpster. He reached in and released the catch, lifted the lid and tossed the sandals in.

"Hey!" screamed Elizabeth. She ran up to the bear dumpster before Henry could let it fall shut and retrieved the sandals.

"Elizabeth—"

"These were mom's." Elizabeth turned away and marched off along the trail. Henry decided not to fight her on this one. He adjusted his backpack and set off behind Elizabeth.

# # #

The Rose Bowl parking lot was empty but not quiet. The ICE Agents with the help of the Army were able to control the Chinese American repatriots after Henry and Elizabeth's escape. A few others had tried to run but were quickly captured. A little over 50,000 Chinese Americans had been processed and now were sprawled out in makeshift tents and cots inside the Rose Bowl, camping on the football field.

One ICE Agent started to wrangle the other agents into place. "He's thirty seconds out," he spoke into his walkie talkie. Momentarily, a black sedan pulled into the parking lot, came to a stop and let Don get out. He carried a manila envelope tucked under his arm. One of the ICE Agents handed him a megaphone.

"You're kidding me, aren't you?" The ICE Agent shook his head no. Don gave back the megaphone. Using the full power of his voice, Don addressed the agents. "We have identified the fugitive repatriots. Central Office is working right now to push the data onto your smartphone. Don held up a grainy security camera photo of Henry. "Who can see this? Everyone? This is Henry Chin. Forty-four years old. Pharmacist. He is still at large and believed to be behind the smoke bomb that nearly led to a prisoner breakout today. We've confirmed a connection with an incident earlier this week that involved a porta potty at a construction site."

Don pulled out a grainy DMV photo of Elizabeth. "This is his daughter Elizabeth. Age 18. Not an exceptional student. We believe she's involved peripherally only because of Henry. These two are the only two repatriots missing from today's roll call."

Don looked around before he calls out, "Palmer!" A young ICE Agent stood up. "You're with me. Gentlemen, it's been a very long day. You may stand down."

Before Palmer could trot over, Babcock raced past him to confront Don. "I want to go on detached assignment to retrieve those two repatriots. I saw them with my own eyes. I was this close to him. It happened on my watch and I feel personally responsible." Babcock leaned in, nearly whispering to Don. "You know I can do a better job than Palmer."

Don nearly betrayed his impulse to chew Babcock a new asshole but somehow managed to maintain his stone faced expression. "Permission granted."

Babcock's jaw dropped. "Really?"

"You've been pestering me for a chance. Now you want to talk me out of it?"

"No sir, thank you sir! I won't let you down!" Babcock bounced away.

Palmer turned to Don. "What did you want to see me about?"

"I just need to be debriefed on what happened today."

"That's it?" asked Palmer.

"That's it," replied Don. Palmer was a smart guy. He was glad to have Babcock out of his hair for the time being too. Don hoped this decision wasn't going to backfire.

Don turned to get into his sedan but a small commotion got his attention. He signaled his driver to wait. Don followed the sound of voices over to the far end of the parking lot. Babcock had rounded up four ICE Agents, Carlos Woteck, Mike Fisher, Charlie Alvarez and Fred Park and was giving them instructions. As Don approached, Woteck spoke up.

"Mr. Director, we're receiving new instructions. Is this under your authority?"

Babcock jumped in. "I need these men to return to Central Office and begin data mining. Woteck, I need you to liaise with Langley. We'll need access to their computer models — the ones they use to profile serial killers. Fisher, I need you to liaise with the Census Bureau. I need ethnic data on his people. Where do they eat, where do they sleep, where do they congregate? Alvarez, I need you to liaise with the IRS. I want to know every bank loan, every paycheck, every mortgage this guy has ever applied for. I want to know everything he's spent a dime on. Park, I need you to write database queries that can cross-tab all this info."

Woteck turned to Don. "Sir?" Quietly, Don whispered, "Do it."

With renewed confidence Babcock turned back toward his new team. "This man may be armed, he may be dangerous. We don't know what kind of threat he represents. All the more reason why we need to find him yesterday. Go!"

As Babcock's team ran off, Don pulled him aside. "The trail is still fresh. You don't think it's a better strategy to commandeer a patrol squad and set out on foot after him?"

"There's something special about this guy. He's not an opportunist. What happened today took some planning and some skill. I want to know everything I can possibly know about Henry Chin before I make my move. If I have to turn over every rock in Chinatown to find him, I will."

Don patted Babcock on the back. "Henry Chin is from Alhambra."

CHAPTER FOUR

Henry and Elizabeth had left the trail about an hour ago to follow a creek across a small plateau. The sun was still high in the sky. Henry looked back along the creek. If anyone were following them, they'd be easy to spot.

The creek cut its way through a large flat formation of sandstone. Henry removed his backpack and sat down. "Take a rest, Elizabeth." Elizabeth brushed aside some of the dirt on the rock.

"Dad, I'm really thirsty."

"No problem," Henry said with a smile. Henry dug into his backpack and pulled out a red, plastic water pump. He liberated a Nalgene bottle from a carabiner and assembled the two. From the pump he dropped a hose into the creek and began pumping water into the Nalgene bottle. Within a few seconds, the liter bottle was nearly full. Henry unscrewed the bottle and offered it to Elizabeth.

"Is it safe?"

"Actually, up here, you could probably drink the water right out of the creek and it would be safe." Henry looked down at the creek, which had a pretty good flow to it. "This creek is probably spring fed further up. This time of year, there's very little snow run off left. It's safe." Seeing she was unconvinced, Henry took a swig of the water himself. "Ahh, it's cold."

Elizabeth took a few small sips, which quickly turned into large gulps. "Easy, easy..." said Henry. "Drink normally otherwise, it'll upset your stomach." But it was too late. Elizabeth drank too much too quickly and her body couldn't handle it. She turned away from Henry and puked the water she drank right back up.

Elizabeth took a moment to recover. Her expression was a mix of anger and humiliation. "I don't really like it up here Dad."

"It'll take a little getting used to." Henry offered her a fresh bandana to wipe her mouth.

"That was really weird."

"What was?"

"I never threw up anything cold before."

"There's a lot of things in life you haven't experienced."

"C'mon Dad, don't go all fortune cookie on me now. This isn't about life."

Henry looked at his daughter. Crumpled, curled up, soft, weak and scared. This was going to be a lot for her to handle. Henry picked up the bottle and reattached it to the pump and refilled it. He turned to Elizabeth. "Want to try this again?"

Elizabeth took the water bottle and this time drank in much more measured sips. Elizabeth looked at the trees off in the distance. "Dad, there are trees over there. Can we walk in the shade?"

Henry took a quick glance. "That won't take us where we need to go. We follow this creek. We can't get lost. We'll always have water."

Elizabeth handed back the bandana to Henry.

"No, keep it."

"What am I supposed to do with it?" Henry reached into his backpack and pulled out another bandana along with a crumpled baseball cap. Henry soaked the bandana in the creek, then lined the baseball cap with it before he put it on his head. The bandana hung down out of the cap, covering his ears and the back of his neck.

"It'll keep you cool and protect your head from the sun." If Elizabeth had a better sense of history, she'd be appalled that her father looked like an old Japanese World War II soldier or someone out of an old French Foreign Legion movie. "You can be quite comfortable if you don't give a damn what you look like."

Just as quickly she shot back, "Then you must really be comfortable." Sarcasm was Elizabeth's normal state of being. Henry never knew that before today. Henry realized then that he had done a real disservice to her. She didn't seem to have any inner sense of courage. That when faced with new and difficult circumstances, she didn't know how to adapt and cope. Sarcasm was her way of defending herself. Sarcasm wasn't going to work very well for her up here.

"How much further?" Elizabeth asked. Henry stood up and gazed off across the plateau. "Past that gully up ahead, there's another plateau. We'll have to cover about five miles before sunset."

"By sunset? I can run five miles in less than an hour."

"On a treadmill, in an air conditioned gym with headphones on, listening to music. This terrain is a little bit more challenging. Which reminds me..."

Henry dug around in his backpack again. "You must think I'm Felix the cat," Henry wistfully chuckled at Elizabeth.

"Who?"

"Felix the Cat? You know, Felix the Cat, the wonderful, wonderful cat. Whenever he gets in a fix, he reaches into his bag of tricks..."

"Stop singing."

Henry cleared his throat as he reached deep into one of his backpack's side pockets until he found what he was looking for: his large, folding hunting knife.

"What are you doing with that?"

"Don't worry, I know how to use this." Henry pointed to a fallen pine branch. "Toss me that."

Elizabeth retrieved the branch and handed it to Henry. With a single motion, Henry flipped open the knife one handed. Elizabeth gasped. "Don't be so impressed," said Henry.

"I'm not," retorted Elizabeth. God, she is quick, Henry thought to himself. Henry shaved down one end of the branch into a short tapered point.

Then Henry reached into his backpack and this time pulled out a hollow steel walking stick tip. He sized it up against the freshly cut taper. Then, he forced it in place over the taper. Once he was satisfied he couldn't push on it any harder with his hands, Henry took the stick and pressed the tip against the sandstone rock with all his might. He tapped the tip a few times to make sure it was secure before he tossed it back to Elizabeth.

"Use this to keep your balance as you walk."

"What am I? Tarzan?"

"C'mon, this isn't so tough. This will be fun."

Elizabeth remained sitting on the rock, holding the walking stick while staring at Henry. "Don't smile, you look so goofy when you smile."

"It's just a couple days like this. That's all I'm asking. Things will be much better in a few days."

"What if they come after us?"

Henry chuckled to himself. "They're not going to come after us. Believe me, we're safe up here. No one is going to care about just one man and his daughter up here."

Henry grabbed his backpack and, in one motion, slung it back on and began walking.

"Yeah, I feel so much better now." Elizabeth stood up slowly and began to follow Henry.

"Don't forget the walking stick," Henry bellowed without looking back. Henry smiled as he heard Elizabeth's footsteps backtrack to retrieve it.

# # #

Babcock raced through the halls of ICE's downtown headquarters. He had called the meeting for 6 p.m. and he didn't want to be late. Babcock didn't want to be late but he was. With his newfound authority, Babcock felt he needed to look the part and stopped off at his home for a change of clothes to something that gave him more of a command aura. In this case, it was a blue blazer and khaki pants to give him a casual and effortless look of being in charge. Babcock pushed open the door to the conference room.

Seated around the conference table were Woteck, Fisher, Alvarez and Park. On the viewing screen behind them was a large blowup of Henry's DMV photo.

"Park, what do you have?"

The Korean American technician began reading from his notes. "Henry Chin. Widowed ten years, one teenage daughter."

"Yes, we know that already. I want to know what his next move is."

"There's a statistically significant probability that he could have changed his name or stolen an identity. It is also possible that he could have gone underground and sought refuge with people sympathetic to his cause. However, between staying put or fleeing, the computer model says it's more likely that he would have fled."

"Again, you have the gift for telling me what I already know. Chin is not here. That means he's gone." Babcock's impatience grew exponentially. "I want answers."

Park fumbled through his notes. "The matrix isn't designed to provide answers like that. It presents patterns based on statistical data based on past actions by those who fit the profile."

"Where did he go?"

Park fumbled through more papers. "Mexico, Canada, Cuba, Ecuador, England, Honduras, Venezuela, Portugal, Bermuda or Guam."

"Which is it?" demanded Babcock.

"The computer says that these are all statistically significant possibilities. It's also a statistically significant possibility that he could have become despondent and committed suicide."

"Why would Chin go to all this trouble to plan an escape just to commit suicide?"

"According to an assessment of his credit card records, he likes show tunes." Park bit his lip before he resumed. "Babcock, the reason why the probabilities are all over the place is because there's nothing very remarkable about him. Part of that is because we simply don't have enough information. But having gone through many 'person of interest' profiles, this guy looks about as dangerous as a substitute teacher."

Agitated, Babcock shoved his finger into Park's face. "That's not your call to make!" Babcock screamed.

Just then, the door to the conference room opened revealing Don. "You're right Mr. Babcock. That's not Agent Park's call to make. It's yours."

"Yes, and I will make that call as soon as these guys give me the information I need!" Babcock slammed his hand down on the table for emphasis.

Don let Babcock's outburst hang in the air for a moment before he broke the silence. "Mr. Babcock, please do not interrogate your colleagues." Don looked around at the other men in the room. "Thank you gentlemen. Get some rest. We've got a busy day tomorrow."

Park, Woteck, Fisher and Alvarez left the room, muttering their good nights to Don. Babcock shuffled through some of the files left behind by Park.

"Tactical question, Mr. Babcock. Why prioritize the background check?"

"I beg your pardon?"

"At the Rose Bowl, the suspect and his daughter created a smoke bomb as a diversion. If they escaped on foot, it was a hot pursuit and you had the resources there to initiate an immediate manhunt. If they had help, then questioning the soldiers about what they saw would have aided in the pursuit. So my question for you is why did you abandon those actions to come back here to assemble a profile when barely an hour ago, we didn't even know his name?"

"Are you questioning my judgment, Director Morgan?"

"Yes I am, Agent Babcock. That is my purview."

"I'm asking you to give me a chance."

"I am giving you a chance. And the first thing you're doing is breaking standard protocol."

"You didn't need to give me the assignment if all you wanted was someone to follow protocol."

"Agent Babcock, you have to demonstrate to me that you can follow the rules before you go and break them."

"The Chinese are an enemy we've never dealt with before. We don't know which ones we can trust and which ones we can't. Before I make a move, before I put the lives of Americans at risk, I need to know everything I possibly can about who we're dealing with. You say Henry Chin is probably unremarkable. Well, he's missing. That makes him remarkable in my book."

"Meanwhile, his trail is getting cold as you conduct your research."

"The one thing we can be sure of is that Henry Chin has no place to go."

"I hope you're right Agent Babcock. What's your next move?"

Babcock was unprepared for that question and struggled to come up with his answer. When he couldn't come up with anything, he relied on his old rhetorical fallback: when in doubt, narrate what just happened. "It was to compile all the information we had on Henry Chin before you dismissed my men."

"Your men? Those are my men Agent Babcock. Don't you ever forget that."

Now, Babcock had to come up with something. He opened his mouth as he prayed for something coherent to come out. "I'll do some data mining." Weak, he thought, but it'll do.

"Agent Babcock, what do you think investigators did before the age of computers?"

"I don't know Director Morgan. What did they do in the good old days?"

Don leaned in nose to nose with Babcock. "I'd be careful about that tone of yours." Babcock matched Don's glare but didn't break eye contact until Don finally ended the mini standoff.

"He has a teenage daughter. You think she can keep a secret? Go talk to some of her friends."

Babcock nodded. "I'll have Alvarez do that."

"No, you do it."

"My team... our team can cover a lot of ground."

"No team, just you."

"Canvassing her acquaintances... that's a bit beneath me," protested Babcock.

"Then it should be very easy for someone who has 'paid his dues.'" Don opened the conference room door. "Shouldn't it?"

Babcock was alone now. He sifted through Elizabeth's file and pulled out her high school class roster. Babcock looked at the photographs of her classmates. Back when he was in high school there was little opportunity for self-expression. Senior portraits required suits and ties for the boys. No facial hair, no long hair, no jewelry. What a difference between the academy he went to compared to public schools today. Babcock felt privileged that he got a good education, which would have been impossible in this ethnic cesspool.

He searched the photos for any teenage boy wearing anything that even remotely looked like a suit. When did individual expression become more important than a good education? He wasn't against public education but Babcock felt that something had changed in the values his father taught him and the values he was seeing today.

People have forgotten that education is a privilege, not a right. If you squander it, or waste it, we have every right to take it away. That this generation of kids seemed unwilling or unable to capitalize on the opportunities they had, galled Babcock. If you won't fight for yourselves, why should I fight for you?

Time was when immigrants took advantage of the opportunities they didn't have in the countries they left behind. Time was when immigrants wanted to blend into America's great melting pot by adopting our customs and the English language.

Mini ghettos like Chinatown disgusted him. Why leave your own country and come to America just to recreate your squalor here? Chinese Americans, Vietnamese Americans, Asian Americans... If you want to come to America, then be Americans.

It was so clear to Babcock that what minorities complained about as racism was the product of an immigrant group's unwillingness to assimilate. Period. End of sentence. He had put up with that attitude his entire life and he was sick of it.

I have nothing against people who come to this country and want to work hard to succeed. Unfortunately, very few immigrants, legal or otherwise, believe that. What guarantee… forget about guarantees… what assurance do we have that minorities are interested in what is best for this country? thought Babcock.

Babcock was sick of people who, and it didn't matter to him if they were minorities or not, advanced quickly in life based on something other than merit. To him, affirmative action was nothing more than grading on a curve and deserving candidates who were mostly Caucasians paid the price. Even though Babcock's career wasn't where he wanted it to be, he believed he was fortunate to have what he had.

Legacy programs that opened doors for Babcock were a necessity against the evil of affirmative action.

Wasn't it obvious to everyone that Director Morgan shouldn't be leading the Southern California District? Babcock believed that Don was nothing more than a calcified artifact from a bygone press conference to please the NAACP. Babcock was ambitious. When did this country start punishing people for their ambition?

Babcock picked up a telephone.

"This is Agent Babcock. I need to get pedigrees on a list of names. Let's start with juvenile criminal records."

§

CHAPTER FIVE

Henry and Elizabeth reached the cusp between the plateau they had just traversed and the canyon ahead. Not quite as large as a canyon but larger than a gully. The creek began to narrow out during this stretch. Henry set down his backpack and found a large boulder to sit down on. He started unlacing his boots. "This is a good place to take a break. Take off your shoes."

"Dad, that's gross." Henry slipped off his boots and removed his socks. He shook them out and hung them on a nearby tree branch.

"Elizabeth, the last thing you want is a blister. Blisters are hard enough to prevent when your shoes fit. Yours don't. C'mon." Reluctantly, Elizabeth sat down next to Henry and began to unlace her sneakers too.

"How much farther?" Henry looked up at the sun and the canyon beyond.

"The place I'm thinking of is about two more miles ahead through this canyon. I figure we'll get there about an hour before sunset. That gives us a little bit of daylight to set up camp before we can rest up for the night."

Henry stuck his feet into the creek and let out a small sigh.

"Dad, that's the water we drink out of," protested Elizabeth.

"The filter will clean it out. Besides, we're heading up stream. My foot water will be in the ocean by the next time we have to refill."

"Give me the bottle now. I want to drink it before you contaminate it." Henry handed her the Nalgene bottle. She took a healthy swig from it. When she was done, she screwed the cap on and handed it back to Henry.

"Here, put some powder on your feet."

"No," said Elizabeth. Henry could tell she was dug in. Ever since her mother's death, Henry had trouble talking with Elizabeth. There was hardly a single conversation they had that didn't end with some kind of an argument. This was more than teenage rebellion. Henry knew she blamed him for something but he could never get her to talk about it. Henry's Brady Bunch fantasy was that he and Elizabeth would have the mother of all shouting matches before she cried and accepted his love for her. Somewhere in Henry's parental value system was a rule that said initiating World War III would be a good thing if it resolved his relationship with his daughter.

Henry reached into his backpack and pulled out an energy bar. He tore it open and offered it to Elizabeth. "Here, you need to keep your strength up." Elizabeth sniffed it before she took a bite and then promptly spit it out.

"That is so nasty." She tossed it back to Henry.

"Believe me, I've had a bunch of these over the years. This is the best tasting one of the lot."

"It's still nasty."

"It's easier to keep your strength up than to regain it," replied Henry.

"Again with the fortune cookie wisdom?"

"Elizabeth, I take full blame for not preparing you for this. I should have taken you on camping trips when you were younger. We should have spent more time together."

"Are you going to tell me stories about all the starving children in China during the war?"

Henry recoiled at Elizabeth's accusation. "That was your grandfather. I was never in a war in China."

"But you're old."

"You've never known life without a cell phone. I remember my first pager. Grandpa had one phone and it had a rotary dial. All your music is digital files. I remember my first CD player. Grandpa listened to the Beatles on vinyl records in mono." As the words came out of Henry's mouth, he knew it was too much but the train was running and he couldn't stop it. "God willing, one day you'll grow up to be old too and tell your kids how hard it was waiting fifteen seconds for your favorite song to download!"

The sound of the gurgling creek was deafening. Henry knew he had lost his temper and was now kicking himself for it. He wanted to say something but his ability to talk was shut down. He needed to hear what Elizabeth had to say first.

Finally, Elizabeth took a deep breath. "You're always right, I'm always wrong. I get it. Now tell me something I don't know!"

For some reason, Henry couldn't say he was sorry. He wanted to apologize but he knew that Elizabeth wouldn't buy it. He had apologized to her before but always seemed to lose his temper again in fairly short order. As many times as they fought, as many times as he punished her, as many times as he lost his temper over and over again, he knew any reasonable person would call bullshit at his apology now.

Elizabeth wasn't going to change. She didn't have to. She didn't know better. Henry did. Henry knew that if they were going to survive, they would have to work together. The only way they could work together was if Henry changed. She was right. She was eighteen now. Henry had to learn how not to treat her like a child.

No, thought Henry, that's the wrong way to think about it. Learn how to treat her like an adult.

Henry shifted his weight on the rock. Out of the corner of his eye, he noticed something in the sand. He stood up and walked over the flat patch of watery gravel for a closer look.

"Come here, take a look at this." Curiosity got the better of Elizabeth. She slipped on the sneakers and trudged over to Henry. Embedded in the sand, about the size of a human hand was a distinct paw print.

"Cougar print," Henry said. Elizabeth was immediately frozen. Her instinct recognized it as the real thing and her impulse to panic had kicked in.

"How do you know it's a cougar? How do you know it's not a bear? Or a wolf?"

"Look at the footprint. The pads are perfectly round. If it were a bear or a coyote, you'd see the claw too."

"Don't cougars have claws?"

"They do. But they're retractable. This is fresh. The cougar probably came by here within the hour."

"Are we in any danger?" Instinctively, Elizabeth gripped Henry's arm.

"Right now? No. We're sitting still. Cougars tend to attack moving targets; prey they can sneak up behind and ambush." Henry realized his words were of little comfort to Elizabeth.

Henry retreated to his backpack. He fished through one of the pockets and found a bright orange bell on a velcro strap.

"I'll attach this bear bell to my backpack. The noise will scare the cougars, bears and coyotes away."

"Won't it let them know where we are?"

"Yeah, it will. But they're wild animals. They're really more afraid of us than we are of them. If they hear us coming, they'll stay away."

"You always talk like you know everything. How do you know you're right?"

How do we know anything? Henry thought to himself. We trust the observations and opinions of people we've never met. Why should my customers at the pharmacy believe me that it's bad to drink grapefruit juice with their medication? 'Because I am right' seemed like an inadequate response.

"I could be wrong," Henry said.

"Now you think you're wrong?" Henry realized he probably picked a bad time to be humble.

"Why don't you take the lead? If cougars are around, they'll attack us from behind. They'll have to eat through my backpack before they hit any vital organs."

"What about me? I don't know where we're going," said Elizabeth.

"Follow the creek. Follow the creek and we can't get lost." Henry wiped his feet dry with his t-shirt before he powdered his feet and slipped his socks back on.

The walls of the canyon rose up high and were fairly steep. There wasn't a clear path along the creek and Elizabeth kept stepping into the water, much to her own annoyance. Behind her was the rhythmic jangle of the bear bell Henry velcroed to the side of his backpack. Elizabeth abruptly stopped.

"Ew!" She pointed to a large pile of feces as she backed away from it. Henry saw the scat and squatted down.

"Are you going to eat it?" asked Elizabeth.

Ignoring her statement, Henry reached out his hand to her. "Hand me your walking stick." Elizabeth handed Henry the walking stick. He poked at the scat with the metal tip. It was moist and didn't fall apart easily. "It's fresh." Henry held his open palm over the scat. "It's still warm. The cougar is close by."

"Is it going to eat us?"

Henry continued to poke at the feces. "I doubt it. You can learn a lot about an animal by what's in its scat. Look."

"I don't want to."

"It's solid and holds its shape. That means it has plenty of water. There's fur and bones in here. Looks like rabbit fur. It's the right color for rabbits up here."

"I don't want to hear it."

"No, sweetheart, this is good news. A cougar would probably only attack us if it were starving. This scat indicates a healthy, well fed cougar. It's not hungry enough to hunt us for dinner. As long as we keep making some noise, it'll be content to stay away from us."

"Is it following us?" Henry looked around.

"Animals are like humans. Following paths is easier than making your own path. This canyon is a natural connector through this area. It's probably well traversed by many species. And it's probably the only source of fresh water for miles. It's probably not following us. We're intruding into its natural habitat." Henry stood up and handed the walking stick back to Elizabeth. Without thinking she wiped the steel tip against the sand.

"C'mon, it's just a little farther up," Henry said. But before they could take a step all the hair on the back of Henry's neck stood up. Without thinking, Henry grabbed Elizabeth and yanked her up along the right side of the gully.

"What the...? Where...?" Then Elizabeth heard what Henry heard: a low rumbling sound. She looked up. On the left side of the canyon were boulders and rocks raining down into the creek. Her legs sudden gave out from under her.

Henry grabbed her and pulled her up the far side of the canyon as hard as he could. "Stay on your feet!" The boulders smashed into the creek below spraying them with water, sand and dirt. Henry shielded Elizabeth with his body. He could feel his backpack being pelted with rocks.

Henry felt Elizabeth curl up underneath him. She screamed but it was the scream that came from helplessness in the face of terror. The rumbling crescendoed and echoed back and forth between the sides of the gully.

Henry tried not to breath in all the dirt that was being kicked up by the rock slide. Henry could feel the ground underneath them shake from the bombardment. Breathe, Henry thought to himself.

As the cacophony of smashing rocks began to die down, Henry allowed himself a small peek over his shoulder. It was like he was watching a slow motion movie. A giant slab of sandstone atop the far side of the canyon cracked away with an ear-splitting squeal. He watched it break away from the canyon wall and freefall into the creek below.

"Don't move!" he screamed at Elizabeth. The sandstone slab pulverized on impact sending a giant spray of water and rock into the air. Henry adjusted his position and tried to cover as much of Elizabeth as he could. Henry shifted his backpack so that his head was covered. A charlie horse would heal but a busted melon... Henry's thoughts were interrupted by a giant smack on his left arm. It felt like a rock. Nothing felt broken. Wasn't a direct hit. Henry kept analyzing what was going on. At least that distracted him from the pain.

The noise slowly subsided. The rain of water and rock ended. Henry looked up. He listened for a second. No new sounds. He rolled himself off Elizabeth who remained curled up and motionless.

Henry looked down at the creek. A haze of dust enveloped the canyon. It was as if the entire eastern wall of the canyon had given away. Henry thought to himself that they were very, very lucky.

"It's over," Henry whispered to Elizabeth. Elizabeth looked up. Her face was covered with a fine rock dust except for where her tears were. Henry offered her his hand and pulled her up onto her feet.

"Take a look. The entire canyon was hit by the rock slide. The direct afternoon sunlight up there must have weakened it. We're lucky we weren't further along in the canyon when it fell. We would have been right in the middle of that."

Elizabeth looked down at the crumbled rock. "So what you're saying is that if we didn't stop to look at cougar shit, we'd be dead?" Henry started to chuckle.

"Yeah, cougar shit saved our lives." Henry looked at Elizabeth. "You okay to walk?"

"Yeah, I'm okay."

"Go ahead, take the lead. Safe bet there aren't any cougars around now."

Elizabeth started climbing over the fallen boulders. Henry gave himself a quick look at his left arm. His tricep had a large black bruise on it. It could have been a lot worse, Henry thought to himself.

# # #

Babcock looked through the two-way mirror into the interrogation room. Eliana Aldana had been sitting there handcuffed for the better part of an hour. Babcock's intent was to let her stew and see how long she could front this tough demeanor. If anything, she looked bored. Out of all of Elizabeth's classmates, Eliana was the only one whose name showed up on a stop and frisk report with her. It was for underaged drinking but Babcock believed that police reports were only the tip of the iceberg when it came to criminal jackets.

Babcock leafed through her file. Mexican, but she was born in the United States. Babcock was willing to bet that she was probably the first in her family to be an American citizen. Threaten her with deporting her parents would be the logical tactic.

Her school records didn't indicate she was a good student. Her grades were middling at best. She had the required courses such as basic English and basic math. A lot of art classes and a typing class were on her transcript. Did they still teach typing? She was definitely going to grow up to be a productive member of society.

Babcock looked at her again. Then he saw the video cameras. He thought about what he was about to do. Probably shouldn't be any tape to go with this, he thought. Some people would decry a White man questioning a minority. Babcock thought about the way things were done in this country and none of it made sense. Black defendants in trials complain that all White juries couldn't be impartial. Yet, when a White person was on trial, the jury verdicts were suspect if the juries were all White. Black juries could be impartial judging a Black man but White juries couldn't be trusted? That was patently absurd to Babcock.

Babcock looked at the paperwork. If he listed Eliana as a 'person of interest' in a terrorist case, a different set of rules kicked in. Rules that didn't require recordings, transcripts or official records. America wanted a clean house, but no one wanted to be the garbage man. Babcock checked the appropriate box.

Babcock straightened his tie and adjusted his jacket. He was about to enter the interrogation room when Don came into the observation room. He looked like he was ready to explode.

"What the hell do you think you're doing?"

"Getting intel."

"Bringing her in for questioning is not what I meant."

"I figured she'd be more willing to talk here."

"I assume you have some evidence?"

"Not yet," said Babcock. "Don't worry, I wasn't going to beat her or anything like that."

"You're not even going to question her at all." Don picks up the phone. "I need an escort, Interrogation One."

"You can't..."

"It's done," ordered Don. "There are still rules we have to follow. We have a tough enough job to do. You know how much the media loves stories about corrupt and abusive law enforcement? That won't happen on my watch."

A dark suited escort entered the observation room. Don turned to Babcock for the coup de grâce. "You're done. I want you sitting at a desk from now on." Don gestured to the escort as they entered the interrogation room.

"My name is Don Morgan. I'm the Director of Operations for the Southern California District. Please accept my apologies, there's been a severe mix up in paperwork. Let me remove those handcuffs."

Babcock couldn't listen to Don's bullshit and left. He paced through the hallway like a wounded animal. Every instinct in his body told him there was something much more to Henry Chin than anyone else was willing to entertain. More than that, he couldn't stand the idea that a keyboard clicking bureaucrat was cock-blocking him from doing his job.

There were two kinds of agents: those who were good field agents and those who were lifers. Lifers were the ones who did things by the book. They advanced because of the time they put in, not necessarily by the quality of their work.

Babcock's father didn't start out that way. He was a decorated soldier who saw plenty of action. What was his reward? A desk job. An administration job. Don had reached the pinnacle of his career. National director wasn't in the cards. Nor was a cabinet position. Don was running out the clock and taking Babcock with him. Babcock was not going to let that happen.

But how?

Henry Chin was the key, of this Babcock was sure. And he was going to need some help.

§

CHAPTER SIX

Henry found the clearing he was looking for. It sat up on a small knoll about thirty feet from the creek. The knoll was surrounded by trees and was fairly flat and level. Henry looked up at the sun and extended his hand to measure the time until sunset. Henry removed his backpack and set it down on the ground. "We'll make camp here for the night. We still have a lot of work to do. Set up the tent, pump some more water and gather up firewood."

Elizabeth sat down on a boulder. Henry couldn't tell if she was tired or mentally burned out. Henry dug into his backpack and pulled out a small folding hand shovel. "Sweetheart, can you look for some firewood? Look for small branches on the ground, about an inch thick?" Elizabeth didn't respond. "Whenever you're ready... probably better to do before it gets dark."

Henry dug a small hole in the center of the knoll. The dirt was dry and tightly packed. Because the shovel was so small, Henry had a hard time getting the leverage he needed. Once he had gotten down about a foot, he searched the area for about a dozen fist-sized rocks, which he placed around the lip of the hole.

Elizabeth didn't move at all while he worked. Henry began searching for kindling and logs for the fire. The area had plenty of deadfall. The question was how long had these branches been lying in the sun. Henry tugged at one of the branches. It broke off easily. Good. These branches will probably get us through the night, Henry thought.

"Elizabeth! Come give me a hand!" After a few seconds, Henry heard her footsteps. "C'mon, a little work now will mean a lot less work later."

"Dad, do you really believe all that motivational speech crap that comes out of your mouth?" Henry pulled on another branch.

"Give me a hand," Henry said. Elizabeth grabbed the branch and together they pulled on it. With some effort, the branch finally snapped off. "It's served me well," said Henry finally answering her question.

"Not everyone can be you." Elizabeth scoured the area for smaller branches. "Everyday you tell me to work hard, study hard."

"Yes."

"But we're up here now. It seems like all that work was for nothing. What good did it do?"

Henry didn't know what to tell her. You could plan all you wanted in life but fate had a way of intervening. For Henry's parents it was a war. For others it was a hurricane or an earthquake that threw a monkey wrench into your life. But how do you explain acts of men? Men who presumably want the same things in life you do?

"Let's get this fire started," said Henry.

"You don't have an answer, do you?"

"Elizabeth, in the right side pocket on my backpack, there should be some hand sanitizer. Can you grab it for me?"

"You can't admit when you're wrong, can you?"

Henry broke off a large piece of bark and cradled some dried grass and kindling in it. He set it down on the ground next to his fire pit. Elizabeth returned with the hand sanitizer. Before she handed it to him she squirted out a dollop for herself.

"No, that's not what it's for!"

"But my hands are dirty."

Henry takes a deep breath. "Toss it over to me." Henry popped open the bottle of hand sanitizer and squirted out a small dollop onto the kindling. "In a pinch, this stuff is a lifesaver. Watch."

Henry took off his glasses and tried to catch what light he could from the setting sun. "Do you know what the main ingredient is in hand sanitizer?"

"Are you asking me?"

"There's no one else around."

"I don't know."

"You put it on your hands all the time. You never wondered what it was?"

"It's sanitizer, Dad. What else do I need to know?"

"It's alcohol. That's why it evaporates so fast and why you need to put lotion on your hands after you use it."

"I do!" Elizabeth was shocked. She never thought about that before. She also never realized it was the hand sanitizer that dried out her skin.

"Alcohol also catches fire very easily... just like this." As if on cue, the kindling on the bark started to smoke. A small blue flame suddenly appeared on the dollop of hand sanitizer. Henry shielded the baby flame with his hands as he gently blew on it. Soon, the kindling started to catch. Henry quickly laid more kindling on top of the flames. Henry kept feeding the flame. Once he was satisfied there were enough twigs aflame to sustain the fire, Henry lifted the piece of bark and slowly lowered the fire into the fire pit.

Henry kept feeding the growing fire progressively larger and larger twigs.

"It's that easy to start a fire with hand sanitizer?"

"Yep."

"Just like at the Rose Bowl?"

"Yep."

"And all those weird colors?"

Henry smiled. He could almost hear the gears grinding inside Elizabeth's head."

"Multi-vitamins have minerals in them. When they burn, they give off pretty colors and a lot of smoke."

Elizabeth stared at Henry. "How do you know that?"

"I'm a pharmacist. We know things."

Then Henry saw a momentary opening. "That's why working hard is important. You never know when what you know will come in handy..."

"Okay, nice try Dad," Elizabeth interrupted. "You really have no idea what you're doing. You just like telling me what to do."

"All right. You caught me. You figured me out."

"Good, you admit it."

"Yep. I admit it." Henry leaned back. "Tell me what to do."

"What?"

"Well, you don't like the choices I've made. Sounds like you've got better ideas."

"Okay. I'm hungry. I want to eat something."

"Food won't be ready for a while. Need to let this fire burn for a bit. Get some good embers going. That's where the real heat comes from. I still need to set up the tent."

"Dad, I'm really hungry."

"I still have the energy bar."

"No. I couldn't spit that out fast enough. There's nothing in your magic backpack?"

"Maybe..." Henry dug around his backpack again. He fished out a black nylon bag. Inside were packets of instant oatmeal, instant soup, freeze-dried foods... nothing that you could eat without adding hot water. He continued to dig through the bag when he heard a clank. "Maybe..." Triumphantly, Henry pulled out a tin of sardines. "Here!"

"Ew! Sardines?"

Henry explained. "These are Portuguese sardines, packed in olive oil and spicy. Probably the best food to have in an emergency. High in protein and high in calories."

"Sardines..."

"Try it." Henry continued to feed the fire as Elizabeth pulled open the tin. The sight of the sardine fillets disgusted her.

"Give it a taste." Henry handed her his camping spork.

Elizabeth took a nibble and made a face. "I need some water."

"The bottle is empty. You'll need to refill it." Elizabeth set down the tin and retrieved Henry's water pump. Henry resumed tending the fire when suddenly he heard Elizabeth scream.

"What? What?" Henry turned in time to watch Elizabeth throw his water pump at a squirrel hovering around the sardines. The squirrel scurried off.

"Elizabeth, haven't you ever seen a squirrel before?"

"I thought it was a rat!"

"You can't tell the difference between a squirrel and a rat?"

"Don't treat me like I'm stupid!" Elizabeth grew defensive.

"If you had a few more A's... no... nevermind. Just get me the pump."

"But..."

"It's gone. The squirrel is gone. There's nothing there that can hurt you."

Elizabeth inched over toward the sardine tin. She peered around and spotted the water pump. She grabbed it and brought it over to Henry.

Henry gently shook it and listened intently as he did. He unscrewed the base and removed the ceramic charcoal filter. Henry nearly cried at the sight of the huge crack in the side of the filter.

"Is it okay?" Elizabeth asked.

Henry sighed. "I hope you like the taste of iodine."

# # #

Little Tokyo was a strange contradiction. Very few Japanese lived in this downtown Los Angeles district anymore. Today, it was mostly a tourist trap for patrons of the newly built sports arena and concert hall. Any resemblance to authentic Japanese culture disappeared a long time ago. Family businesses here have long been replaced by national chains capitalizing on Orientalism: Samurai Steakhouse, The Geisha Tea Room, and The Ginza Hotel.

Babcock liked it because his favorite karaoke bar was a few blocks away from ICE's Central Office building. It was on the second floor in the Japanese Village Plaza. At any given time of day you could hear 80s pop music bleeding out into the streets. Babcock had a hard time feeling nostalgic for an era that never really went away.

Paper lanterns hung from the ceiling. Rough hewn wooden tables were smoothed over with a thick layer of clear polyurethane. Behind the maitre d podium was a prominent sign that declared "Japanese Owned and Operated."

Before the economy went south, this place used to be jam packed with an eclectic mix of businessmen, civil servants and college students. Now it was just college students, specifically trust fund kids and there weren't many of those anymore.

Babcock sat in a booth with Park, both well into their third beer while a Madonna wannabe belted an off key rendition of Respect Yourself.

"I dated this Chinese girl with body image issues," began Babcock. "She asked me if I was bothered by her small breasts and I said..." Babcock held his mouth opened as he muffled his voice, "'I don't care.'"

Park laughed. "I don't have that problem with Korean girls." They both take a swig of beer.

Babcock pointed at the stage. "Did you pick out a song?"

"Nah... pipes just aren't what they used to be."

"Were they ever?"

"Hey, I got more game than you do, White boy," Park retorted good-naturedly. Park looked around for the waitress. "You want another beer?"

"Before we do another round, I wanted to ask you a favor."

"What's up?"

Babcock leaned in and spoke in a hushed whisper. "I need a stat analysis on Henry Chin."

"I'd love to help you. Boss says you're out of the loop on this. There's no way I can run that without setting off alarms all over the system. Don is a by the book kind of a boss. I'm a by the book kind of a guy. Boss says no, boss says no."

"Sometimes you gotta break the rules. Sometimes you have to work on instinct."

Park looked around. Babcock's paranoia was catching. "That may be good for you but it's not something I can live with. Chain of command, following orders... there's a reason why we do things the way we do it. It's not like our job is to find bombs before they explode in playgrounds."

Babcock sized up his friend. When they first met, Babcock had run a secret background check on Fred Park and turned up nothing remarkable. With all the unrest between the United States and China, any person with an Asian face would naturally draw suspicion. Babcock needed to know about the men who had his back. Park fit the stereotype. Good at math, bad at sports. Park wasn't a Christian but Buddhists had a reputation for being peaceful people.

"Look, I'll tell you what I do know about him," whispered Park. "He's a hapless father with a teenage daughter. So we let two slip through the cracks. Out of the fifty thousand we processed today, that's not bad."

"Are you willing to take a chance that the one that got away was the bad guy?" pressed Babcock.

"It's not like we captured him on the battlefield, or his name came up in a wire tap or even if his bank accounts had unexplained money in them. This guy was a nobody."

"How can you be so sure? Henry Chin is Chinese. You're Korean. How can you be sure you're being objective?" Park puts down his beer. "It's a fair question," Babcock emphasized.

Park studied Babcock's face. "A White militia man shoots up a playground full of school children. Could you be objective if you were put on his jury?"

"Of course," Babcock answered.

"You're White, he's White. You can be totally objective?"

"It's not the same thing."

Park waited for the clarification that he soon realized would not be forthcoming.

"Okay, I'm waiting to hear why," he prompted.

"It's just not," Babcock said defensively. "Why do you think White people can't be objective?"

"Because you asked if me, being an Asian, could I be objective dealing with another Asian."

"Can you?"

"If it's not even a question for you, then why is that even a question for me?"

"C'mon Park, we profile people all the time."

"Then why not profile White people when a White person commits a crime?"

Now it was Babcock's turn to study Park's face.

"Virginia Tech was the work of a lone gunman and yet dozens of Asian students were questioned by police."

"A sensible precaution," countered Babcock.

"But if they were looking for a conspiracy, why did they limit themselves to the Asian students? Couldn't the shooter have had White friends?"

"I'm sure they were ruled out right away."

"Because they were deemed to be one of us. And the shooter was considered one of them."

"The shooter was one of them," shot back Babcock defensively.

"Am I one of them?" baited Park. "Or would you stand up for me if any questions arose?"

"Of course, Park. You're one of us. I'd stand right by your side." Babcock took a sip of his beer. "What you need to do is stop fixating on your race."

Park started laughing. "Interesting."

"You've got a problem dealing with race," emphasized Babcock. "You're always talking about Korean Americans. There is no such thing. You're either Korean or American. You can't be both. The fact you keep talking about being Korean makes me wonder how American you consider yourself if the shit ever comes down."

"And you're okay with that? Wow."

"What's 'wow'?" asked Babcock.

"You. You couldn't win with logic or reasoning so you attack me with an unprove-able accusation. It's Rhetoric 101. If you don't like the premise, change the argument."

Babcock tried his best to recover. "I guess we'll have to agree to disagree."

"Why? You didn't even try to persuade me."

"I don't have to."

"You should. Sometimes the 'givens' aren't always given." Park finished his beer. "How are you holding up?" Park asked. "You must have set the record for the quickest promotion and demotion in department history."

"In the movies, no cop ever solves the crime until after he's been suspended. I feel like I'm right on track. You want another beer?"

"Nah. I've got to get home. Thanks for the beer." Park tossed down a few dollars for the tip and headed out the door.

Babcock wanted another beer. He needed a moment to calm down. He silently congratulated himself for not losing his temper. He always hated it when people assumed he was wrong. He had a good education, just as good as anyone he worked with. But racism was destructive and had poisoned many of the basic principles the country was founded on. At some point, minorities had to stop using it as an excuse for their own failure.

Like it or not, China was our enemy now. This was the new reality. He would be failing in his duty if he ignored that. Babcock waved his hand, trying to get the wait-ress's attention.

There was a commotion outside. Babcock thought he heard Park's voice scream-ing. Babcock flashed his badge at the maitre d as he ran out of the karaoke bar.

On the street Babcock saw Park lying face down. Two Army privates had Park's hands bound behind him with plastic ties. They were methodically going through his wallet when Babcock flashed his badge at them.

"I'm Babcock. ICE."

Park called out, "I wasn't lying. I was just with Agent Babcock."

"Yeah, I'll verify that. He's one of ours."

One Army private spoke up. "He refused to submit to a random blood test."

"I tried to explain but they wouldn't listen."

The Army private continued, "But if he's one of yours, we'll release him into your custody."

Babcock hesitated. "No, rules are rules. If his number came up, his number came up."

"Babcock, what are you doing?"

"These men are just doing their jobs. Relax." The Army privates pulled Park up into a sitting position. A medic came over with an electronic bullet syringe.

"Hey, Babcock..."

"You have nothing to hide, right?" Babcock could see the fear in Park's eyes turn into rage.

"You're a sonuvabitch, Babcock." The medic used the bullet syringe to draw a blood sample from Park.

"If it'll make you feel any better, I'll submit to a blood test too."

The lights on the electronic bullet syringe started flashing. The medic read the results off the small LCD screen.

"Mitochondrial DNA test positive. He's of Chinese descent."

Park protested. "What? I'm Korean! I'm Korean!"

"Yeah, that's more than enough," said the medic.

"One drop of blood, Park. One drop of blood," taunted Babcock.

"I'm Korean!"

Babcock sized up his former colleague. "I don't know what you are."

The Army privates pulled Park up on his feet and escorted him to a waiting van.

Babcock continued, "But I do know you're an illegal."

As the Army privates put Park into the van he turned back and yelled to Babcock, "Go fuck your mother!"

Self-satisfied, Babcock responded, "A White man would have said 'die mother-fucker!'" The Army privates closed the doors to the van and went about conducting more random blood tests.

Babcock returned to the karaoke bar and settled his bill with the maitre d. Babcock found himself unnerved by Park's betrayal. Agitated was more like it. He had worked side by side with Park since he came to work for ICE. He had his suspicions but he saw the way everyone treated Park so he figured he must have been thoroughly vetted by Homeland Security.

When you're sworn in as a federal employee, part of your oath is to protect America from all enemies, both foreign and domestic. It didn't matter if you worked for ICE, the Treasury Department or mopped floors at the V.A. hospital, that oath meant something sacred.

Babcock took a seat at the bar and ordered another beer. Babcock tried not to pay attention to the singer who was commemorating the arrest outside with a rendition of China Girl. Good thing the song doesn't have any high notes or else I'd have to shoot you, Babcock thought.

The beer went down quickly. Babcock still couldn't quite calm himself so he ordered another one. The bartenders must have changed shifts. A tall, wispy Japanese girl tapped this beer for him. She wore a black tank top exposing her tattooed arms.

"You just start your shift?" he said trying to make his small talk seem as casual as possible.

"Been here all night," she responded without even making eye contact.

Babcock grabbed one of the cocktail napkins and scrawled something on it. He slid it over to the bartender.

"What is this?"

"You should give me a call if ever you're in a jam."

She gave him a smile. Babcock took out some bills to pay for his beer but she waved him off. "It's on me."

Babcock still put down a few dollars for a tip. "What time does your shift end?"

"I close tonight but my boss has very strict rules."

"We all have rules to follow."

She batted her eyes at him and held up the napkin. "If I ever have to call this number, who should I ask for?"

"Nick. My name is Nick Babcock. And yours?"

"Everyone here calls me Sasha."

"That's not a traditional Japanese name."

"No, it's not. Nick Babcock? Should I call you Officer Babcock? Or Detective Babcock?" she flirted.

"Agent Babcock," he confessed.

"Well Agent Babcock," Sasha started, "I'll be sure to keep this in a safe place." She tucked the napkin down her bra. "Good night."

Babcock didn't quite know how to react. He thought things were going so well. He was going to have to deal with his agitation some other way. He finished his beer and left.

As soon as he was out of the bar, Sasha took the napkin and tossed it in the trash. "Asshole," she muttered to herself.

§

CHAPTER SEVEN

Henry finally had a chance to sit down. The tent was standing and he had strung a clothesline between two trees to hang their clothes and equipment on. His backpack was carabinered to the clothesline so it would stay off the ground.

The campfire provided some warmth but little light as Elizabeth huddled close to it.

Henry clicked on a small, battery-operated lantern as he searched his backpack for his mess kit. Once he found it, he clicked off the lantern.

"Can you leave that on? It's dark."

"I want to conserve our batteries for as long as I can." Henry picked up his mess kit began to walk over to the creek.

"Where are you going?"

"Just getting some water."

"Keep talking so I know you're there." Henry started singing an old show tune from The Music Man. "I said talk, not sing," Elizabeth complained.

"My singing will keep the wild animals away," Henry joked.

"Keep singing then."

Henry returned with a pot full of water. He set it down gingerly on the rocks over the fire. Henry added an iodine tablet to the water before he sat back down. Then he crumbled a Flintstones vitamin into the pot.

"What's that for?" asked Elizabeth.

"Vitamin C helps kill the taste of the iodine. Let that sit there and come to a boil."

Elizabeth asked, "Don't you have a stove?"

"I do, but we have a fire now. We may as well use it and save the fuel for later. I don't know how long we're going to be up here and I want to be prepared in case Uncle Clyde can't get us everything we need."

Henry looked at the daughter he hardly knew. He wanted so much to talk to her, to get to know her better but where to begin?

"Read any good books lately? What about TV shows? Music?"

"Why do you think you can act like my father now?"

"I am your father."

"I wish you weren't. Eliana told me her family was willing to hide me. I wish they did."

"Then you would be in the repatriation camp right now and her family would be under arrest."

"You don't know that. You keep talking like you know everything but you don't know anything."

"Elizabeth, I wasn't put here on earth to make your life more comfortable. My job is to prepare you for being a grown up. Okay, I admit I haven't done the best job but I haven't given up."

"I'm eighteen. Your job is done. Honestly, I don't know what mom ever saw in you."

As if on cue, the water came to a boil. Henry fished out a packet of freeze-dried beef stew from his backpack. He tore it open and poured the boiling water into the packet. He resealed the packet closed to let it steep. The campfire continued to quietly crackle.

Henry started humming quietly to himself, however after a few bars, he couldn't help himself and started singing. "Dream of now, dream of then."

"Dad, stop singing."

Henry paused for a moment but then decided to continue. "Dream of a love song, that might have been."

"Dad, stop it. You're embarrassing me."

"I'm embarrassing you? In front of whom?" Elizabeth instinctively looked around. Henry continued, "Are you so concerned about what other people think about you that you'll freak out even when there's no one else around?"

"Dad, you don't understand what it's like. It's hard enough to fit in."

"What is it like?" asked Henry.

Elizabeth was exasperated with her father. Finally, she blurted out, "Don't you own any clothes that fit?"

"That's it? Most of the clothes I buy, I buy when they're on sale. But, by the time they're on sale, all the normal sizes are gone. You can be very comfortable if—"

"If you don't care what you look like," Elizabeth finished. "Yeah, yeah, you already said that. Is the food ready yet?"

"Another minute or two." Henry poked at the fire. Henry wanted to tell her a story but couldn't pull anything out of his memory, so he just started talking.

"Years ago my buddies and I were looking for a new watering hole because the bar we usually go to was shut down for serving minors." That last part was a lie but Henry felt obligated to protect his moral standing as her parent.

"We found this karaoke bar. It was great. All we did was drink and make fun of everyone who sang. One night a woman caught my eye. I tried to strike up a conversation with her. She wouldn't say a word to me. She wouldn't let me buy her a drink. So I got up and sang that song to her. Oh, my buddies let me have it. They heckled me worse than anyone we had seen up until then. But afterwards, that woman let me buy her a drink. That woman was your mother."

"Yeah, I kind of figured that out."

"You're here because I don't give a damn about what other people think about me." Henry opened the freeze-dried. "Stew is ready."

Henry handed Elizabeth the bag and a plastic spork. Elizabeth took a bite. The meat was chewy and the vegetables had no taste. "Eat what you can, I'll finish the rest."

Elizabeth ate silently. The night was quiet except for some chirping crickets and the crackling fire.

"You don't have a TV set in your backpack, do you Dad?"

"If I did, I wouldn't be able to get cable." Henry wondered what was going through her mind. At home she always had the TV on, or was listening to her iPod or was watching the latest video of something or other on YouTube, or was engaged in a Facebook chat. Henry had often wondered how a human being could exist with so much noise around them. When did she have time to be alone with her thoughts?

"You really want to check your email, don't you?"

"Dad, nobody emails anymore. It's all text messages."

That cinched it for Henry. His daughter was jonesin' for an info fix. He had seen it in some of his younger co-workers at the pharmacy. Anytime there was a lull or a pause, they'd check their phones to see if there were new messages or updates. Henry was alarmed at the frequency they checked. He liked to stay informed as much as the next person but the need for information stimulus was almost addictive. Henry wondered if kids today have an over-inflated sense of importance. All that information was fleeting. What was important yesterday was long forgotten by today. Henry believed his daughter was going through information withdrawal.

Henry watched Elizabeth struggle to eat a few more bites of the stew. "I think I have some Tabasco sauce if that helps."

"I don't like spicy foods."

Henry started to accept the fact that he probably lost Elizabeth for tonight. Emotionally, socially he could sense that she had withdrawn inside herself and there would be little chance of breaking through her defenses.

"Here, you can have the rest." Elizabeth handed back the bag of freeze-dried stew to Henry.

"Eat up. I've had an energy bar and a tin of sardines already today."

"No, I can't eat anymore. I want to go to sleep."

"The tent is all set up. Just take off your shoes before you go in."

Without a word, Elizabeth stood up and walked over to the tent. She unzipped the tent and stepped inside with her shoes still on. Henry was about to say something but suppressed the impulse. He felt bad for her. He had convinced himself that escaping with Elizabeth was the only choice they had. What if he was wrong? What if she was better off in the repatriation camps? Henry quickly pushed the thought out of his head. Self-doubt was an indulgence he couldn't afford.

Henry knew that the Japanese internment camps the U.S. had set up during World War II were hardly fun and games. Many young Nisei men died in Europe on the battlefield to prove their loyalty to a country that treated them as enemy collaborators solely by virtue of their race. The ones that couldn't fight suffered in their own way: depression, addiction and suicide.

Inside the tent Elizabeth felt her way around. She had a little bit of light from the campfire glow. On the ground was a thin foam pad, a sleeping bag and a large bath towel Henry had laid out for her. Elizabeth rolled up the towel to use as a makeshift pillow. Then she climbed into the sleeping bag and tried to fall asleep.

She couldn't get comfortable curled up on her side because the ground was too hard. Every time she rolled over, she heard a weird noise, like tin foil crinkling. She patted herself down and found a receipt in her pocket from something she had purchased a while back. Great, she thought to herself. Everything that's important to me is in three suitcases at the bottom of this mountain and what do I get to keep? A receipt from the mall.

She didn't want to lie flat on her back because she felt too exposed. She was never a back sleeper anyway. She was miserable. The only comfort she wanted was to sleep curled up in a ball. She closed her eyes and did all she could to keep from crying.

Henry could hear her toss and turn inside the tent. Henry finished the stew. He could taste the iodine but he was used to it from all his times camping. He sealed the empty freeze-dried bag and folded it up as small as it could go. Henry tossed it into a plastic bag he had hung from the clothesline as a makeshift garbage bag. Then he licked the spork clean. He would have to rinse it off in the creek before the next time Elizabeth would need to use it. Henry set aside the pot of water for tomorrow morning.

Henry grabbed a bivvy sack out of his backpack and laid it down on the ground. He found the walking stick and placed it about an arm's length away. He washed his socks in the creek with some camping soap and wrung them out as best he could. Using clothespins he fastened his socks to the clothesline to air dry. These would have to make due, Henry thought. Elizabeth is wearing all my spare socks. He then took off his pants and boots and hung them up. He looked at his hiking boots. Not as durable as the Corcoran's he wore in the 82nd but they held up well.

Henry shook as much dirt and dust off his feet before he crawled inside the bivvy bag. Using his baseball cap and bandana as a pillow, Henry lay flat on his back and closed his eyes. He took off his glasses and held them in his hand as he folded his arms across his chest.

Henry counted slowly to himself as he inhaled through his nose, feeling his chest rise and fall. Henry was surprised at how much tension he was holding in his body, especially in his shoulders, neck and jaw. He would have to pay more attention to how much stress he was holding onto and consciously let it go.

Henry took a few more deep breaths. He could hear Elizabeth tossing and turning in the tent. He knew that as tough as it was for him, it was much worse for her. Yes, Henry thought to himself, this is the right choice. To Henry, anything was better than living with that feeling of complete helplessness. It was a lesson he hoped Elizabeth would learn.

Elizabeth's tossing and turning continued. Henry began to quietly hum. Henry noticed Elizabeth's tossing and turning had abated slightly. Henry repeated the melody, humming quietly until he heard Elizabeth snore softly.

# # #

The street lights had been turned off to conserve energy. Babcock silently cursed that decision because it made the street signs nearly impossible to read at night. His badge was still good enough to get him past the checkpoint but this entire neighborhood was now a ghost town. Babcock had to point his car's headlights at the street signs so could read them. After twisting his way through this residential area, he finally found the house he was looking for.

Babcock parked his car and searched the glove compartment. He was sure he had a flashlight but he couldn't find it. He popped open his trunk figuring he had one in his emergency kit but no luck there either. Screw it, Babcock thought to himself.

Babcock walked up to the front door of Henry Chin's house. The door was unlocked. He pushed it open and stepped inside. He let his eyes adjust to the darkness. The house hadn't been empty for long but already, it had a stale, musty odor to it.

Babcock reached for the light switch and flipped it. Nothing. They must have taken the entire neighborhood off the power grid. Babcock fished a cigarette lighter out of his pocket and gave it a flick. The way the light from the flame danced on the walls gave the house an eerie haunted feeling.

Babcock spied the family portrait. He wiped the dust off it. Henry's wife was White. That was good to know. That explained why his daughter looked so strange. Not really strange. Exotic.

Babcock let the flame go out on his lighter and let his eyes adjust to the darkness again. Boxes were everywhere, strewn about haphazardly. Babcock would have to move slowly so he wouldn't trip over anything. As he climbed up the staircase, every step creaked beneath him.

He turned into the first bedroom at the top of the stairs. This was definitely a girl's bedroom. Anything that was store bought had been hand decorated with beads, buttons or paint. It was as if the owner had to customize everything. On her desk were cups filled to the brim with colored pencils and magic markers. Scattered about was a menagerie of origami creatures. Butterflies seemed to be her favorite.

On the nightstand next to the bed was a photograph of mother and daughter. Elizabeth was a little bit older in the photograph. He could see the family resemblance more easily in this picture. This was an odd family, Babcock thought. Unusual, not typical. To each her own.

Babcock reached into his pocket and pulled out his cell phone and hit the speed dial. He got dumped directly into the voicemail system. "Hey, it's me. Was thinking about you. Haven't talked to you in a while. We should catch up." Babcock was about to hang up the phone when he saw that it already had. Unsure if his message went through, Babcock hit redial.

"It's me again. I left you a message just a moment ago but wasn't sure if it took. Just wanted to make sure you got it. In case you didn't I was just saying we haven't talked in a long time and we should catch up. Give me a call when you get a chance. I'd really like... would love to catch up." Babcock listened for a moment before he hung up the call. He wasn't any surer if the second call went through but he let it go. Another try and she'd probably think he was stalking her.

The long day and all the beers were starting to catch up with Babcock. I'll stay here a little bit longer, thought Babcock. At least until she calls me back.

He wandered out of Elizabeth's bedroom and into the master bedroom. Henry's room was at the opposite end of the spectrum. There was virtually nothing personal in view. No photos, no jewelry. Austere and undecorated. It was as if all Henry did was come here to sleep.

"Henry Chin, who are you?" muttered Babcock out loud.

Babcock opened the dresser drawer. Socks, t-shirts, underwear. Nothing unusual. An American flag pin. How could he leave that behind? wondered Babcock. Babcock yawned. A jewelry box with cufflinks. Henry didn't seem like the cufflinks kind of guy. Babcock opened the box but now fatigue had caught up with him. His eyes couldn't quite focus.

Babcock sat down on the bed... and then put his feet up. Before he knew it, he was snoring. He hadn't fallen asleep so much as he passed out from exhaustion.

In the jewelry box was exactly the clue to Henry Chin that Babcock was searching for. His realization would have to wait until morning to register. For now, Babcock drifted off into the kind of sleep that was more akin to a coma that healed physical injuries rather than the kind of sleep that restored the soul.

Babcock had intended to use this exercise to see if he could get inside Henry's mind and anticipate his next move. Maybe it was the exhaustion that wore down his normal defenses. He felt his emotions were very close to the surface and was surprised about what he felt.

Babcock was jealous. Henry's wife was beautiful. He had this house while Babcock could barely afford his studio apartment. It didn't seem fair that Henry had all this being Chinese and all. Babcock momentarily felt weird coveting something that a criminal had. When he thought about all the special breaks that Henry must have had that helped him in his life, Babcock felt a small amount of rage from the pit of his stomach.

Why am I not entitled to this? Why am I not married to a beautiful woman and living in my own house? That thought locked itself into a repeating loop in Babcock's mind as he finally drifted out of consciousness.

Babcock's arms succumbed to gravity and fell down by his side. The cufflink box fell out his hand and hit the floor but the noise wasn't enough to stir Babcock awake. With his other hand, he clung to his cell phone almost willing it to ring.

The jewelry box lay open on the floor, its contents jarred loose and sitting nearby on the floor.

The ambient light coming in through the window glinted off Henry Chin's Airborne Infantry combat pin.

§

Chapter Eight

The rumble of the C-130 transport plane was deafening. Private Henry Chin sat wearing his full compliment of battle rattle. It was barely six hours ago he was rousted out of the barracks in the pre-dawn hours at Fort Bragg along with the rest of his company. If there was any shit going down in the world that involved the United States, the 82nd Airborne was a ready deployment team, prepared to be anywhere in the world within 24 hours. 'Death From Above' was their motto and Private Chin was ready to live up to that.

Private Chin ran through the various scenarios in his head. Even though they had been in the air for an hour, it was still possible this was still a training exercise. Military pilots needed to log in hours just like the rest of them. Training missions were conducted like the real thing. Equipment check, buddy check, two hours on the tarmac, weapons issued. Pallets full of ammo, rations, GP-Mediums and other equipment were stacked high in the cargo section of the plane. All these elements suggested the real thing. However, no one was issued parachutes. If this were a training mission, why not go all the way? After all, they were the 82nd Airborne.

Private Clyde Wilson leaned over and whispered to Private Chin. "Do you think we'll finally get to fight Russians?"

Private Chin thought about it. "I doubt it. If this is a real deployment, we're not leaving the hemisphere."

"How do you mean?"

"If we were going to engage the Russians somewhere in Eastern Europe, they would have short hopped us over to Langley and put us on a bigger plane."

"Makes sense," concurred Private Wilson. Every American lived with anxiety about 'the bomb,' or 'mutually assured destruction,' or any euphemism that described the end of life as we knew it. Before he graduated high school, Private Chin had applied for an appointment to West Point. During his interview he was asked, 'If you had to push the button, would you do it?' Private Chin wondered if his answer had cost him the appointment. It was a question that private citizen Henry Chin was unprepared for so he ended up telling the truth. "If I was ordered to push the button, I would push the button."

"And if it were your decision?"

"I don't know," said Henry. He didn't get the appointment so he enlisted. Henry wanted to serve. He needed to prove himself. If two men run a foot race and one comes in first, there is very little room to complain about preferences and favoritism. Henry believed the U.S. Army was where he could be judged solely for his abilities. Henry wanted that chance.

Just then, the company XO, Lieutenant Morris came out and gave them the signal. When they had boarded the plane, they were given sealed envelopes with their orders that they weren't to open until they got the signal. Private Clyde Wilson tore open his envelope. He was shocked at what he read.

"Panama?" he said. He turned to Private Chin. "Fucking Panama?"

"Good thing we did all that Arctic weather training," quipped Private Chin.

"Fuck, this is a real mission," complained Private Wilson.

"Fuck, we're not going get our stars for jumping into a combat zone." The entire company of about sixty guys were now all visibly annoyed about their deployment into Panama. They were young guys, under the age of twenty, and all with a surplus of testosterone. They were all arrogant, cocky and had an air of indestructibility about them. Not only had all of them passed basic training with flying colors, they had to be distinguished enough to be recommended for the 82nd Airborne where they had to pass an even more rigorous training course just to qualify. Everyone on this plane was an elite soldier. Everyone on this plane was disappointed.

Private Chin was just like everyone else in his company. He had proven his physical abilities and was recently made leader of his squad. He had that swagger but wanted to test himself in the shit. He wanted that chance but wasn't sure if he would get it in Panama. He could see everyone's disappointment and decided to do something about it. Private Chin stood up and led the company in a call and response chant:

"Airborne Daddy's gonna take a trip,
C-130 rolling down the strip.
Jump up hook up shuffle to the door
Jump right out and count to four.
If my chute don't open wide
Tell my momma I really tried.
Pin my wings upon my chest

Bury my ass in the front leaning rest!"

They kept up the cadence for a few more rounds before they nodded off for the rest of their flight to Panama.

The company unloaded the cargo onto the tarmac. The sun blazed down on them. The humidity was worse than Florida and the bugs were going to be an issue. Two hours they sat. Two hours of 'hurry up and wait.' They got flack from some passing Navy Seabees calling them 'Hollywood soldiers." They kind of were. They had their M-16s and their full battle rattle but hadn't been issued ammo yet. They looked the part but couldn't do shit.

The C-130 was refueled for its return flight back to the states. Private Chin watched the soldiers board the plane for America while body bags were loaded into the cargo section. Private Chin leaned over to Private Wilson. "When we go home, we're sitting up front. We're ain't riding in the back."

"Amen," said Private Wilson.

The light started to play tricks with Henry's eyes. The sky was the wrong color. Henry stared up and squinted before he realized what the problem was: he was in that state between asleep and awake. He thought about his breathing and tried to keep it slow and steady. Something was wrong and right now, he had the advantage because, to the casual observer, he was still asleep.

Henry was curled up on his side when he opened his eyes. His lids were gummed shut but he still managed to force them open. It was probably about a half hour before sunrise. They sky was glowing with light but everything was blurry: the rocks, the trees. But they moved naturally with the gently sway of the wind. He slowly put on his glasses.

Coming into focus was a rattlesnake coiled up, flicking its tongue at Henry. Henry took a slow, deep breath as he reached behind him and felt the ground. He found the walking stick and wrapped his hand around it tightly. Once Henry had his grip on the walking stick, he held his breath as he swung it around.

Elizabeth woke up. The blue and white colors of the tent glowed brightly in the morning sun. It wasn't a nightmare, she thought. This is really happening. She could hear her father moving about outside. Her shoulder was stiff from sleeping on the hard ground. She scratched her head and wondered when was the next time she'd be able to take a hot shower.

She stretched out her shoulder to get the blood flowing. She unzipped the tent and stepped out. She rubbed her eyes. Henry had stoked the fire back to life and was boiling water in the pot.

"What are you making?"

"Good morning Elizabeth. Just made some ramen noodles. You want some?"

"Smells good. I'm so hungry." Henry handed her the pot and a spoon. She gingerly took a bite. She found a small piece of over cooked chicken and bit it. "This tastes good."

Henry offered her the bottle of Tabasco sauce. She took it and shook out a few drops. "I normally don't like spicy food but I just have a huge craving for it right now." Elizabeth ate the entire pot.

"Do you want more?" Henry offered.

"Yeah. Is there anymore chicken?"

"Chicken?" Henry asked.

"This is chicken, isn't it?" Henry didn't say anything. Then Elizabeth saw it. Over the fire pit, Henry had built a small rotisserie and was roasting a rattlesnake.

"We had a visitor this morning," Henry said sheepishly. Henry couldn't tell what emotion was on her face, if it was anger or horror. Finally Elizabeth handed Henry back the pot.

"Can you make some more for me?" she asked.

"Of course." Henry took the pot over to the creek and refilled it. He set it down on the fire pit, making sure that it was balanced properly.

"It'll take a few minutes for it to come to a boil," said Henry. He stood up. "I'm going to break down the tent. We've still got a good long hike ahead of us today."

Elizabeth sat and stared at the pot of water. Without a television, without a radio, without her cell phone, this was the most exciting entertainment available.

Henry unzipped the tent and took off his shoes before he climbed inside. He knelt down and began to roll up the sleeping bag and tie it up. Henry's lower back was giving him problems. I'm getting old, Henry thought to himself. He stretched his arms upward to try to loosen his lower back when his hand hit something. Henry looked up. Hanging down from the apex of the tent was a paper receipt folded into an origami butterfly.

#

Don sat at his desk shuffling through papers. The first thing a casual observer might notice about his office was that there was no computer sitting on his desk. The giant CRTs had gone the way of the dinosaurs and so had the flat screen LCD monitors. Most agents were issued their own data tablets. Don had one but kept it locked in his bottom drawer. Don told people that he was an old schooler, preferring to read actual paper books rather than buying an e-reader. Or that he preferred ink and newsprint over pixilated data pushed onto an iPad. He didn't mind coming across as an antisocial curmudgeon throwback but the truth was he didn't have the patience to learn computers. He spent a week with IT to learn how to read emails on his smartphone but he never hit reply. Instead, he'd call the person back. The benefit of working this way was that he had dozens, if not hundreds, of phone numbers memorized. Also, it was easier to read a person through a phone conversation than through an email. Besides, Don was the director of his region: Rank has its privileges.

Don's secretary buzzed him. Don knew he was old school. He never got used to calling secretaries 'Administrative Assistants.'

"Agent Babcock here to see you sir," said the disembodied voice on the intercom.

"Send him in," replied Don. It's too early in the morning for this shit.

Babcock dropped a military personnel file on Don's desk. "What's this?" Don opened it and was greeted with an 8x10 color photo of a very young Henry Chin in his full dress Class A uniform, posed before an American flag.

"Corporal Henry Chin, 82nd Airborne, 274th Division, Fifth Battalion, Charlie Company. This man has the training to be a domestic terrorist and we were the ones who trained him."

Don looked down at the file and quickly scanned through the pages. How did we miss this? he wondered. Why didn't his military record show up in the background check? "How did you figure this out?" Don asked.

Babcock dropped Henry's combat wings on Don's desk. "I found this in his house."

"You searched his house?"

"It was the logical place to look."

Don continued to scan Henry's service record. "I assume you've looked through this. Any indication that he could have turned? I'm seeing a clean psych eval, no reprimands for insubordination, no gigs of any kind. According to this Henry Chin was a rock soldier."

"You know as well as I do, a man's service record doesn't always tell the whole story. Turn the page," Babcock said smugly.

Don did. The next dozen or so pages of Henry's service record were heavily redacted. Not only did Henry's service record not tell the whole story, it told no story at all. Don reached for the telephone and dialed.

"This is Director Morgan. I need access to military personnel records." Don leafed through Henry's file searching for any clues. "Yes, Corporal Henry Chin, 82nd Airborne, 274th Division, Fifth Battalion, Charlie Company." Don continued to scan the pages and found what he was looking for. "Operation Blue Spoon." Don waited for the reply. "Director Donald Meyers Morgan. Authorization foxtrot, kilo, lima, eight, five, two, juliet, whiskey." Don waited for the forthcoming reply. "Thank you. Route the data to terminal..." Don looked up at Babcock.

"Five five nine," Babcock finished.

"Route the data to terminal five five nine. Thank you." Don hung up the phone and sighed as he addressed Babcock. "Tell me what you find."

"Yes sir," said Babcock.

"Hang on a sec Babcock," signaled Don. "Tell me, what happened to Fred Park last night. What's his disposition?"

"Sir?"

"Don't play dumb with me. I know you were with him when it went down."

"Director Morgan, census archives confirmed that his maternal grandmother had a Chinese surname that could also be Korean. Lab results confirmed the field test. Fred Park is Chinese."

"She died before he was born. Maybe he never knew," corrected Don.

"Doesn't matter. He lied to us. That alone is grounds for dismissal."

"Agent Babcock, he probably didn't know. How far up your family tree can any of us go?"

Babcock turned and faced Don directly and spoke with grave seriousness. "Phineas Babcock came to America on the Mayflower. Ignorance is no excuse. Is that all?"

"Get out of here," muttered Don. Don knew he had to remain impartial and emotionally detached from his job but that task was getting more and more difficult.

Babcock fired up Terminal 559. The confidential information protocol was counter-intuitive like most aspects of government bureaucracy. Sensitive and classified information was routed to a communal terminal in the middle of the bullpen so that the requestor would be conspicuous to the rest of the team. This was to deter agents from discreetly pulling up DMV records of suspected cheaters. Of course, that didn't stop anyone who happened to be walking by from glancing over your shoulder.

Babcock keyed in his user name and password and up popped the splash screen for Operation Blue Spoon. It wasn't a black ops mission or even a covert op. The U.S. had committed troops to protect international ships in the Panama Canal from civil unrest. And yet it was a classified mission. There had to be a reason.

Babcock pulled up the service records of the men who were part of Blue Spoon. One by one, he clicked through them until one happened to catch his eye. It was the photo of a young, wirey, African American soldier. Something about this man rang a bell. Babcock pulled out his laptop and turned it on. After logging in, he pulled up the records at the Alhambra checkpoints. On the morning that the Chinese Americans had to report to the repatriation assembly centers, Henry Chin was visited by an African American male. Babcock pulled up the surveillance photo and compared it to the service record in front of him. The logs confirmed his suspicion. He had found the connection.

Babcock raced back to Don with the news. He pushed past his administrative assistant and burst into Don's office.

"I found the connection," Babcock announced.

"What is it?"

Babcock glanced quickly around the room and didn't see Don's computer. "Follow me." Babcock led Don out of his office and back to the bullpen.

"Private Clyde Wilson. Basic training at Fort Dix, same as Chin. 82nd Airborne, Fort Bragg, same as Chin. Both deployed to Panama for Operation Blue Spoon. After he was discharged he lived in Florida, same as Chin. Moved to California, same as Chin. Once they met in basic training, these two have been as thick as thieves, never living more than twenty miles apart from each other."

Don was still skeptical. "That doesn't necessarily mean..."

"Operation Blue Spoon, Private Chin had forty seven confirmed kills. This man is a trained killer and he has a partner. There's your conspiracy."

Don felt his body instinctively kick into 'cover your ass' mode. If Chin and Wilson were behind any more violence, he would have a lot of explaining to do. It would probably mean his job.

Don gently ushered Babcock aside and took his place at the terminal. "Look away for a second," Don requested. Babcock looked away as Don logged onto the terminal. Don accessed the security alert screen and upgraded Henry Chin's threat level to 'Imminent.' He then added Clyde Wilson's name and information to a new security warning and set his threat level at 'Imminent' as well.

Don turned to Babcock. "Go pick him up."

Babcock smiled. "Yes sir!"

Echo Park is one of the older sections of Los Angeles. Clyde's house probably could have used a new coat of paint and some Scott's Turf Builder to fix the dirt patches in his front yard. The houses here were small, much smaller than houses in other, more affluent Los Angeles neighborhoods. Most of the people who lived on this street had been living here for over thirty years, raised families and entertained grandchildren on the weekends.

A Department of Water and Power utility truck pulled up in front of Clyde's home. Hidden from view was SWAT leader Officer Sonya Yamamoto. Conspicuously Japanese, she wore her hair in a long ponytail. She signaled to her team, five guys with MAC 10s and waited.

Babcock climbed out of the truck in his meter reader disguise. As casually as possible, he walked up the front walkway.

Inside the garage, Clyde tossed a case of bottled water into the back of his cargo van when he spotted some movement in his front yard. Something was wrong about this meter reader. His body language was all wrong. He had the wrong build and the wrong face for this kind of job. Out of the corner of Clyde's eye, he noticed the DWP truck out front but he also spotted the moving shadows of all the feet underneath it.

The doorbell rang. "Shit!" Clyde said out loud as he realized his home was about to be raided.

Babcock looked back at SWAT Officer Yamamoto and gave her a subtle nod. She gave her men the signal and they sprung into action. They converged at the front door with a battering ram.

BAM!

Clyde heard the crash as he shoved the key into his van's ignition and turned over the engine.

Inside the house, SWAT Officer Yamamoto heard the engine start. "The garage!" she screamed. She and her men made it out the front door just in time to watch Clyde's white cargo van smash its way out of the garage and screech down the driveway. The tires squealed as Clyde turned the cargo van away from his house.

The SWAT team drew their weapons but couldn't take the shot. There were too many innocent bystanders on the street that could end up in the crossfire. Babcock ran out into the street. His weapon was drawn. He wanted to shoot someone but couldn't.

SWAT Officer Yamamoto finished talking on her walkie. "He just blew through our roadblock."

§

CHAPTER NINE

Henry led the way up the incline. There wasn't an established path up here as they kept close to the creek. Henry had managed to pack up their camp quickly so they could cover as much distance as they could before the sun got too high in the sky. Early morning and late afternoon were the best times for covering a lot of ground.

"Dad!" beckoned Elizabeth.

"It's not time for a break," responded Henry.

"Dad..." repeated Elizabeth.

"What?" Henry turned around. Elizabeth had her knees pressed together and was dancing that dance. "Okay." Henry stopped and removed his backpack. From a side pocket he pulled out a Ziploc bag with a roll of toilet paper in it and offered it to Elizabeth.

She didn't take the toilet paper immediately. "Umm..." Henry got it. He gave her his hand shovel. She stared blankly at the toilet paper and the shovel.

"Find a tree and lean up against it. It'll help you keep your balance."

"I've never..."

"Taking a dump in the woods takes a little getting used to."

Elizabeth looked away. "What's wrong?" asked Henry. She couldn't look at him. Henry ran through the possible scenarios in his head. "Have you ever even used a public toilet?"

Elizabeth turned and walked away. "Don't look." Henry was about to say something smart ass but held his tongue. This was difficult for Elizabeth. He shouldn't make it any harder than it was for her.

"Elizabeth!" he called out. She turned and looked at him. "Come here!" She approached him as he dug into his backpack. He tossed her a stick of Chapstick.

"What's this for?" she asked.

"Smear some it under your nose. It'll help offset the stink."

As she left, Elizabeth signaled for her father to turn away. Henry obliged and turned his gaze upward toward the mountain's summit. He did keep one ear trained in her direction in case she needed help... he hoped she wouldn't need help. He really didn't know how he could help her.

Henry stared up at the ridgeline. They wouldn't be able to reach it in time to set up a campsite before sunset. They could definitely make it there by sometime tomorrow morning. After they crested over the ridgeline then it was the better part of a day's walk to descend to the bottom of Colby Canyon and, hopefully, their rendezvous with Clyde.

The glare of the morning sun made it difficult to pick out details but there was something moving against the grain up there. Maybe it was a deer. He heard some rocks tumble down the hill but didn't recall the tell tale sound of a deer hoof hitting it first. Was that a glint of metal up there?

Elizabeth wandered a few hundred feet away from her father. She looked at the trees but didn't know how to pick one for the upcoming task. How do I choose? she wondered. She touched the bark on one tree and found it rough to the touch.

"When you dig the hole, leave the dirt right next to it!" she heard her father yell. It must be so that all she would have to do is kick the dirt over her poop; so she wouldn't have to bend down and shovel the dirt over it. To hell with it, she thought and started digging.

It didn't take her too long to dig the hole. The ground right at the base of the tree was soft and gave way easily. She smeared Chapstick under her nostrils before she squatted down into a sitting position and let herself fall backward against the tree. She undid her blue jeans and glanced around before she slid them down to her knees. A breeze blew by reminding her of how exposed she was.

She opened the Ziploc bag and balanced the roll of toilet paper on her lap. Okay, she thought to herself. Concentrate. Relax. Here it comes.

She took a breath and bore down. A second later came the unmistakable sound of a wet, splattery crap. A look of horror came across her face as the reality of what just happened sunk in.

"Dad!!!" she screamed.

Henry stood in the creek, barefoot with his pants rolled up to his knees. He poured liquid camping soap onto Elizabeth's pants and rubbed it into the fabric as vigorously as he could. Her spray covered a large area. Henry felt compelled to be as thorough as he could cleaning it up.

Standing by the creek, wrapped from the waist down in a towel was Elizabeth. Henry couldn't resist. "It's like potty training you all over again!"

"You don't know everything!" she yelled back. It wasn't her usual sarcastic retort. She was really hurt by this. Probably humiliated. What teenage girl would enjoy what she's just been through? Henry figured it was best to preserve his daughter's pride as much as possible.

Henry stepped out of the creek and laid her pants down on a large rock. He retrieved his rope and stretched it out between two trees in as much direct sunlight as he could find.

"I'm going to need your help," he said to Elizabeth.

"How?" she whined. Henry reached into his backpack and found a pair of nylon shorts. "It has no lining."

"In this light, your pants should dry out in about an hour." She slipped on the shorts but kept the towel wrapped around her waist.

"Here," said Henry. He handed her the leg part of her pants.

"What do you want me to do?"

"Just hold it as tight as you can. We're going to wring as much water out of your pants as we can." She did. Henry began twisting. Elizabeth was amazed at how much water came out of her pants. "Take a guess at how much water that is."

"What do you mean?"

"You said your pants were heavy. Take a guess how much water they soaked up."

"Why?"

Henry continued wringing. "I really don't know very much. But what I lack in raw knowledge, I make up for with deductive reasoning." He could tell she resented the schoolroom treatment but decided to risk irreversibly pissing her off for the rest of the day and continued.

"Let's make it easy," he said as he continued to wring her pants. "How much would a gallon of water weigh?"

"I don't know."

"You have enough information in your head to figure it out."

"I don't know what the answer is," she protested.

"I'm just saying that if you think about it for a few minutes, you could probably figure it out through deductive reasoning, just like Sherlock Holmes."

"Whatever."

"My Nalgene bottle holds a liter of water. That should help you figure it out."

"We didn't study the metric system in school."

Henry gave her an incredulous look and shook his head. "At least you've heard of the metric system." Henry redoubled his grip on her pants. "Hold on tight. Let's give it one more twist." Satisfied that he wouldn't get any more water out of her pants,

Henry clipped them to the clothesline and for a moment, allowed himself to admire his work.

"Now what?"

"We'll take a break here for an hour until your pants are dry enough to continue. I'll make us some lunch."

Henry didn't go to the trouble to dig a fire pit or start a campfire here. He pulled out his single burner liquid fuel stove and boiled some water.

"Okay, your choices for lunch today are spaghetti and meat balls or beef stroganoff."

"Spaghetti and meat balls? In there?"

Henry looked at the package. "I've had this before. It's more like spaghetti and meat ball."

"Let's have that. I've never heard of beef stroganoff."

"Well, we'll probably eat all of this stuff eventually. When did you become so shy about trying new things?"

"C'mon Dad, just give me a break. There's nothing wrong with the way I do things."

Henry filled his pot with water and fired up his single burner stove. They both sat in silence for a few minutes, watching the pot, waiting for the water to boil. Finally Elizabeth spoke up.

"So Dad, if our goal is Canada, what are we doing up here?"

Henry instinctively looked around to try and spot eavesdroppers.

"There's no one else up here," Elizabeth insisted. "Are you so concerned about what other people think that you're afraid to tell secrets when there's no one else around?" It was a close mimic of Henry. Henry felt he had to confide in her now.

"We're not going straight to Canada. I thought it was best for us to hide up here for a while. If Chinese Americans were going to escape, now would be the time to do it. Now would be the hardest time for such a plan to succeed. So we hide out until the heat is off."

"How long will that be?"

"I don't know."

"Wow," said Elizabeth. "Finally, something you don't know."

"I'll have a better idea when we meet up with your Uncle Clyde. He'll tell us what's been going on and we'll adjust our plans accordingly."

"And if says things are okay, can we go home?"

"Sweetheart, I really need you to get used to the idea that we'll never be able to go home again."

"What makes you so sure about that?"

"I've got a few years under this belt. Over time, you understand things better. Over time, it's easier to see the changes. Even in your life you've seen changes."

"What changes?"

"Well, by your senior year you had to carry your student I.D. with you all the time. You didn't have to do that freshmen year, did you?"

"Nope."

"And your friends Caridad and Esperanza? They had to carry I.D. too."

"Yes..." said Elizabeth suspiciously.

"But what about your friends Katie and Brooke?"

"How do you know who my friends are?"

Shit, Henry thought to himself. "The point is that the school treated you like an outsider—"

"Stop! Stop! Stop! Answer my question. How do you know who my friends are? Have you been reading my text messages?"

Henry tried valiantly to stay on topic. "The point is that that we're all U.S. citizens and yet—"

"That is so creepy, you reading my text messages. What else do you know?"

Henry was cornered so he thought he might as well put all his cards on the table. "You don't need a boob job."

Elizabeth glared at him. "I hate you." Elizabeth stomped off toward the creek.

Henry tended to the pot of boiling water while muttering to himself, "I'm so glad we have this time together."

Henry finished letting the freeze-dried spaghetti steep in the bag. He called out to Elizabeth but she ignored him.

"The food is ready. I'm leaving it here. I'm going to go take a nap." Henry saw Elizabeth cock her head. Henry kept his word and vacated the area.

Henry grabbed his bivvy bag out of his backpack. Henry didn't know why but he decided to go through his backpack's outer pockets again. He found a small ditty bag that didn't look familiar. He squeezed it gently and recognized the objects inside. Clyde you're a lifesaver, Henry thought to himself.

Henry found a shaded spot a distance away from Elizabeth. He had to push his way through some underbrush. With a little effort, he could crane his neck and spot her but if she decided to come search for him, he'd definitely be able to hear her coming.

Henry laid the bivvy bag down on the ground and sat on it. He leaned back against a tree. He checked one more time to make sure that Elizabeth was staying put where she was before he opened the ditty bag.

Inside was a small Ziploc bag with a fresh marijuana bud, about the size of his thumb. Henry opened the bag and inhaled. Clyde had always said he was going to get a Cannabis prescription. He finally followed through. This stuff was medical grade.

Getting a script was never an option for Henry. He was drug tested regularly at the pharmacy and a positive result for THC would be looked upon poorly by his employer. Henry examined the glass pipe. Clyde must have cleaned it recently. The screen was brand new too. Clyde even included a cigarette lighter. Henry broke off a small piece of the bud, set it in the pipe and lit up. Tasty, Henry thought. Once he got it fired up, he took a long toke, closed his eyes and leaned back.

Medical grade Cannabis is much stronger than the shit we smoked in high school, Henry thought before he drifted off.

# # #

The bomb squad gave the 'all clear' at Clyde's house. Babcock reentered the house and took a good look around. All the furniture was covered with bed sheets and with good reason. Babcock lifted the sheets to reveal old worn out furniture. The upholstery had gaping holes in it but the stuffing was held in place by duct tape. Despite the crappy furniture, there was a huge flat screen plasma television hanging on the wall.

Just then, Don entered the house. "What the hell happened," he demanded.

"SWAT team screwed up. They didn't have the perimeter set up. He got away." Before he knew it, Babcock suddenly had SWAT Officer Yamamoto in his face. "Get it right doughboy. You knew the perimeter wasn't secure when you gave the order to approach."

"Hey hey hey, don't call me 'doughboy.' That's racist!"

"I'm not calling you doughboy because you're White. I'm calling you doughboy because you're soft! I don't get what your fucking hurry was. We had the element of surprise on our side."

"It didn't seem to help Officer," barked back Babcock. Don stepped in front of Babcock and addressed Officer Yamamoto.

"What makes you so sure, you had the element of surprise Officer…"

"Yamamoto," she finished. She pointed to a glass pipe sitting on the coffee table. "His pipe was still lit when we got here. You don't smoke Cannabis if you're in a hurry."

LAPD Lieutenant Baumberger entered the room and signaled to Babcock. "Agent Babcock? I've got something to show you."

Baumberger led Babcock and Don into the garage. "Lieutenant, let me introduce you to my boss, Director Don Morgan."

"Pleasure," said Baumberger. He turned to one of his men. "Go ahead, tell them what you told me."

The uniform policeman cleared his throat. "We counted three crates of M-16s. Matching ammo was found in these crates. A few thousand rounds. Serial numbers indicate they were legally bought over time. He must have been stockpiling them. We must have caught him in the middle of loading his vehicle."

The uniformed cop pointed to an empty spot on the floor. "There's no dust or dirt there. Something sat there recently."

"Like what?" asked Don. The uniform cop grabbed a wooden crate and placed it perfectly in the clean spot. He took a crowbar and pried the crate open. Inside were hand grenades.

"Holy shit," exclaimed Babcock.

The uniformed cop continued. "You figure he's gotta have at least one crate of this. Who knows how much he had in here originally."

SWAT Officer Yamamoto entered the garage and saw the hand grenades. "Jesus Christ," she blurted at the sight of them.

Babcock signaled Baumberger. "Lieutenant, arrest Yamamoto."

"What?" she said as she turned to Babcock. He placed his hand on his sidearm.

"Take one more step and I will drop you." Babcock turned to Baumberger. "The charge is sedition."

"I don't believe this," she protested.

"She fouled up this operation. If it's not incompetence, then there must be another reason and I want to know why. Lieutenant, once she's in custody I want her tested."

"For what?" Officer Yamamoto already knew the answer.

Babcock leaned in. "I hope you have one drop."

Baumberger intervened. "Officer, take Officer Yamamoto outside and wait for me." Once they were gone, Baumberger addressed Babcock. "She's a good officer. Don't fuck with my people."

Babcock went nose to nose with Baumberger. "Under the Repatriation Act, you must comply with my orders." Baumberger threw a glance at Don. "I hope your man knows what he's doing."

After Baumberger left the garage, Don turned to Babcock. "That wasn't necessary, dressing her down like that. Every division likes to mete out its own discipline. If she did screw up, it was her CO's place to call her out, not you."

Babcock threw an accusatory glance at Don. "That's the problem today."

"You better be sure you want to say what you're going to say," warned Don.

"Nobody values field experience anymore. You're all so concerned about following the rules. Following the rules perfectly isn't the goddamn prize!"

"No, it's not the prize," rebutted Don. "But it is the only thing that keeps us from anarchy. Babcock, I know your kind. You're impatient and you're ambitious. You look at me and think to yourself, 'I'm never going to be like him. I'm going to be different.' Son, that strategy never works. I understand you need to make your bones, but without patience and discipline, you are going to get someone killed."

Don pointed to the crates of weapons for emphasis. "What if he knew you were coming? The street would now be littered with dead police officers."

Babcock couldn't believe what he was hearing.

Don continued, "You have a penchant for making the wrong decision."

"Director Morgan, it was her screw up."

"I heard what her CO said about her. He has more credibility with me that you do. Agent Babcock, I'll need your credentials and your sidearm. Now."

It was a humiliating act for Babcock having to surrender these things in front of strangers. This was a power play by Don and he was the pawn. Babcock didn't have a choice. He handed them over to Don.

You racist sonuvabitch, Babcock thought to himself.

# # #

It had been a rough day for Private Chin and the rest of Charlie Company. After an hour drive from basecamp into the jungle, they spent the rest of the day setting up the rear garrison. GP-Medium tents for their barracks, GP-Medium tents for the mess hall and GP-Medium tents for equipment storage. The work was grueling under the hot, Panamanian sun but it wasn't anything they couldn't handle.

Once everything was done, the garrison commander was notified and came out to address his men as they all stood in formation. Battalion Colonel Windsor was a full bird colonel. He laid out for them their mission and the rules of engagement.

"Our job is to neutralize the guerillas attacking the canal and make it safe for civilian ships to transit. The men we're looking for are thugs. Calling them guerillas is too good for them. We don't know how many there are. We don't know where they are. However, we have superior training and superior weapons. Don't let me down."

Cut and dry with little fanfare but it was the go ahead for them to be issued ammo. 'Now the shit begins,' thought Private Chin.

They got busy in a hurry. The next day Private Chin's six man squad was assigned a three day LRRP. It was time to put that training to the test.

A LRRP was the Army's acronym for Long Range Recon Patrol and was pronounced 'lurp' as in 'slurp.' A squad was assigned an area on the map to patrol and was under orders to take out any hostiles they came across.

The first thing that Private Chin learned was that a three day LRRP was rarely ever three days. If it was a three day LRRP, you could count on it lasting at least five days before basecamp would radio you to return. Private Chin learned this on his first LRRP.

The radio was a bulky piece of equipment that had to be carried in lieu of your own equipment. Your buddy had to help you out by doubling up on his equipment.

Because they were packaged in cardboard, the batteries were prone to leaking. If they did, they often left acid burns on your back.

Radio communication wasn't like talking on a telephone. You could be assured that hostiles were scanning the different frequencies, monitoring for any chatter. Private Chin's communication protocol was to check in at appointed times over the radio. Three clicks over pre-assigned frequency at the appointed time were to indicate that they were carrying out their mission without incident. The enemy would have to be listening at the right time on the right frequency to hear the clicks. And even if they did, the clicks, in all likelihood, would have been shrugged off as merely background noise. Three clicks in response meant that they were to continue until they received different orders. Any additional orders would be given in Morse code.

Today was the fifth day of their three day LRRP. No hostiles encountered yet. When they began their mission, each man carried a gallon of water. The sun's heat had been unrelenting and their efforts to dig for moisture or recover condensation had failed. Every man was now rationing their last drops. Water was heavy and their canteens were rigid and affected the way they walked. One day Henry was going to have to calculate for himself how much water was the most efficient to bring on one of these LRRPs.

Every man was on his last MRE. As a squad, they had run out of cigarettes and each man was secretly hoarding his secret stash of toilet paper.

Private Chin unfolded a topo map as his men crowded around it. Private Wilson spotted something right away. "There's a water buffalo about five clicks away. We can make it there before sunset." Private Wilson seemed almost relieved at the discovery.

Private Chin was less jubilant. "To get there we'll have to snake through this canyon. We don't have access to the high ground from here. We'll be sitting ducks as we make our way through there."

"Are you gonna scrap the mission?" asked Private Taylor.

"No, I'm saying that if we're gonna get shot at, this is where it will happen. Eyes and ears guys. Let's move out."

They used duct tape to secure anything hanging off the side of their gear to minimize noise. They moved slowly through the bottom of the canyon in single file. Private Chin led the way. Private Wilson brought up the rear. Private Chin scanned upward looking for movement or shadows or anything that was even remotely out of place.

They were a third of the way into the canyon when Private Taylor tapped him on the shoulder. Private Chin stopped and looked back over his shoulder. Private Taylor pointed back to Private Wilson who signaled he heard something off to the east. Private Chin hand signaled his squad down into a crouch. Ever since basic training,

Private Chin and Private Wilson made a good team. Private Chin had great eyesight. Private Wilson had great hearing. This time Private Wilson heard something before Private Chin saw anything.

From their position, every man was now on high adrenaline, with their attention trained at the rocky steep Private Wilson had pointed to. Private Chin was hoping that Private Wilson had heard the enemy before the enemy spotted them.

The squad remained still. If the enemy had seen them, they were sitting ducks. Private Chin spotted a small grove of trees and hand signaled his men to move there for more cover.

As they began to move, Private Chin huddled near a tree to get a better look up at the bluff when suddenly a tree branch near his head exploded in a cloud of splinters. Everyone hit the ground. Private Chin cocked his weapon and prepared to return fire.

But there was something strange about the sound of him pulling back on the charging bolt. It sounded too clear. Like it was only a few feet away. The images of Panama faded away as Henry realized he was in a dream. Every muscle down his back tensed up. He was holding his breath.

Henry opened his eyes to find an AK-47 rifle pointed at his face.

"What the hell are you doing up here Chinaman?" asked the man in camouflage.

§

CHAPTER TEN

The parking lot for the Colby Canyon trailhead was deserted. Clyde didn't expect anyone to be up here on a weekday. This area was for day hikers only who would come early in the morning, scale to the summit and return here by sundown. If you wanted to reach the top, you had to do it that way because you couldn't leave your vehicle here overnight without incurring a hefty fine.

Clyde parked his cargo van and looked around. There was a cloud of dust approaching from the main road. Clyde decided to hold here for the time being until he could figure out what the situation was. No sense in drawing any more attention to himself than necessary.

As the cloud of dust grew closer, Clyde could see it was a park ranger truck. It was a white, customized Ford F-250. The truck pulled up right beside Clyde's van and parked. Ranger Eleanor was in her fifties. If she were White, she'd be considered dark skinned, but light skinned if she were African American. Her skin was so weathered by the outdoors and a two pack of cigarettes a day habit, it was hard to tell what ethnicity she was.

Clearly her best days were behind her. No one could imagine her rappelling down into a ravine to rescue a stranded hiker. She wore her long salt and pepper hair in a braid. As she walked over to Clyde, she took a quick look in the van.

"You know you need an Adventure Pass to park here." She pulled out her book and started writing him a ticket.

"I have one in the van," Clyde said. He had to stop her from writing that ticket. Once she got back to the station and put it in the system, this place will be crawling with... with whomever that was back there who invaded his house.

"You should have hung it up," she admonished. She looked up at Clyde with a puzzled look. "What are you doing up here?"

Clyde tried to shrug it off. "Just up for a quick hike."

Clyde wasn't dressed like a typical hiker. He was wearing basketball sneakers, not hiking boots. He was wearing blue jeans, not shorts. He was wearing a polo shirt, not a t-shirt or tank top. As far as Ranger Eleanor was concerned, he wasn't up here to hike.

She banged the side of the cargo van with her fist. "Open it up," she ordered. A windowless cargo van up here during the week could only mean one thing to her. Illegal dumping. She was going to nail this litterbug.

Before she knew it, Clyde had thumped her in her solar plexus with the palm of his hand knocking all the wind out of her. As she doubled over, Clyde gave her a karate chop behind her ear, sending her to the ground unconscious. Clyde immediately recoiled at what he had done.

"I'm so sorry, I'm so sorry," he repeated over and over again. "God, I didn't want to do that, I'm so sorry." Clyde quickly checked her vitals. She was breathing but unconscious.

Clyde gently picked her up off the ground and sat her in the drivers seat of his cargo van, safely buckling her up with the seat belt.

Clyde swung around to the back of the van. He grabbed two M-16s and stuffed a few boxes of ammo and spare clips into his pockets. He looked at the unopened crate still sitting in the back. Clyde tore the lid off. Inside, nested in individual pockets of shock-proof foam, were a dozen hand grenades. Even though Clyde didn't have room for anything more, he grabbed two grenades and squeezed them into his back pockets. He shut the back doors and returned to the front seat.

Ranger Eleanor's breathing remained regular. You're gonna wake up with a bad headache, Clyde thought. He patted her down and found her truck keys. He reached over her, released the emergency brake and threw the van into neutral. The van coasted forward slowly as Clyde steered it off the parking lot and into a drainage ditch. Clyde threw a few branches over it to hide it as best he could but it was still easy to spot from a distance away. Then he hurled Ranger Eleanor's keys as far as he could. Clyde figured he had until the end of the day before anyone would notice Ranger Eleanor was missing. He had to make some good time.

Clyde headed over toward the far end of the parking lot and past a sign that marked the Colby Canyon trailhead. Clyde turned away from the path and started up the incline following along side a creek.

Clyde calculated in his head that Henry and Elizabeth would be at least a day's hike away, assuming they had kept a steady pace since he originally dropped them off.

Clyde hiked for nearly an hour straight at a crisp pace without any rest. Clyde knew he had to take it easy. His sneakers weren't giving him the traction that he needed on the slippery rocks.

Clyde looked down at his clothes. His polo shirt was soaked through with sweat. Clyde needed to take a break.

He knelt down by the creek and splashed some cold water on his face. He concentrated on slowing down his heartbeat. He cursed himself for not being prepared for that raid. Another hour and he would have been gone, only with everything he would need to survive with Henry and Elizabeth.

Don't punish yourself, Clyde thought to himself. Don't become your own worst enemy. You escaped. You're still useful to Henry. You can still help him. If you were caught, you'd be useless right now. Worse than useless to Henry.

Clyde took a moment to listen to the world around him. He needed to get used to hearing what this area sounded like normally so he'd know if something was amiss. Once he got his heart to slow down and could hear past his own breathing, he listened. Clyde heard a steady wind rustle through the trees. He could hear the persistent gurgle of the nearby creek. He heard a raven caw. He heard a woodpecker pecking at a tree. He could hear scrub jays singing to each other.

His heart was beating normally now. He could hear the hum of a hummingbird's wings. This is what normal sounds like, Clyde thought to himself. He lifted up his head and with his eyes closed, he let out three quick whistles, just like the sound Henry made back at the Rose Bowl. Not much of an echo, the trees were too close and were absorbing all the sounds. Clyde let loose one more triplet and listened for a reply. A few seconds later, nothing.

I hope you're on schedule, wished Clyde as he resumed his press upward.

# # #

The creek was hypnotizing. Elizabeth wondered how long she had been staring at it lost in her thoughts. Her mind kept drifting back to the last days she spent with her mother. The hospital wouldn't let her up into her room because she was too young but one day they did. Now that she was older she understood why. Veronique's time was coming to an end soon and it was now appropriate for her to see her mother and say goodbye.

But it wasn't a satisfactory goodbye. In the final days before Veronique passed, the cancer had taken over nearly her entire body. She had wasted away to less than ninety pounds. What was most heartbreaking for Elizabeth was that her mother had long stopped being her mother when the cancer reached her brain.

Veronique lay still in her hospital bed. Elizabeth spoke to her and even took her hand but there was no reaction. Henry tried to comfort Elizabeth but there was no consoling her.

Elizabeth always sensed that there was something different about her mother. She spoke differently than all the other parents. She always carried herself like an aristocrat in a movie. She never seemed to lose her temper and always knew the right thing to say. It was like having all the characters Julie Andrews played for your mother.

Elizabeth always felt her mother harbored some great secret that she would share with her someday. The fantasy that recurred the most was that her mother was a forgotten queen and that Elizabeth was heir to a kingdom. That fantasy was how Elizabeth endured all the teasing she got in school. She didn't fit in with the Asian kids nor did she fit in with the White kids. She always felt more comfortable around her Latina friends. They were the first ones to come visit her after her mother died.

Henry had asked Elizabeth if she wanted to say anything at her mother's funeral services. They didn't have many friends so it wouldn't be like a big public speaking engagement. Chances were that she knew everyone that would come. Elizabeth was barely eight years old but she wanted to do it. She wanted to say out loud the words her mother never got to hear.

The day before the service several men in tweed suits came to the house. They said there would be no service tomorrow. They had come to take her mother back home. She remembered her father yelling at one particular man: a man she would later find out was her grandfather, Sebastian Colville, a thick bodied, gray haired man. He had flown all the way to the United States to take Veronique back to their family estate in France. Henry wanted her buried here where they could visit.

Elizabeth didn't understand all that was going on at the time. She could hear them fighting, shouting at each other, very angrily. She wanted her father to stop. She wanted her grandfather to tell her that she was a princess and that he was taking her home to her kingdom. She was eight years old and so desperately wanted to hear those words.

She couldn't really understand what they were fighting about, but suddenly the screaming stopped and she watched her grandfather stomp his way to the front door. Just before he left, he turned to her father and declared, "My daughter would be alive if it weren't for you."

Elizabeth stared at him. Colville suddenly realized her presence. There was such hatred in his eyes. She was instantly afraid of him and backed away. Before he left, Colville spit at Henry's feet.

She always blamed for father for everything after that. That accusation stuck with her and constantly bubbled underneath everything. My daughter would be alive if it weren't for you. Colville had said it with such force, it must have been true.

Veronique's body was taken back to France. Elizabeth never got to speak at her mother's funeral. She never got to say the words she wanted to say. She also never got the proclamation that she was an heir to the throne. No secret identity to ever be revealed. And somehow, she was wired to blame her father for all that. Blame him for what? She was nothing more than a teenage girl, sitting on a rock next to a creek up in the mountains, dreaming of a hot shower.

Elizabeth returned to the clearing. Her pants were dry now. She took them down and slipped them on. The pot was still sitting on the single burner. How strange, she thought. Her father was usually so anal he would have cleaned that pot already... and told her that her pants were dry... and taken down the clothesline.

She stood there puzzled when she heard a rustling nearby. She pushed her way through some thick underbrush when she looked up to see the same man in camouflage that attacked Henry.

Then she saw her father, on his knees with his bandana stuffed in his mouth and his hands behind him, held by plastic ties. Instinctively, she called out, "Dad!"

The man in camouflage turned and ran right at Elizabeth. She was frozen in place. Fear gripped her legs and she couldn't run. Before she knew it, the man in camouflage tackled her and had pulled out another plastic tie to secure her hands.

Elizabeth could feel the ties tighten around her wrists. It was painful but she was pinned down. The man was sitting on top of her, pressing her face into the dirt. As he stood her up, Elizabeth got a good look at this man. He face was all bruised up and he was bleeding from his lip and nose. He didn't get her father without a fight.

Before he was blindfolded, Henry was able to figure out the man in camouflage's name. He was Tom Lynch. It was written in black magic marker on his camouflage t-shirt. Best Henry could figure out was that he was in his mid 30s. White, definitely. Both Henry and Elizabeth were blindfolded. Despite being blindfolded, Henry could pick out his daughter's footsteps behind him. He could hear her grunting. Lynch had muffled her with a bandana too.

Henry could feel the warmth of the setting sun on the back of his neck so he knew they were going east. That was corroborated by his sense they were walking uphill. Henry felt dirt beneath his feet. Dirt indicated they were on a well-worn path. If he felt the crunch of dried grass under his feet, they would be pushing through a virgin area.

Henry was also listening to Lynch's footsteps. In addition his rhythmic steps, there was a stutter that indicated he didn't lift his foot completely off the ground when he brought it forward. Henry began to deliberately drag his foot in the dirt timed with Lynch's idiosyncrasy. Only Henry dug his foot in deeper than Lynch's. Hard enough to leave a rut in the dirt but not loud enough to draw Lynch's attention.

Thinking back, Henry realized that Elizabeth must have surprised him. This was important to know. Whoever Lynch was, he wasn't law enforcement and he wasn't military. This guy had no training whatsoever. Henry was pretty sure he knew whom he was dealing with.

Henry counted silently to himself to measure the passage of time. He figured that they had been walking for nearly an hour. Henry calculated that it was just around dusk. He anticipated he should be able to feel the temperature change. Distance wise, he figured they were about two miles due east of where they were.

It would be night soon. He would have to figure out his bearings if he could only get the blindfold off. Henry tried to remember which phase of the moon it was. He kicked himself for not paying closer attention. This was something he should know.

Finally Henry felt the ground flatten out. He could tell by the difference in Lynch's pace that they had reached their destination. Lynch made them sit in the dirt, cross-legged before he removed their blindfolds and gags.

"Where are we?" asked Elizabeth.

"Quiet!" ordered Lynch.

Henry had called it correctly. It was exactly dusk. From the glow in the sky, he roughly knew which way was west. Once the stars came out, he'd find the North Star and confirm it. No sign of the moon. Means the skies will be darker. A full moon or anything near it would be visible by now.

Then Henry had a chance to look at the surroundings. Large canvas tents were set up. Army surplus. Looked like GP-Smalls of the hexagonal variety. There was camping gear available that was much lighter and durable than what was here.

Camouflage netting hung between the trees, hanging low over the tents. These guys didn't want to be seen from above. There was a perimeter around the site made up of sandbags and trenches. However, these trenches did more than limit access to the campsite, they were defensive positions.

Then Henry saw what confirmed all his suspicions. Dangling from a low hanging tree branch was a flag. It had the red and white stripes of Old Glory but where there should have been a blue field of stars was a coiled snake against a yellow background.

"Uncle Eldridge! I'm back!" Lynch cried out. There was some movement. The man who appeared was about sixty years old. Gaunt, balding but wiry strong. He walked using forearm crutches. His legs were intact but were held in place by braces. On his shirt was a service ribbon. A small rectangular bar colored with blue, green and white stripes. Henry recognized it as a military medal of some kind but couldn't pull the information out of his head at that moment.

"What the hell is this?" Eldridge demanded.

Lynch snapped to attention and saluted. "I found these enemy combatants snooping around the plateau."

Eldridge couldn't hide his exasperation. "And you couldn't leave them well enough alone? Cut them loose now!" Lynch flicked open a knife. "Easy! Are you stupid?" Eldridge turned to Henry. "I have to apologize for my nephew."

"Yeah," said Henry. "I was pretty sure this was one giant misunderstanding."

"My name is Eldridge Mason. You've already met my nephew Tom Lynch."

"Pleasure. I'm Henry and this is my daughter Elizabeth," said Henry.

"You have to understand our surprise seeing you up here. We like this spot precisely because no one comes up here. Guess seeing another human being startled my nephew," said Eldridge. "What were you doing on the plateau?"

Henry rubbed some feeling back into his wrists once Lynch cut off the plastic ties. "Just camping. Always wanted to bring my daughter up here."

"Camping, huh," offered Lynch. "That's quite a pair of canoes you've got." Elizabeth self-consciously crossed her arms across her chest.

"What do you mean?" she asked.

"You've got very large feet," said Lynch with something halfway between smart-ass and a leer in his voice. Eldridge quickly took back control of the conversation.

"You're a long way's off from the plateau. You must be hungry. Holst! Rigby! Front and center!"

It remained silent for a moment but then Henry heard the sounds of feet shuffling in the dirt. It sounded more like staggering. Holst and Rigby were well into a bottle of Johnnie Walker and were having a little trouble standing up.

"Guys, what did I say? No hard liquor until after sunset." To Henry, Holst and Rigby didn't seem to practice this rule on a regular basis. Both men were well into middle age, heavy set and wore something a little thicker than a five o'clock shadow on their faces. Holst and Rigby were startled at the sight of Henry and Elizabeth.

"Go and see if Mess Daddy has anything left to eat." Eldridge turned back to Henry and Elizabeth. "We'll rustle up something for you to eat."

Holst reached over to grab Henry by the shoulder when Eldridge held up his hand. "They are our guests."

As Henry and Elizabeth were escorted over to the mess tent, she leaned over and whispered in Henry's ear, "Should we be scared?"

Henry looked at Elizabeth and shook off the notion.

Once they were out of sight, Eldridge called Lynch over. "Why didn't you leave them where they were?"

"I couldn't take a chance they were coming up this way."

"So you blindfolded them and brought them here?"

"I didn't think I should kill them. They might have information we could use," said Lynch.

"Kill them? We don't kill unless we have to. Grab some guys and clear out the work tent."

"Why?"

"Because you brought them up here after sunset. I'm not sending them back out in the dark and if we escort them, there's half a chance you numb nuts won't find your way back."

"You can't let them go free, Uncle Eldridge. They might report us."

"Did you notice that they're Chinese?"

"I did notice. I'm not stupid."

Eldridge squelched his impulse for the obvious joke. "Who are they going to report us to? They're not supposed to be out here running free. Just let them go and be done with it."

"Maybe there's a reward. You know how you're always saying we need to raise more money."

"So we go to the feds, turn them in and in the process of collecting this reward, how do we explain what we were doing up here? You're all chewed up with the dumbass. I'll talk to him after they eat. I'm sure both of us would be more than happy to pretend that today never happened."

As Henry and Elizabeth were escorted across the compound, Henry took in as much detail as he could. He counted four GP-Small tents set up in a semi circle around a central fire pit. All were hexagonal tents that came to a point. They could sleep about six men comfortably, which is good considering it takes at least four guys to set it up. More, if they didn't know what they're doing.

Henry knew that each tent weighed about two hundred pounds. That was a lot of equipment to hike all the way up here. Henry doubted that couch potatoes Holst and Rigby had a secret identity as pack mules. They had to have some vehicles up here, something with a flatbed but something that could maneuver in this terrain: and they would need a few because one ATV with a flatbed tow could only handle one tent.

They entered one of the GP-Smalls. This tent looked like it was a dedicated mess hall. There were two long plastic folding tables that could comfortably seat a dozen guys. No benches or chairs. It was probably bring your own chair. The kitchen equipment seemed like pretty standard camping gear, a Coleman two burner gas stove, a Weber gas grill, a water station set up on a small folding table. These guys are dialed in, thought Henry. This isn't a weekend camping trip. These guys have been up here a while and weren't leaving.

Mess Daddy looked like he had just finished cleaning up. He was drying off what looked like a stack of a dozen blue enamel plates. Holst called out, "Hey Mess Daddy, got some grub for our guests?"

"Jeez, I just got done cleaning. It wouldn't kill you guys to help me wash dishes once in a while." Then Mess Daddy caught himself. "My name's Walsh but everyone calls me Mess Daddy." Henry and Elizabeth curtly introduced themselves before Holst explained their dinner situation.

Mess Daddy scratched his chin. "Hmmm... these guys cleaned me out of today's rations but I got something I was saving for a special occasion. You eat pork?"

"Do we look Jewish?" Henry baited. Lynch took the bait.

"Hell, if you were Jewish you wouldn't..." Mess Daddy loudly cleared his throat. "I have some vacuum packed pork chops I can throw on the grill and I have a spare can of corn. Sorry to be so chintzy, these guys eat a lot."

"We really appreciate your hospitality." Elizabeth followed Henry's lead and smiled too.

Mess Daddy knew what he was doing. The pork chop was grilled medium, juicy and well seasoned with a bit of cayenne pepper for a nice little kick. The canned corn was... well, canned corn. Henry watched Elizabeth eat. She should have been hungry but he guessed it was her nerves that kept her from devouring the pork chop.

"Eat up," suggested Henry. "You're going to need your strength."

"I'm sure you will," interjected Eldridge as he came into the tent. Henry marveled at Eldridge's agility at moving about. Obviously, he had a lot of practice at it.

"Don't stop, please," Eldridge continued. "Finish eating." Eldridge took a seat next to Henry and laid his crutches on the ground. "We've cleared out a tent for you and Elizabeth to spend the night here. I'm sure you'll agree that it would be a lot safer for you to return to your campsite tomorrow morning when it's light out."

"Thank you. That's very considerate of you," replied Henry as he studied every nuance of Eldridge's face.

"You know, people come up here for lots of reasons," began Eldridge. "Some of those reasons are obvious. It's beautiful up here, you can get away from the noise of civilization. Get away from those who would meddle in your private business." Eldridge paused to gauge Henry's reaction.

"I hear you," said Henry.

"I'm pretty certain you probably have a lot of the same concerns we do."

"It's not unlikely," countered Henry.

"Life goes on. Live and let live is our philosophy."

"Mine too," said Henry.

"Good. I'm glad we understand each other." Eldridge stood up. "We don't have a lot up here, but we do have a shower."

This caught Elizabeth's attention. "A shower?"

"We don't have hot water but it's warm. You look like you could use one. I'm pretty sure we could find a clean towel for you."

"Thank you," said Elizabeth.

"Come on outside when you're done. A few of us will be jack-jawing by the fire. Hang out with us for a bit. We'll promise to keep the conversation rated PG-13."

"Sure," responded Henry.

"Carry on." Eldridge gave Henry a salute. Eldridge had caught Henry off guard. A soldier is supposed to stand and salute a superior officer and Henry nearly gave in to that reflex. Eldridge carried himself with the cadence and rhythm of a man who served in the military. Henry wondered if Eldridge noticed his reaction. If he did, he didn't show it as he left the tent.

Henry and Elizabeth were alone. Mess Daddy had finished cleaning everything and presumably was sitting outside by the fire.

Elizabeth leaned in toward Henry as if to say anything but Henry shook his head before she did. "Are you done eating?" Elizabeth nodded.

Henry and Elizabeth stepped out of the mess tent. The night air had a slight chill in it. The weather was changing and Henry was worried it might include some rain.

"Hey, come join us. Pull up a chair. Rigby, you got an extra stogie?" Rigby began searching his pockets.

"Thanks for the offer. I don't smoke." Henry looked around. Eldridge sat in a folding camping chair. Next to him was Lynch, Rigby and then Holst and then about four more guys that Henry hadn't seen yet. Mess Daddy Walsh was nowhere to be seen.

"It's been a long day," continued Henry. "We're both pretty tired. We're going to get some rest. Give my compliments to Mess Daddy."

"Will do," responded Eldridge. He watched Henry and Elizabeth retire to their tent. He tapped Lynch on his elbow. "See, he did exactly what I told you he'd do."

The tent was lit by a battery-operated lantern hanging from a stand. Two cots were set up for them with bedrolls. A long, folding table was left behind. Henry looked at the ground. There were a ton of fresh footprints. Henry counted six pairs of footprints. There was a lot of recent activity here moving things around.

Elizabeth sat down on one of the cots as Henry checked out the folding table. "I really could use a shower," said Elizabeth.

Henry ran his finger across the table and tasted the residue. "We have to get out of here as soon as we can."

§

CHAPTER ELEVEN

Babcock sat in his car with the window cracked slightly open. He had gone through about a half a pack of cigarettes waiting for the sun to come down. This was a quiet neighborhood in Glendale. People came and went in their cars and generally minded their own business. There was not a lot of foot traffic, not even the occasional pet owner taking their dog out for a walk.

The static crackle of Babcock's portable police scanner seemed to push the cigarette smoke out of the car. Babcock resented Don for taking him off the case. The reasons were so transparent it made him angry. It was his investigation that led to Clyde Wilson but it was trusting another law enforcement division that allowed him to escape. Babcock believed that Don was looking for any reason to dump him now that they got their big break. Maybe Don was more ambitious than he gave him credit for. Maybe Don was eyeing a position in the President's cabinet. Babcock was fuming that Don was going to grab all the credit for his hard work. If the police catch up with Clyde Wilson, Babcock wanted to be there before Don. He wasn't going to let go of this case quietly.

Babcock's eyes kept drifting over to one particular townhouse searching for signs of movement.

His patience paid off. Shortly after sunset, a light came on up on the second floor. Babcock turned off the police scanner and tossed his cigarette out the window before he stepped out of the car.

Babcock wasn't looking for a confrontation. He felt like his world was spiraling out of control and he needed a friendly voice to talk to and the cell phone wouldn't do. He rang the doorbell. After a few seconds, the porch light came on and the front door opened.

"You don't know how to respect boundaries." The voice belonged to Natasha Cho, a tall, lithe woman with long straight black hair. She stood in the doorway in her bathrobe with her arms crossed waiting for the slightest provocation to throw Babcock back onto the sidewalk.

Babcock tried to diffuse her anger. "I'm working on a new case right now and it's got me—"

"Excuse me," she interrupted. "Do you see a sign on my door that says 'therapist'?

Babcock tried another tactic to calm her down. "There's a chance you might be in danger." This statement got Natasha's attention.

"What do you mean?"

"Things are a little crazy right now," began Babcock. "Average people might not be able to tell the difference between Chinese and Korean people. If you and I were together—"

"You don't know a thing about me!" Natasha was on the verge of losing her temper. She instantly resented the idea she needed Babcock to vouch for her as if she needed him for validation. "All you know about me is that I'm Korean and sometimes you even get that wrong!"

Despite her anger, this was their most meaningful conversation since their break up three months earlier. Natasha had tried to shut Babcock out of her life completely but he still persistently tried to contact her... not enough that would make the police intervene but enough to annoy the shit out of her. Babcock believed that she had dumped him because he was White and he figured this might be the last chance he'd have to tell her so.

"You always bring up the race issue. I don't care about race. If you didn't bring it up all the time, it wouldn't be an issue."

"My family is Korean. We talk about Korean things."

"But you don't have to do it front of me all the time. You're in America. You can talk about American things too."

Now Natasha found herself yelling at him. "You're the one who keeps bragging about how your family came over on the Mayflower! You don't see anything wrong with that?"

Babcock continued to press his point. "You're the one who needs to examine why this is such a big problem." Just then, Babcock saw something move inside her place. "Who's in there?"

Before Natasha could answer, Babcock crouched down and shouted, "Federal agent! I need to see your hands now!"

Stepping forward was Berlin Tanaka. He was Asian, but sported bleached spiked hair. He came to the door bare-chested with a towel wrapped around his waist. Babcock had never seen such a muscular Asian before... at least not one that appeared to be pure Asian.

"Federal agent?" asked Berlin. He turned to Natasha, "Is this your psycho ex?"

"I'm going to need to see your I.D." Babcock ordered.

Natasha shoved Berlin back into the townhouse. She turned back to Babcock. "Lose my number," she ordered before she slammed the door shut on him.

She's so unreasonable, Babcock thought to himself.

Babcock retreated back to his car. He looked back up at Natasha's townhouse. The lights were off now and he could see the curtains move. Babcock took the hint. He figured he had less than two minutes to drive away before she called the police.

He wasn't very worried. He opened his glove compartment and pulled out his dupe badge and credentials. He wanted to arrest Natasha's boyfriend but wasn't sure what he would tell the police if they came. He didn't believe Natasha would call the police but who knew about her boyfriend? He could be imbalanced. As a precaution, Babcock clicked on the police scanner and lit a cigarette. The static voice of the police dispatcher came over it.

"Tango Alpha Four, Code Three."

"Tango Alpha Four, Code Three, go ahead."

"Respond to a single vehicle injury accident. Big Tujunga Canyon Road, Colby Canyon. Vehicle is a white delivery van. Bus dispatched to the twenty."

"Copy. Confirm. En route, Code Three."

Babcock nearly jumped out of the drivers seat. His first mistake was not rolling down his window before trying to flick his cigarette away. He had to get out of his car and toss that lit cigarette properly before he could drive off.

On his cell phone Babcock speed dialed the direct number for the ICE watch commander's desk. "This is Agent Nick Babcock." Babcock held his breath hoping that Don would have waited until tomorrow morning to officially list him as inactive.

"Go ahead Babcock," came the reply. Babcock knew he was going to catch hell for what he was going to say next, but he was convinced Henry Chin was a domestic terrorist loose somewhere in the mountains. Now was the time to trap him up there. Surely Don could appreciate the lessons learned from the last time a terrorist was trapped in a mountain region and escaped.

"I need a task force detailed to the Angeles National Forest under Director Morgan's authority. Authorization foxtrot, kilo, lima, eight, five, two, juliet, whiskey."

The Colby Canyon trailhead parking lot was full of military vehicles. Floodlights were set up and practically turned night into day. A tow truck was pulling Clyde's cargo van out of the drainage ditch. Medical personnel were tending to Ranger Eleanor.

The Army had set up a command center under a canopy in the center of the parking lot. A giant topo map was spread out on a table with search grids demarcated and labeled.

In the center of it all was Babcock. He was a living example of the axiom that said that if you act like you're in charge, people will treat you like you're in charge. He had exceeded his authority to bring these men out here. He knew he would need something extraordinary to show for it.

"I need an update!" he bellowed.

ICE Agent Alvarez ran up to him. "I spoke with Ranger Eleanor. Her description of her assailant matches the description of Clyde Wilson."

"We could have guessed that," said Babcock brusquely. Then he remembered that maintaining high morale was important. "Very good. Carry on."

ICE Agent Alvarez didn't know what to make of Babcock. Under Don, he always knew what he was supposed to do and why. Everything Alvarez had done so far up here was on his own initiative. It was like Babcock was waiting for someone to bring him a good idea.

"Babcock," began Alvarez, "Any word on Director Morgan's ETA?"

"He left me in charge," shot back Babcock. Alvarez recognized Babcock's classic evasive non-answer answer.

"Maybe I should check—"

"You have work to do. Do it!" barked Babcock. Alvarez knew something was not right but he had to respect the chain of command and pray he was doing the right thing.

Babcock pounded his fist on the topo map. "This isn't going to do us shit. I need satellite images now! Where's the lieutenant?"

Lieutenant Campbell came over to Babcock when one of his men told him about Babcock's demand.

"Are you Babcock?" queried the young Lieutenant.

"How come your men haven't provided me with satellite image data yet?"

Lieutenant Campbell wondered what bad espionage TV show Babcock came from.

"Agent Babcock, my men were deployed here to assist apprehending an armed fugitive—"

Babcock's impatience took over. "That armed fugitive is aiding a known domestic terrorist. The next time a building explodes or a subway gets shot up, do you want your name mentioned each time as the man who didn't get the terrorist when he had the chance? I'll make sure that happens. We don't know how widespread the conspiracy is. Now I need satellite images and I need them now!"

Lieutenant Campbell worked his way over to his communications tech officer who had overheard the entire exchange.

"He knows only the Pentagon can authorize satellite imaging, right? He knows that real time satellite imaging is almost impossible at night?"

"Yeah, I know," responded Lieutenant Campbell. "I don't think this pencilneck knows the difference between a Key Hole satellite image and a screenshot from Second Life."

"Wanna test that theory?"

"You read my mind," said Lieutenant Campbell.

But they didn't get the chance. Over the walkie talkie came some new intel. "Footprints, grid five!"

"Lieutenant Campbell," yelled Babcock. "Deploy your men to grid five!"

Almost immediately, Lieutenant Campbell ordered his men up the trailhead, but detouring to follow the path along side the creek.

# # #

Clyde had crested over the ridgeline right about at dusk. He considered himself fortunate. Any later and he would have lost any of his remaining sense of direction. He knew where Chilao was and was fairly certain he could recognize it from the ridgeline. If he had arrived any later, it would have been too dark to see.

Clyde drew an imaginary line connecting Chilao and where he was standing on the ridgeline. Along this line was his best guess where Henry and Elizabeth were. He hypothesized that if they were still hiking up, they wouldn't be too far off that line. He used the distant mountains to help him keep his bearings as he began descending toward the Chilao area.

It was a moonless night. Clyde's only hope was that Henry and Elizabeth had set up camp for the night and had a fire going. Maybe he had the lantern on and was telling ghost stories to her, Clyde thought. Otherwise, it would be impossible to find them, let alone see your hand inches in front of your face. Clyde would have to depend on his hearing to find them.

Clyde soon crossed the imaginary threshold that marked in his mind the farthest up the mountain Henry and Elizabeth could have reached. He stopped and he listened. Crickets. There was an owl. No sound of deer moving or even a coyote howl. However, there was another layer to the noise. Off to the west, Clyde heard the gentle gurgling of a creek.

Clyde deduced they would follow the creek, or at the very least, stay close to it. By now, the sun had completely set and the night sky was pitch black. Clyde looked up at the stars and used them to orient himself.

The ground was covered by coarse pebbles, forcing Clyde move cautiously. Clyde measured his steps with his breathing all the while listening. If Henry and Elizabeth were in stealth mode, he'd never find them. Then Clyde remembered that Elizabeth was a teenager and unlikely able to operate in any kind of stealth mode.

Clyde took another few moments to reconnoiter himself. If he could make his ears reach out and grab sounds out of the air, he would have.

I haven't been operating in stealth mode myself, thought Clyde. Maybe Henry heard him coming and is laying low. Maybe Henry thinks I'm an approaching hostile. Clyde whistled three sharp whistles. He waited. There was no reply. Only silence.

All this silence and darkness was feeding Clyde's paranoia. What if something happened to Henry? What if it was a bear or a cougar? Clyde removed one of the M-16s off his shoulder. In the Army, Clyde had taken advanced weapons training. In practice he should be able to load an ammo clip and attach it to his weapon in complete darkness. Hell, he would be able to do it underwater. The old muscle memory was still good. He had that ammo clip filled and locked in place in what seemed like only a few seconds. Clyde hoped he wouldn't have to use the M-16 but it was always better to be prepared for bear but find a rabbit rather than the other way around.

Clyde calculated that he should travel another half hour down the mountain before he would try to signal for Henry again. He had been running at just about full speed since he left the Colby Canyon parking lot... Clyde couldn't figure out how many hours ago. He needed to rest and conserve some of his strength in the event he wouldn't be able to find Henry tonight.

Clyde walked over to the creek and washed his face. He scooped some water into his hands and took a sip. The water was cold and refreshing. Clyde backed away from the stream and began looking for a rock to sit on.

His face hit something.

It startled Clyde. Whatever it was, it was rough against his skin. He threw up his hands in a defensive posture and then realized what he walked into: Henry's clothesline.

"Henry?" Clyde called out. No response. Clyde followed the clothesline to where it was tied off around a tree.

Clyde felt down the tree and found Henry's backpack. Hallelujah! thought Clyde. He patted down the side and found one of Henry's battery operated lanterns and clicked it on.

Not much of a campsite, thought Clyde. The tent wasn't set up, neither was the water station. Clyde spotted Henry's single burner stove. Next to it was an empty bag of freeze-dried and Henry's spork. This is wrong, thought Clyde. Henry wouldn't leave out garbage like that. Something must have happened. Something that caught Henry by surprise.

Clyde was satisfied that there wasn't anyone around. This can't be a dead end, Clyde thought. Henry wouldn't have left a cold trail. Clyde was sure of that.

Clyde knew he had to be methodical. He set down the M-16 and found what he believed to be the center of Henry's campsite. He kept his eyes focused on the ground as he moved further out from the center. Clyde was careful not to disturb anything on the ground if at all possible.

He recognized the imprint of his sneakers that Elizabeth was wearing. He found two different sets of boot prints. He figured the smaller one had to be Henry's. Strange, Henry was ambushed by one person? wondered Clyde. Henry had more skills than that.

Whatever happened, Clyde found himself standing in the epicenter. Henry would have left a clue. Henry would have left a clue. Clyde would just have to find it.

And he did.

It was subtle but Clyde spotted it. The shadows from the lantern had betrayed their appearance. Henry had dug a rut in the dirt with his foot pointing in the direction they went. East. Okay!

Clyde looked around the campsite. We can't come back here. Tactically, that would be a mistake. Clyde scrambled and packed everything back into Henry's backpack. He had emptied his pockets of the ammo and the grenades and stuck them in the backpack's outer pockets for easy access. He managed to strap the M-16s across the top of the backpack to take some of the pressure off his soldiers. As advanced as the Army was, they still didn't know how to make a shoulder strap that didn't dig into your chest.

Clyde knew that he wouldn't be able to use the lantern to track Henry without giving himself away. Clyde hoped that Henry's Mini Maglight was still in one of the pockets. When Clyde found it he couldn't help saying out loud, "Thank God something's gone right today."

Clyde immediately rebuked himself for that utterance. Can't think like that. Wherever Henry is, he's in trouble and I'm the only help that's coming.

# # #

Henry lay back in his cot staring up at the top of the tent. Elizabeth had finally fallen asleep. Henry figured it was best to let her get what ever sleep she could have. Henry was trying to rest as best as he could without falling asleep. He kept his ear on the jack-jawing around the campfire outside his tent. In Henry's mind there were two possible outcomes: One, they would get tired and call it a night or; Two, they would get drunk and pass out. As long as they kept talking Henry and Elizabeth were trapped but safe.

Henry looked over at Elizabeth. For the first time, he truly questioned his decision to go on the run. If they had stayed in the repatriation camps, they would be prisoners but they would be safe. Their lives wouldn't be in jeopardy.

Eldridge seemed like he had a military background. He could have been in charge of men. If Henry had to guess, Eldridge was an officer, but not a career officer. It's not in his bones, it's not in his walk... what's left of his walk. He didn't have the gravitas that comes with experience. Maybe he was a lieutenant who was injured early in his career. Maybe that's why he didn't trust him. It's not that Henry thought Eldridge was a dishonorable person, he felt that when push comes to shove, Eldridge wouldn't be able to control his men, especially Lynch.

Henry had seen Lynch's type before. A cancer, sowing seeds of discontent who rarely had an original, constructive idea of his own. He was the type of man who always acted as if he knew something his commanding officer didn't know. Lynch was the man Henry didn't trust. Henry didn't like the way Lynch looked at Elizabeth.

That was always a tough call for Henry. The line between protecting Elizabeth and letting her live her life was a constantly moving target. In this case, Henry wanted to protect her. That's why he didn't share his concerns about Lynch with Elizabeth. He hoped that Elizabeth would have noticed the stares and offside looks Lynch gave her and know that she would have to do more than just say no.

But Henry also had withheld from her what he was able to deduce about these men. The flag hanging over their camp was a White militia flag. These men weren't up here for the weekend for a camping trip, this was their secret training ground. The last straw for Henry was the pseudoephedrine residue he found on the folding table. These guys were cooking meth, probably to sell to raise money. They were definitely suspicious of outsiders, probably paranoid.

And it didn't help that Henry and Elizabeth belonged to a race of people these men held responsible for their nation's woes.

Henry didn't tell Elizabeth any of this. He honestly didn't know her well enough to predict how she would react. Henry hoped that was the right decision for now. He knew he wouldn't always be able to shield her. He would have to teach her how to see the world as he saw it. But he couldn't help wanting to be her overprotective father for just a little bit longer.

The noise outside had died down. Henry climbed out of his cot and gently woke up Elizabeth. "It's time to go."

Henry motioned to Elizabeth to follow him as he pushed his way through the tent flap.

The campfire had died down. There were a few empty bourbon bottles lying around but it looked like all of Eldridge's men had turned themselves in for the night.

Henry looked up at the night sky. There was no moon out. The stars lit up the night sky like Christmas lights. Henry quickly got his bearings and pointed west.

"This way," he said to Elizabeth. Holding her hand, he pulled her along to the perimeter of the campsite.

"I don't understand why we have to leave now," she protested.

"Shhh!" Henry continued to pull her along after they had left the camp. Henry was about to breathe a sigh of relief when suddenly he was blinded by a bright spotlight. Once your eyes have gotten used to pitch darkness, any light is painful.

"On your knees." The voice unmistakably belonged to Lynch. Henry gestured to Elizabeth to kneel down and she did so. Lynch turned to Holst and said, "Go wake up my uncle. Tell him he did exactly what I said he'd do."

Lynch secured Henry and Elizabeth with plastic ties on their wrists and marched them back into the campsite. Eldridge, having just been rousted out of his rack wasn't looking very happy.

"I caught them trying to escape," announced Lynch.

"Why the hell didn't you let them?"

"Who were they in such a hurry to see?" countered Lynch with an overly self-satisfied look on his face.

Henry knew that Lynch would test the men's loyalty to Eldridge. He was going to make his case soon. Henry decided to take a chance and try to expose Lynch's treachery before he had a chance to make his case for mutiny.

"You guys love to run around up here and play soldier when you don't have half the stones of a girl scout," taunted Henry.

"What the fuck did you say?" said Lynch.

"Look at your shirt, look at your pants. A soldier in the U.S. Army would have a helluva lot more pride in the way he looks. A soldier in the U.S. Army wouldn't buy his fatigues from K-Mart. You guys aren't soldiers. You guys are second rate Blackwater wannabes."

"What army did you serve in motherfucker?" screamed Lynch.

"I served in the 82nd Airborne, 274th Division, Fifth Battalion, Charlie Company." Elizabeth was startled at his admission.

"Wait," intervened Eldridge. "What was your mission?"

"Operation Blue Spoon," replied Henry.

Eldridge glanced over at Lynch. "Heard about what you did in Panama. That was pretty bad ass."

"You don't believe him, do you uncle?"

"I had some friends that were down there. The name Operation Blue Spoon was known only to the guys who were there. Let him go."

"What? He's the enemy! We're going to be at war with China any day now and you want to let him go?"

Eldridge stood up to face his nephew. "He's not the enemy, he's one of us."

Lynch matched his uncle's stare, "He's the fucking enemy and if you can't see that, then why are you in fucking charge?"

"Let them go," ordered Eldridge as forcefully as he could.

"No." Eldridge was shocked. He and his nephew had their differences before but this was more than defiance. This was outright disobedience. This was mutiny.

"Rigby, take my uncle to his tent and make sure he's comfortable there."

"What the hell are you doing?" asked Eldridge.

"What we're doing up here is a good thing. It's a necessary thing and I can't let you screw it up because you've lost all your sense of reason. Rigby, take care of my uncle."

Rigby took Eldridge's arm. Eldridge stood up and let Rigby escort him away. Henry knew he had miscalculated. Eldridge was far weaker than he thought. Henry's potential ally was now a prisoner too.

Lynch walked over to Henry and smacked him in the face with the butt of his rifle. Elizabeth screamed.

"You," said Lynch addressing Henry. "You're gonna answer some questions now."

As they dragged Henry into the tent he felt relieved that he made one right decision. He hadn't told Elizabeth anything. He didn't know how much protection this afforded her but he knew she wouldn't have to lie to save his life.

Henry hoped with all his might that Lynch would direct all his wrath and paranoia at him and not Elizabeth.

§

CHAPTER TWELVE

Eldridge sat in his tent. Normally he would pace around but Lynch took his crutches. He was pissed at his nephew. He was also pissed at his sister. He had tried to be the good uncle taking a major role in Lynch's life after his nephew dropped out of high school. What Eldridge didn't expect was Lynch showing up on his doorstep with a suitcase the day after he turned eighteen. As soon as Lynch was of legal age, his mother kicked him out of the house, sold everything she had and moved to Indiana to live with a retired refrigerator assembly line worker. She was fed up with Montana and wanted the exciting life she felt she had been cheated out of.

Eldridge always had a strong sense of duty ever since he was in the Marine Corp. He had lost the use of his legs to a stray sniper bullet while stationed in Korea guarding the DMZ. He lived near Camp Pendleton after his discharge but couldn't bear watching the various regiments deploy, going off to do the things he couldn't do anymore.

Moving to Los Angeles was a mistake he would later conclude. He was discouraged by how the city had been overrun by Mexicans, Blacks and Asians. He never felt safe in any of those areas and he was a Marine. He ended doing some volunteer counseling at the V.A. in West L.A. and discovered an entire subculture of veterans who chose to live off the grid. Most of these guys were suffering from some form of PTSD and Eldridge tried his hardest to have them come in and stand down.

In V.A. parlance, a stand down was a recreation of the ritual of a veteran's discharge. The hope was that the ritual would somehow reboot his sense of reality and stop living as if his life were under siege.

It worked for some of the guys, but most refused and eventually died from exposure. It was during this time that Eldridge truly began asking himself, Is this what I was fighting for?

It didn't take long for Eldridge to find like-minded people. They all shared survivalist fantasies of the coming apocalypse. Not the religious kind of apocalypse with angels and devils but a 7.0 earthquake in Westwood. There would be chaos, there would be rioting, there would be looting and most of all, there would be a lot of unnecessary deaths.

Eldridge became their de facto leader because of his military Survival, Evasion, Resistance and Escape training. It was better known in the popular culture as SERE. Eldridge seemed to have found his new calling in life and even though he may not have been happy, he was content.

Until the day his nephew showed up on his doorstep.

Even though Lynch was his flesh and blood, he had to face the reality that he was a bad kid. Right away, Eldridge noticed that some of his belongings went missing. His cufflinks, his gold watch given to him by his father when he graduated from the academy and small amounts of cash. There was no doubt in Eldridge's mind that Lynch was stealing from him. He was positive that his guns would have disappeared too if he wasn't so anal about keeping them locked up.

The weekend training jaunts became problematic for Eldridge. He wanted to go but was afraid Lynch would rob him out of house and home. If he vanished afterwards, it might have been worth it but Lynch seemed content to stay, perpetually mooching off his uncle.

At first, Eldridge was encouraged by Lynch's participation in these weekend getaways. Not only was Lynch interested in surviving a catastrophe, he wanted to be able to assume authority in the event there was a leadership vacuum, as what happened in Louisiana.

Soon Lynch started bringing his own friends to these camping getaways. These men were aggressive, confrontational and lazy. They would pick a fight with you about anything. Who should have been the NFL's first round draft pick, who should have won the World Series... but they all shared a deep hatred for the federal government. These men scared away Eldridge's buddies and soon took over the camping trips.

But wishing for the destruction of the federal government doesn't make it so. For all their bluster, they didn't know the first thing about military tactics.

Not only that, they barely knew anything about camping. What began as a weekend for a few old timers to drink beer and complain about women turned into drunken target practice.

Eldridge continued to host these camping jaunts despite his conscience because he felt it would make a difference in his nephew's life. He felt compelled by his sense of duty to his nephew.

Lynch made it known that not only did he want to be prepared for the apocalypse, he wanted to incite it. To do that he would need money.

Through an old quartermaster buddy, Eldridge was able to procure military surplus equipment at heavily discounted prices. The mountains were an ideal place to set up a base of operations. With the federal cutbacks, the national forests and parks were short handed. Cooking methamphetamine was the quickest way to turn a fast dollar.

Eldridge was against it until the economy tanked. For some of these guys, cooking meth was their only source of income. Some had families to raise. Eldridge agreed to it conditionally until the economy picked up and they could get regular jobs.

It bothered Eldridge that he wasn't close to his nephew. He knew Lynch was a born whiner and complainer with little ingenuity to think or do things for himself. He was a natural leader only in the sense that he was good at getting other people to do his work for him. These were not the values that were taught to him by the Corp and he was very angry with himself for letting his nephew get away with it.

Eldridge realized that his devotion to his nephew was born out of duty and not love. That at a time when Lynch needed a father figure, Eldridge gave him a commanding officer. Eldridge considered his failure the result of his lack of experience leading men. His military career ended too soon and maybe he unconsciously tried to make up for it by the way he treated Lynch.

Maybe there was still a way to reach Lynch. Eldridge searched his heart and realized that despite everything he did love his nephew and he would tell him so.

Eldridge looked up as Lynch entered the tent.

"Tom, I have something to say—"

"I don't want to hear it," interrupted Lynch as he raised his handgun and fired a bullet through Eldridge's forehead.

# # #

Private Chin determined the general direction the incoming shots were being fired from. Private Wilson had made sure their six was clear. Even though the enemy had the higher ground, none his men had been hit but Private Chin knew that good luck was fleeting. Private Chin and Private Wilson laid down suppressive fire so his squad could flank right to find some cover behind rocks and under denser foliage. Once some of his men were there, they laid down their own barrage of suppressive fire so Private Chin and Private Wilson could join them.

Secure for the moment from enemy fire, they considered their next move as two of Private Chin's men returned fire.

"I count about eight or nine different weapons," began Private Chin.

"I count twelve," said Private Wilson.

"Okay, twelve it is." Private Chin trusted Private Wilson's hearing far more than his own. "They definitely outnumber us."

Private Chin began to outline his plan. "There's no way they can advance and assault us directly from that position. There's a path down from that ridge to the south. That's where they will try to outflank us. Keep the enemy engaged at full tilt for about ten minutes then taper off for the next ten. Make them think they're picking you off one by one. Private Wilson and I will set up a kill zone along this path." Private Chin turned to Private Wilson, "You still got both your Claymores?"

Private Wilson smiled.

Private Chin turned his attention back to the rest of his men. "Wait for the big boom. I figure they won't fire on you after that. Feel free to come join us. Got it?"

"Yes sir!" came the reply.

"Okay, lay down some suppressive fire for us."

His men did as they were told and laid down a barrage of bullets so he and Private Wilson could slip away.

The path down from the ridge was exactly where the topo map said it was. It was overgrown but still there. Private Chin counted off the time in his head. It took them four minutes to get here. Only six minutes left to set the kill zone. Private Chin signaled to Private Wilson. "Go farther up. About one hundred feet. Then circle back counter clockwise." Private Wilson nodded before he headed up the trail.

The Claymores were idiot-proof. Written on the front of the mine were the words Front Toward Enemy. Private Chin dug a hole in the middle of the trail and partially buried the Claymore and covered it with some palm fronds. He set the blasting cap and attached the detonation cord. Private Wilson was one hundred feet further up doing the exact same thing. He kicked dirt over the electric detonation cord as he moved up along the right side of the trail. He knew that Private Wilson worked about as fast as he did and was mirroring his movements on the other side of the trail.

Because Claymores were command detonated (as opposed to being on a fuse or timer), he could retrieve them later if they didn't need to be used. Once Private Chin had both his Claymores set, he retreated to higher ground behind them.

He scanned the other side of the trail for Private Wilson. He saw the rhythmic flash from Private Wilson's pocket mirror. He knew he was set too. Now they waited.

Private Chin could hear the gunfire dying down. The distinct sound of the Army issued M-16 was all but gone. The enemy had at least one pump action rifle, a few .22 caliber rifles, and a handgun. Private Chin wouldn't bet his life on this assessment. Private Wilson was so much better at it.

Clearly his squad had superior weapons however, Private Chin chose this tactic because he believed his squad was out numbered. Once he heard the firefight die down, he knew he'd have his answer soon.

He could hear movement. Approaching footsteps, lots of them. He saw them cross over the point where Private Wilson set his Claymore on the path and began to count. Five, ten, fifteen, twenty, twenty-five, twenty-seven! Twenty seven was more than double what they thought were there. As far as Private Chin could tell, only the front eight or nine were carrying weapons.

This is a pathetic group, Private Chin thought. There was nothing romantic about this band of guerillas. No uniforms, no camouflage, no boots or standardized equipment. What a bunch of rag bags. Dirty white t-shirts, shorts, flip flops. More machismo than training. That's what gave Private Chin the advantage. After a few more seconds, all twenty seven guerillas were inside the kill zone. Private Chin waited until the first man was less than ten feet away from the Claymore he buried in the trail before he detonated it.

Imagine your grandfather's 12 gauge shotgun. It's hardly a weapon of finesse. You wouldn't win any accuracy contests with it, but at close range it would have enough power to rip the flesh off a man's body. Now imagine that instead of using gunpowder, you used C-4 as your propellant.

The first Claymore took out about ten men easily. The rest of the men instantly panicked, turned and ran back the way they came (as Private Chin had predicted). They ran smack into Private Wilson's Claymore, which he detonated, also killing about ten men.

The remaining men couldn't go forward and couldn't go backwards. They decided their best bet was to get off the trail as fast as they could, but that decision led them straight to the two remaining Claymores. Private Chin detonated his and a few seconds later, he heard Private Wilson detonate his. Once the smoke cleared, there was only one guerilla remaining. He was a kid about twenty years old. He didn't run off the trail. He had been paralyzed by fear and stood his ground. Now he was covered in dirt, blood and pieces of flesh from his compadres. He bent down and picked up a rifle and pointed it aimlessly.

Private Chin had a bead on him. "Drop your weapon now!" The kid started firing in his direction. At this close range, Private Chin could tell that rifle hadn't been cleaned in a long time. The kid kept shooting round after round blindly until he dry fired. Realizing he was out of ammo, he tossed the rifle aside and threw his hands up in surrender. Private Chin was mad. How dare you fire your weapon dry and then surrender. You don't get to shoot at me for free motherfucker. He took aim and shot the kid in the fleshy part of his thigh.

The kid fell to the ground screaming as he gripped his thigh. Then Private Chin heard it. It was so clear to him, he knew that Private Wilson heard it too. The firefight between their squad and the enemies on the bluff had escalated. Private Chin and Private Wilson came down from their positions all the while checking the area to make sure it was clear and that no one else was approaching.

Private Chin grabbed the kid by the throat. In Spanish, Private Chin demanded, *"¿Cuántos más hombres?"* The kid continued to scream in pain. Private Chin shook him. *"¿Cuántos más hombres?"* he repeated.

"No sé! No sé!"

Private Chin drew back and punched him in the face and then put his knee on the kid's bullet wound.

"Bullshit! *¿Cuántos más hombres?*

"No sé! No sé!"

Private Chin drew his M-16 on the kid and pointed it at his face. The kid stopped screaming and threw his hands up in the air. Private Chin repeated his question one more time but much slower. *"¿Cuántos más hombres?"*

"No sé!" the kid insisted.

Private Chin let go of the M-16 and grabbed the kid's face. He put his thumb between the kid's left eye and his nose and began to slowly dig into his eye socket. The kid screamed in pain as Private Chin increased the pressure.

"Treinta! Treinta hombres!"

"¿En todos?" demanded Private Chin.

"Sí, en todos," the kid responded. Private Chin pushed the kid into the ground. For a moment, it looked like Private Chin was going to back off but suddenly he swung the butt of his M-16 around and knocked the kid unconscious.

Private Chin took long deep breaths to slow down his heartbeat. His adrenaline rush was abating.

"Thirty men?" ask Private Wilson as he secured the unconscious kid with plastic ties.

"Yeah," confirmed Private Chin. "We walked our squad right into a motherfucking ambush. We gotta go back."

Private Chin and Private Wilson returned to the trail. The stench of human excrement leaking from the dead guerillas was overpowering in the tropical heat. If Private Chin and Private Wilson had bothered to look, they would have seen the damage done by their Claymores. The guerillas that were closest to them when they discharged had limbs blown off while most had their torso flesh shredded off. There was no point in administering first aid, anyone hit by the shrapnel of the Claymores in that close a range would bleed to death in seconds.

But Private Chin and Private Wilson had bigger worries. Their squad was pinned down in this small canyon. They couldn't go back because they needed water. They couldn't go forward because there were still thirty armed guerillas firing down on them. They would need some help.

When Private Chin and Private Wilson returned to their squad they found them huddled down behind a large boulder. They laid down a barrage of cover fire to allow the squad to move to a more protected location. The update was grim. One man had taken a bullet in the shoulder and couldn't hold his weapon anymore. They were all running low on ammo.

Private Chin took control of the radio. "Hammer Lock, this is Key Stone, come in, over."

"Key Stone this is Hammer Lock, over."

"Under fire. Enemy in grid oscar six, five. Request airstrike. Over."

"Confirm, enemy in grid oscar six, five. Over."

There was silence over the radio for a few seconds. The guerillas continued to fire at them.

"Key Stone, this is Hammer Lock, request granted. ETA two minutes. What's your color? Over."

Private Chin looked over at Private Wilson. "Green."

"We'll be popping green, over." repeated Private Chin.

"Confirmed. See you on the other side. Over and out."

Private Chin ordered his men to take cover. "We have less than two minutes!" They huddled up next to rocks while lying prone on the ground. Before Private Wilson secured himself, he handed Private Chin a smoke bomb. Private Chin kept track of the time. With thirty seconds left, he popped the smoke bomb and tossed it a few feet away out into the open. It spewed out a huge cloud of green smoke.

Then they all felt it. It began as a low vibrating rumble radiating out from the center of your chest before it turned your entire ribcage into a timpani drum. The first flyby was low to determine the target's location. The second released a single missile on the enemy's position.

The explosion was deafening. The ground shook and for a few seconds, dirt rained down on everything. The explosion echoed back and forth throughout the canyon for a few seconds before it died down to an unnatural silence. No more gunfire, no sounds of nature either. No sounds of birds or insects. Only the sound of the ringing in your ears.

The green smoke had done its job identifying the position of the squad so the flyby would know where not to fire.

Private Chin regrouped his men and circled up to the top of the bluff. The missile had uniformly cleared the area of all topography and left behind a deep layer of loose, freshly turned dirt. As you walked through the area, your feet sank easily into the soft dirt.

There were probably thirty men up here. There were enough charred body parts lying around. Private Chin didn't bother to count. Others would mourn for these men, Private Chin wouldn't. Even though these guerillas had superior numbers, the superior position and even tried to outflank them, Private Chin's squad fought them to a stalemate before calling in the airstrike.

Private Chin radioed in. "Hammer Lock, this is Key Stone, area secured. We're on the other side. Send our regards. Over."

"Key Stone, this is Hammer Lock, message received. Over and out."

Private Chin was mad. He stared at a disfigured head lying partially buried in the dirt. One eye was pushed down toward the nose. The other eye was missing as was the rest of his forehead.

The enemy should have bugged out instead of holding their position for so long. Private Chin had called the right play but didn't anticipate there would be so many guerillas. Intel said they moved in bands of less than five men.

They should have given up. Didn't they know we'd respond with overwhelming force? The guerillas should have given up.

For a moment, Private Chin lost his temper and flipped off the safety on his M-16. Private Wilson saw him and grabbed his arm.

"It's over," said Private Wilson. "Your weapon's hot and there's no one around except us. It's over. You can't make them even more dead."

Private Chin bottled up his rage. He needed to learn to control it. At this moment, he was furious at the world and fought to keep it under control. But for this moment, he couldn't. He pulled his arm free and fired a round at the one eyed head.

Henry heard Elizabeth scream. Henry tried to move but a dull, nauseating pressure inside his skull kept him where he was.

"Daddy, are you awake?" Elizabeth was sitting in a chair right next to him. "Daddy, you have to wake up." He couldn't open his eyes, but he could feel her squeezing his hands.

The smack on his head had left him woozy but not unconscious. Everything around him was like a black fog. It was as if his mind had been severed from his body and then coarsely reattached. He knew he wanted to say something but he couldn't move his mouth. He knew he wanted to sit up but couldn't move his arms. He began to feel the fog closing in on him again.

"Daddy, you have to wake up! Please, Daddy, wake up!" He could feel Elizabeth gently patting him on his cheek. It broke his heart to hear Elizabeth begging like that. Henry fell back on his training and tried to concentrate on his breathing, only he couldn't feel himself breathe.

"Daddy, they just shot someone," she whispered in his ear.

Henry tried to focus. The black fog faded in and out. Henry tried to imagine music but there was too much pain. Henry thought this was a good sign, feeling pain instead of nothing. The pain wasn't there before. Henry felt he must be getting closer.

Henry had no capacity to measure the passage of time. The fog seemed to get thicker but the pain remained constant. Henry began to concentrate on his daughter. He saw her face in the fog. He repeated her name in his mind. He used her name like a mantra to focus his energy.

He had a sense of his arms and legs now. They were heavy, leaden. He could feel his mouth now. Dry, cracked and painful to move. Henry was certain he was able to grunt. Then all at once, the black fog dissipated.

Henry opened his eyes. He had no idea how much time had passed. He was inside a tent. His vision was slightly blurry. He didn't have his glasses anymore. He tried to open his mouth but his jaw hurt and his throat was dry. He tried to lift his hands but they were bound. So were his legs. He was on a table lying flat on his back.

The table was on a small incline so his feet were higher than his head. Oh great, Henry thought. These guys really are Blackwater wannabes.

Henry managed to look around the tent. If Elizabeth was there, she was out of sight and silent.

"Elizabeth!" called out Henry in the loudest whisper he could muster. He forced the panic down into the lowest part of his gut. He was certain that as terrified as he was, Elizabeth was even more scared and that she was relying completely on him.

Henry tested his bonds. Nothing. No give. He tried to tip over the table but it was spiked down into the ground. He knew the soil up here was dry and rocky and wouldn't hold a spike for long if tested. He began to gently rock himself from side to side knowing eventually the soil would give. Small amounts constant pressure would eventually do it even though for the first hour or two it would feel like nothing was happening. It was exactly the same principle behind a wood shelf: leave enough books on a wood shelf long enough and the shelf will eventually snap. Henry could only hope he would have enough time.

He didn't.

Lynch entered the tent followed by Holst and Rigby. Blackwater wannabes indeed. Holst and Rigby carried in towels and jugs of water.

Lynch stood over Henry looking down at him. "You're awake."

"Where's Elizabeth?"

"She's okay."

"I want to see her."

"We've got some things to talk about first. I have a hard time believing you were in the military, let alone the 82nd Airborne."

"I doubt there's anything I could say that would convince you."

"So you admit you were lying?" pressed Lynch.

"I'm telling you the truth. I'm just saying you'll never believe it."

Lynch leaned in. "You people come to my country and you shit all over it. You have no respect for the people who are already here. It's nothing short of an invasion."

Henry had heard this rant before and other variations of it. Which flavor of White discontent did Lynch believe?

"I hate that you minorities have more rights than I do. I can't get a job. You people have taken them all. And now, my government has seen fit to give you free room and board because your feelings got hurt. China is our fucking enemy. We should put all of you on a boat and send you back if I had my way."

The alarm bells started going off in Henry's mind. "What about my rights?" continued Lynch. "You all got your Gay Pride parade and your Chinese New Year parade and streets named after Martin Luther King. I'm all for that. But why can't White people celebrate White pride with our own parade? We are the only people in this country you can legally discriminate against. I'm a real American. Does that sound fair to you?"

Henry knew the bug that was up Lynch's ass. Lynch was one of those guys who would never believe he lost a fair fight to anyone, let alone a minority. He was a slacker, sick of disappointment. It bugged him that minorities had things he felt he deserved. He had to get him off that topic for Elizabeth's safety.

"It's so fucking simple. Why doesn't anyone get it?"

"I'm an American," began Henry. "More American than you I'll bet."

Henry cleared his throat.

"I was a solider in the United States Army, 82nd Airborne, 274th Division, Fifth Battalion, Charlie Company. My father served in the Marine Corp in Vietnam. He came back and met my mother while marching with Dr. King from Selma to Montgomery. His father served in the U.S. Navy during World War Two and later was a military translator in Korea. His father was the first Chinese to practice law in Oakland. His father survived the San Francisco Earthquake of aught six. His father was a laundryman during the Great Depression of 1873. His father came to California for

116

the gold rush and helped build the Transcontinental Railroad. Eight generations of my family have lived in this country. How many generations have you been here?"

"Do you have any idea what it means to be an American? My uncle lost his legs because of people like you. Vietnam, Korea and the Japs? I cry for all the veterans who spilled blood fighting you people and now you walk around my country like you belong? America first. You people need to wait your turn. We should have killed all you zipperheads when we had the chance."

"Lynch, you've never worn the uniform. You don't get to speak for us who did." This got a laugh from Holst and Rigby. Lynch didn't find it amusing at all.

"You're not American. You don't get to speak for real Americans," countered Lynch.

"Ask your uncle. He'll know. If he was in the military then we know a lot of the same things."

"My uncle can't answer any questions now."

Henry instinctively knew what Lynch meant. Eldridge's medal that Lynch wore confirmed it in his mind. Lynch never served, that was obvious to Henry. Lynch was crazy and he had a camp full of followers. Why do they always seem to follow the crazy ones?

"I know you're lying about serving in the 82nd Airborne."

"I'll bet you don't know what that medal is you're wearing," interrupted Henry. He looked for Lynch's reaction. "It's a Joint Service Commendation Medal. Your uncle must have done something pretty good to earn that. Do you have any idea? Do you even know where he served? Vietnam? Lebanon? Africa? Iran? Wait, you said he lost his legs because of people like me. Your uncle's a Vietnam vet?" Henry searched his mind for other Asian operations toward the end of the Cold War. "Cambodia? Korea?" Henry kept staring at Lynch. "You don't know, do you? You have no idea what your uncle did to earn that medal."

"It's my medal now. I wear it to honor him," retorted Lynch.

"But if people think it's yours, you're not going to correct them, are you? Let me talk to your uncle."

Lynch nodded over to Holst and Rigby. They exited the tent but return moments later, dragging in Eldridge's body. They let it fall to the ground. Henry tried to study Lynch's face to spy any weakness, anything at all that would give him an advantage. But Henry saw no remorse, no shock, no regret in Lynch's eyes. Lynch was proud and confident, possibly for the first time in his life.

"Why are you up here? The truth this time."

"I am telling you the truth," said Henry.

"No, you're not." Then Lynch's voice dropped an octave. "I had a nice conversation with Elizabeth. How is it possible that your own daughter has no knowledge of you serving in the military?" Henry's mind raced. How long had he been unconscious? How did Lynch talk to her? Is she okay?

"I never told her about my military service."

"See, something as massive as being in the 82nd Airborne? I would have told everyone. You know how many free drinks I would have gotten? One for every man I killed."

"If you'd been through what I'd been through, you'd understand why I didn't tell her."

"If things weren't the same, they'd be different. Mumbo jumbo bullshit." Lynch opened a canteen and took a swig from it, imitating the casual sadism he'd seen in many war fantasies. "I've had enough of your bullshit. I know for a fact there's no way you could have served. You chinks are all tiny little weak men. You couldn't beat anyone in a fair fight. Guess what? We can beat you even in an unfair fight."

Lynch leaned in nose to nose with Henry.

"Now, I want to know why are you up here?"

Henry held his tongue. Whatever was going to happen next, Henry would have to outlast him in a way entertaining enough for him to leave Elizabeth alone.

Suddenly, Lynch slammed his fist into Henry's stomach. Sucker punch, thought Henry. His eyes welled up with tears from the pain.

"It's time someone finally taught you people a lesson," said Lynch.

A towel was pulled over Henry's face. Here it comes, the bad Blackwater recruitment video: how to waterboard your friends and neighbors. Henry's breath grew shallow as the towel became saturated with water. These guys are total amateurs, thought Henry. He knew the chances were good that they'd screw up and accidentally drown him.

"Why are you up here?" demanded Lynch.

They didn't disappoint him. Henry choked on his tongue as he inhaled a mouthful of water. As the black fog returned, his soul was filled with regret for failing to protect Elizabeth.

§

CHAPTER THIRTEEN

Babcock wished he had a pair of sturdy shoes. He was sure his black Kenneth Cole wing tips were all but destroyed by this rigorous mountain hike. There was no clear path along side the creek and his foot found the bottom of it many times already. His jacket was torn and his shirt was soaked through with sweat. His black dress socks gave his feet no cushioning and he was certain he had a blister. It took all his effort to keep up with Lieutenant Campbell and his squad of a dozen men.

At one point, Lieutenant Campbell caught Babcock eyeing his combat boots.

"You wouldn't have a spare pair of those lying around I could borrow? Size 10?"

"No such luck," said Lieutenant Campbell.

"I'll give you a hundred bucks for yours," joked Babcock.

"My Corcorans cost a lot more than that," said Lieutenant Campbell as he subtly accelerated his pace.

Geez, thought Babcock. It was just a joke. Aren't we all on the same side?

Babcock didn't have his own flashlight. He was depending on the spill from the soldiers equipment. The sense of urgency he had instilled in them came from his own sense of imminent danger posed by two ex-military men on the loose when in truth he needed to wrap this up before someone called Don and woke him up.

The soldiers took their position at the ridgeline. They were certain that Clyde Wilson had made it this far up. His footprints were clear and fresh. In fact, he had made no effort to hide them. He had hoped that they would have caught up to him by now, but Clyde Wilson had such a good head start that seemed unlikely.

What was beginning to bother Babcock was Clyde Wilson's motivation. Why come up here? White delivery vans were so common in Los Angeles, the chance a random stop would have found him were close to nil.

Babcock was having a very difficult time navigating the last hundred yards or so to the ridgeline. Then he figured out why. The soldiers had turned off all their flashlights and were now lying prone, reconnoitering the next valley with night vision goggles.

The men had grown eerily silent. Babcock noticed the sounds of the night for the first time. A gentle wind rustled the leaves in the trees. Crickets sang. Off in the distance, he could hear an owl hoot. He didn't know what kind of owl it was but it was loud.

Babcock walked up along side Lieutenant Campbell and tried to take in the valley below.

"Hey hey hey, get down. You're like a shooting gallery target if you stay standing up," admonished Lieutenant Campbell. "Beyond this ridgeline is a great place for a bogie to set up."

"How much longer will it be before we catch up to him?"

"With his head start we won't be able to catch him unless one of two things happened. One, he stopped to rest for the night. Two, he's lying in wait to ambush us. If he stays on the move, we could be tracking him for a few days. We're ready for that scenario." Lieutenant Campbell gave Babcock a quick once over. "Apparently, you're not."

Just then, Corporal Wesson signaled. "L.T. we got a heat signature further up the ridgeline."

"That must be where he is," offered Babcock.

Lieutenant Campbell trained his night vision goggles upward to where Corporal Wesson had pointed. "That's a strange signature."

"What do you mean?" asked Babcock.

"There's a lot of heat, but not a lot of light. As if it were camouflaged."

"That shouldn't be unusual."

"But that amount of heat for that amount of light means there's a lot of camouflage... It doesn't make sense. There's no way one person could create all that."

"But it's got to be him, right?"

"If your man is ex-military, he's trained in light discipline. He could be here in our field of view but if he's running in stealth mode, we wouldn't see him, even with night vision. I don't think that's him up there. I don't think it's a bunch of campers either. That's a mystery up there."

"Then it must be him."

"I'm saying that it doesn't necessarily have to be him. Why do you have such a hard on for this guy?" asked Lieutenant Campbell. "I just told you I don't think it's him up there."

"Who else could it be?"

"That's a very good question. One that's worth spending a little time and effort to figure out. Corporal Wesson."

"Yes sir?"

"You and Private Hooper, flank that area to the north. See what's up there. Structures, people, equipment. Standard recon protocol. Get in, get out, don't let them know you were there."

"This guy's a real bad apple. The sooner we get him the better off our country is."

"With all due respect to your expertise," began Lieutenant Campbell, "I saw their jackets, both men you're looking for. If they were conspirators, they would have blown up something a long time ago. If the cheese came off their crackers, they would have ambushed us at the first chance they had. Who you think they are, doesn't make sense."

"These men are domestic terrorists. The sooner we have them in custody, the easier Americans will be able to sleep at night." Unconsciously, Babcock pulled out a cigarette and lit it. Before he knew it, all the air was removed from his lungs by a sharp thump to his solar plexus from the butt of the Lieutenant's hand.

"We have to exercise light discipline too... sir."

"Okay," began Babcock as he struggled to regain his breath. "This is a direct order. We are going to continue our pursuit."

"That would be inadvisable," countered Lieutenant Campbell. He pointed in the direction of the heat signature. "That doesn't make any sense."

"What else could it possibly be? Lieutenant, I'm not repeating myself again. Continue the pursuit."

Lieutenant Campbell signaled his men to move out. Babcock had already worked out the logic in his mind. It had to be Henry Chin up there. He had a head start and plenty of time to set up a basecamp. If it was a family out camping, then Chin could be hiding out with them. Even if Chin was armed, Babcock had a dozen armed men with him. Babcock was comforted by the idea that in the event of a confrontation, he had the overwhelming force.

"I haven't had an In-N-Out burger in three months," whined Peck.

"Don't do this to me," said Milburn. "I don't ever want to eat beef jerky again as long as I live."

"If I close my eyes I can almost smell a Double-Double."

"Keep talking and I'm going to shove a handful of dirt down your throat," threatened Milburn. "You can eat that crap day in and day because you're young. I can't eat cheese anymore." He continued to train his night vision goggles toward the western horizon.

"Where do you think they're gonna do with Eldridge's body?" Peck shifted his legs in his foxhole.

"Don't know. Don't care. Not my concern. All I care about is getting my money and going home. This may be all fun and games for you. I need a bed to sleep in and a toilet to shit in. I'm fifty years old. I think I've earned that."

"That's what's wrong with this country," complained Peck. "Nobody wants to fight for anything anymore. You reach a certain age, and you think you're entitled to something."

"Hey asshole, I fixed cars for twenty years. And then they started adding computer chips to the engine. Do you how much an authorized diagnosis computer costs?"

"You had your own shop for twenty years and you weren't able to keep up? Why do you blame them for making a better car?"

Milburn resisted the urge to pop Peck in the mouth. "The hell's your problem? You don't know what it's like to invest your entire life in your own company and then watch some new tech make you obsolete. You don't know what it's like watching weak politicians give away our jobs to foreign countries."

"And what did you do about it? Nothing. You don't want to send a message. You don't want to fight. You just want your bed and your toilet. You don't have the right to complain. You can't expect something for nothing," accused Peck.

"Are you deaf? I said I had my own shop for twenty years. That counts for something."

"No, it doesn't. Every day that you draw breath, you have to earn your keep. You want to bank some credit, you do on your own. It's nobody else's responsibility. I never bought this retirement bullshit."

"Wait twenty years, see how you feel then," said Milburn.

"My point is that only the strong survive. That's what made this country great. You say the politicians are weak? If you don't fight them, then you deserve what you get."

Milburn suppressed his anger. He was perpetually mad at people who always seemed to get unfair breaks or preferential treatment: especially women and minorities. He didn't believe in handouts. He believed that a day's pay was a day's pay. A man should earn his keep but shouldn't have to work like a dog until the day he dies.

An owl hooted. For some reason, this got their attention. Both Milburn and Peck had spent their fair share of time in the fortifications around the campsite performing night guard duty. That owl hoot sounded out of place. Milburn pointed southward up into the hill overlooking the campsite. Peck pointed his night vision goggles and scanned the area.

"I don't see any—"

"Shhh," hushed Milburn.

"I think that was an owl."

"Shhh."

"I've never seen an owl with my own eyes."

Milburn leaned against the sandbags and began scanning the horizon. "You'll never see them. They move too fast and they don't make any noise." The hairs on the back of his neck stood up.

"Do you see the owl?"

"Fuck the owl. I got a weird sense we're being watched."

"No shit?"

"Holy—"

"What?"

"You missed it. There was a heat flare on the western horizon. There, to the west."

"Where?" asked Peck.

"There, about eleven o'clock."

Peck pointed his night vision goggles up toward the sky.

"No, no, no! Eleven o'clock on the horizontal," rebuked Milburn.

"I don't see any flares."

"It was there for a second. Like someone lighting a cigarette. You see that?"

"There's movement. There's people out there," confirmed Peck.

"Yeah, I see it. The ground looks like it's moving. I see one dude. He looks like he's standing up."

"I got the same thing. Holy shit. It looks like about a dozen guys."

"So far I've counted eight. Maybe there's four or five more. Go get Lynch. Tell him we got about a dozen bogies coming our way."

Lynch was pissed. This just confirmed in his mind that there was no possible way this Chinaman was ever a soldier. No American soldier would have passed out so quickly. The water pooled in Henry's mouth. Lynch wondered if he should give him CPR or just let him die.

Holst and Rigby stared at Henry.

"What do you want to do?" asked Holst.

Just then, Peck burst into the tent. "We spotted bogies approaching from the west. Two or three dozen.

Lynch didn't bat an eye. "Wake everyone up. Call battle stations. We're at DEF-CON Five!" Peck ran out of the tent. Before Peck left, he hesitated. He wasn't sure if he should tell Lynch that DEFCON Five represented the least amount of impending threat. But when Peck saw Eldridge lying on the ground with a bullet in his forehead, he thought better of it.

"What are you waiting for?" barked Lynch. Peck ran out of the tent. He knew Eldridge was dead but he had never seen a dead man before with his own eyes. He had trouble accepting the idea that the dead body on the ground was someone he ate with, drank with, shared stories and, for the most part, respected. For just a brief moment, he wondered where Eldridge's soul had gone.

Lynch turned to Holst while pointing at Henry. "Wake him up."

Holst and Rigby loosened the straps that held Henry down and turned him on his side to let the water drain out of his mouth. Lynch couldn't help but crow.

"If it's one thing that chinks got, it's a lot of friends. Uncle Eldridge, you should have listened to me."

Holst squeezed Henry's belly and a spout of water shot out of his mouth. Rigby turned Henry onto his stomach and slapped his back. More water sputtered out. Both Holst and Rigby were hoping that Henry would come to before Lynch ordered mouth-to-mouth resuscitation. Neither one was in a hurry to draw that straw.

Rigby lifted up Henry and gave him the Heimlich maneuver. Unfortunately, Lynch got the full spray out of Henry's mouth.

"Watch it, you fucking moron!" screamed Lynch. But his anger was shortly lived as Henry started coughing. He was having the worst headache he could remember. Huge globs of mucus and phlegm hung out of his mouth as he tried to expel it from his lungs. Each cough was painful, ringing in his head as well as in his chest. Henry was grateful to be alive. As long as he lived, there was always a chance.

Lynch kicked Henry in the abdomen. A glob of phlegm hit the dirt with a splat. That was the last of it. Henry could breathe now without drowning.

"Who are your friends?" asked Lynch.

Henry had no idea what Lynch was talking about. Open your mouth, say anything. "Christians, Jews and Muslims."

Henry felt Lynch's fist impact on his cheek. "Who followed you up here?" Henry felt a strange sense of joyful irony. Lynch was clumsily torturing him like a bad scene from a Rambo movie and yet his outbursts were giving Henry all the intel he needed. Men are approaching. He's running out of time. I will get my chance soon.

They let Henry fall to the floor. "Tie him up, we may need him as a hostage," said Lynch as he left the tent.

Lynch picked up his uncle's AK-47. He had waited a long time to hold it in his hands. It wasn't an ordinary AK-47. His uncle had modified it so it would fire full automatic. Lynch had always wanted to fire it but his uncle wouldn't let him. Not even up here. What also made this AK-47 special was the grenade launcher attached to the underside of the barrel. It could easily propel a grenade the length of a football field.

He tucked two thirty round banana clips in his belt and threw off the safety. We're gonna see some shit tonight.

Lynch joined his men in the sandbag-fortified trenches on the west side of the campsite. Milburn handed him his night vision goggles.

"See? Even though they're moving their way down into the valley, they're heading in this direction," reported Milburn.

"How many you figure?"

"I counted a dozen men," said Milburn.

"That's it? Not two or three dozen?"

"No." Milburn was a little surprised at the disappointment he sensed from Lynch.

"Do they know we're here?"

"They have to. They're making a beeline almost straight for us."

"Twelve guys. We got twelve guys. But we know they're coming. We're going to do Bunker Hill."

"You don't literally mean by the whites of their eyes, do you?" asked Milburn.

Lynch chuckled. "That's exactly what I mean. I want to wipe them out completely. They'll never know what hit them."

# # #

Clyde couldn't believe the set up. Even though the camouflage netting obscured his view, from his vantage point he could see four GP-Small tents. How the hell did they get all this crap up here? He could smell the smoke from their campfire. He could hear men snoring. It was several men at least.

He was trying hard to stay focused. He was bordering on complete exhaustion. He wasn't sure if he could trust his senses. He thought he had heard a single gunshot earlier but he had stopped to rest and was half asleep when he heard it. He didn't know if the gunshot was real or from his dream. He couldn't even remember his dream.

Strategically, Clyde decided that it was a real gunshot and to adjust his approach accordingly. He was tired. He was making mistakes and mental errors. He wished Henry were here so they could switch off taking naps and standing guard.

That was the hardest thing about the army for Clyde. Not the constant physical training or the endless drills. It was sleep deprivation. Anyone could complete an obstacle course when they were fresh. Try doing it after being on patrol for forty-eight straight hours with no sleep. That was Clyde's weakness. That was Henry's strength.

Suddenly, Clyde felt every muscle tense up. If these guys were military, they would have a patrol up here watching for anyone approaching. Clyde had been moving in stealth mode. It was slow and time consuming but he had to ensure his invisibility. Whoever was down there outnumbered him. He had no idea if they were armed. The snake flag hanging from the tree wasn't a good sign. Clyde had to be very careful. He couldn't underestimate these guys.

Clyde watched the campsite. Even in this darkness, he could spot movement. There was none. Something's not right. If these guys were military, someone would be on patrol making sure the area was clear and secure. If these guys were civilians, someone would be jack-jawing.

Clyde was certain that Henry and Elizabeth were here.

If he were on a routine recon patrol, he'd exercise patience. He'd study their routines, count how many men, and see what equipment and supplies they had. This could take hours or it could take days. Clyde's instincts told him that he didn't have that time. He waited a few more minutes to see if there were any changes happening below. Nothing.

Clyde used his hands to partially obscure his mouth. He inhaled and hooted like an African Wood Owl. Henry would recognize it as a bird that wasn't native this area.

Clyde held his breath as he listened. Movement. Voices. Low, indecipherable. He waited for any return signal from Henry. Nothing. Clyde spotted some movement on the western side of the camp. Clyde kept his head low. Then he spotted him. A man. Not Henry's build. Larger. Standing up. Clyde watched to see what he would do. He could see his head move as if he were scanning the area. He could see his arms pointing up in his direction. Dang it. I was too loud, Clyde thought to himself.

Even with a head start, they'd catch up to him quickly. He decided that he would make his stand here. If they chose aggression, he would defend himself. Clyde looked around. Maybe over there behind that rock would be a better place to defend, he thought. His weapons were loaded. All he had to do was get over there. He wouldn't commit to the move unless he was sure.

Then he saw it.

One lone man running across the campsite. He came from the western most edge. He ran into one of the tents. Counting clockwise, it was tent number three. Clyde exhaled slowly. He would only have the advantage for a short amount of time. Another moment later, he saw the man run to tent number one and roust the others up from their sleep.

Clyde adjusted his position. He had a clear line of sight into the center of the campsite. He had his M-16 cheeked and set on semi-automatic. He figured if he could take out one or two men with precision, quality shots, that would make the men down below think twice about coming up here. The men emerged from the tent.

Clyde held his breath as he waited for the men to enter the clearing. They didn't. Clyde lifted his head in time to watch all the men run toward the western edge of the campsite. They were all armed but not making any provocative moves or advancement toward Clyde. Something else must have spooked them.

Clyde waited another moment before he saw another man emerge from tent number three. Clyde could tell from his gait that he was in his thirties. He didn't have the extra puppy energy of the first man but hadn't learned the art of conserving his movements like a man Clyde's age. He strode into tent number four. How odd that all the other men ran and he didn't, thought Clyde. After another moment, he emerged from tent number four with an AK-47. He jogged to join the rest of the men. He must be the leader, concluded Clyde.

Clyde quickly ran through the math in his mind. Tent number one is where the rank and file were billeted. Tent number four is where the ranking officer bunked. Tent three was the center of attention for the moment. Tent two was an unknown.

Clyde returned the safety back on his M-16. Something had gotten their attention and Clyde was going to take advantage of it. If Henry was here, he would have left a clue. Tent number three would be the place to start. Clyde swung his M-16 back onto his back, pulled out Henry's hunting knife and descended into the camp.

Clyde could hear movement inside tent number three. He crouched on the eastern side of the tent, out of sight from the western edge of the camp. He could hear two distinct sets of footprints shuffling around. One guy, Clyde could jump and neutralize without a making a sound. Two guys, no. Their comrades were men with lethal weapons ready to use them.

If there were only the two men in the tent, he could easily put a bullet in each of their heads before they knew anything, but he would be giving up his invisibility. It would also be a matter of seconds before they'd hear the shots and be on him.

Clyde decided he needed to risk a peek into the tent. If he could get his intel without engaging these men, he could keep his invisibility. Clyde crawled over to the tent entrance and pulled aside one of the flaps just enough so he could see inside.

Two heavy-set middle-aged men. Both had their backs to the tent entrance. On the ground was a man with a bullet through his forehead. Not Henry, thought Clyde. It bothered him that the corpse was lying there uncovered. Not that Clyde was squeamish about that sort of thing, he had seen his fair share of bodies. But friend or enemy, letting the body lie there uncovered was a sign of contempt for the deceased.

They were working on something on a table. As one moved to the side, he saw what was it was.

Henry was unconscious. His face was pale and bloated but he was still breathing, barely. The ground around the foot of the table was mud. It wasn't too hard to figure out that they were waterboarding Henry. Why? wondered Clyde. Henry doesn't know anything. Clyde couldn't fathom the entire picture. A dead guy on the ground, dead, execution style. Henry being waterboarded, it didn't make any sense. It was in that moment that Clyde decided that these men didn't deserve to live.

Clyde shucked off both M-16s and the backpack. He kept Henry's hunting knife. He had to neutralize both men as silently as possible. At least one of them was going to die.

Clyde got into a squat with his weight evenly split between both legs. He shifted his position so he was on the left side of the tent opening. He kept low so any movement was below their eye line. He held Henry's open hunting knife in his right hand and waited. He was waiting for the two men to split the table: one on the far side facing the tent opening and one on the near side facing the opposite direction.

Clyde could see they were tying Henry down onto the table. That made no sense, thought Clyde. Unless they were going to waterboard him more. But Henry was already unconscious. These men were taking their time, as if they didn't want to join their comrades. No matter, I'm more patient.

Then Clyde got his opportunity. Holst never knew what hit him. The hunting knife flew across the tent and found its mark at the point where his throat and chest met. The last thing he felt was his warm blood flood up into his mouth before everything went black.

By the time Rigby turned around Clyde had an arm across his neck and a hand on the back of his head. He was pulled backwards as he reached up to grab the arm. He had no choice but to give in to gravity as his face slammed into the dirt. His head felt like it was going to explode from the growing pressure inside. He could feel his arms grow limp just before everything went black.

The man was unconscious, but Clyde couldn't take any chances and cold cocked him in the face with his elbow. He was going to hurt badly but he would eventually wake up with a broken jaw. Better than his buddy's fate, which was that he wasn't going to wake up at all.

Clyde pulled his weapons and backpack into the tent before he tended to Henry. He retrieved the hunting knife and wiped it clean on Holst's pants before he cut Henry free from the table. He gently patted him on the cheek to wake him up but Henry remained unconscious. Clyde pressed down on Henry's abdomen and water spurted out of his mouth. Clyde leaned Henry's head down over the edge of the table and tried to drain his lungs as best as he could.

He rolled Henry back up onto the table and checked his airway. No blockage. He checked Henry's carotid artery for a pulse. If there was a heartbeat, it was very weak. He gave Henry five quick sharp and shallow chest compressions. Clyde had to get Henry breathing again. Clyde gently lowered Henry's jaw and pinched his nose closed and began to breath slowly into Henry.

Clyde watched Henry's chest slowly rise and fall with each breath Clyde gave him. He intermixed the breathing with some chest compressions. Five, six, seven, eight more breaths. The pulse was still there but Clyde had to reboot Henry.

I hate to do this. Clyde wound back and slapped Henry across the face as hard as he could. There was no change in Henry's breathing.

Clyde began to feel panic grow in the pit of his stomach. In his mind, Clyde began to punish himself for not running up the mountain faster and for waiting too long in the trees before coming into the camp. Or for taking too much time to pack the van, allowing himself to be ambushed back at the house. But if they hadn't surprised him, Clyde would be waiting down at the trailhead for Henry, not searching the mountains for him. There were too many 'what ifs' for regrets. Fate, God or destiny had put this situation in his hands. He had to wake Henry up.

Slap! This time Henry coughed, expelling clear slime from his lungs. Henry tried to sit up as Clyde grabbed his shoulders.

"Clyde?" gasped Henry.

"Can you stand up? You have to get on your feet."

Henry opened his eyes. "Where's Elizabeth?"

Just then, from outside the tent, came the sound of gunfire. A barrage. Whatever was coming up the mountain, these guys were shooting at it.

"I don't know," responded Clyde. "Can you stand up?"

"Where's Elizabeth?"

"If you can stand up, we're going to go look for her." Clyde held out an M-16 for Henry. Henry took it and pulled back on the charging handle.

"You got an extra magazine?"

"Of course," replied Clyde tossing him a thirty round clip. Henry tucked the magazine into his belt and flipped the safety off on his M-16. Clyde threw on the backpack and holding his M-16 low, led Henry out of the tent.

They swung around to tent number four. Clyde had guessed right. It was an officer's tent. Two bunks, a makeshift desk out of wooden crates. Clyde and Henry swept through it quickly before moving on to tent number one.

Clyde guessed right again. Here is where the men were billeted. This style tent could hold eight guys with their gear comfortably. It looked like they crammed at least double that number in here. It didn't help that it looked like they were all slobs. Henry wanted to call out for Elizabeth but wasn't sure if she'd be able to hear him over the gunfire.

Henry and Clyde finally hit tent number two. This was the mess tent. The tables were in a different configuration than Henry remembered. They were pushed over to the sides of the tent and knocked over. The dirt in the center of the tent had been greatly disturbed. There were many fresh footprints circling the center.

Henry knelt down and examined the dirt. It looked like someone had crawled away from the center. Henry drew his weapon and followed the trail outward to behind one of the tables. Henry signaled to Clyde who aimed his M-16 at the table.

Henry yanked the table aside. To their horror, they found Elizabeth. Her face was swollen, bruised and bleeding. Her blouse was torn. Her blue jeans and panties were pulled down to her knees.

She had been raped.

§

CHAPTER FOURTEEN

"EVERYONE DOWN!"

Lieutenant Campbell's order came just a fraction of a second before gunfire erupted from near the summit. His men threw themselves safely to the ground. Lieutenant Campbell wasn't as fortunate. His men were trained to follow his orders to the letter without hesitation. They did. Babcock didn't. Out of the corner of his eye, Lieutenant Campbell saw Babcock remain standing and dove for him knocking him to the ground. Babcock ended up with a mouth full of dirt while Lieutenant Campbell took bullets in his upper back, left shoulder, and behind his left ear.

Babcock heard himself scream as he covered his head with his arms as bullets impacted on the ground around him. He felt a hand grab him by the shoulder and drag him across the dirt into the bushes. The gunfire continued. The soldiers returned fire. Babcock drew his gun but didn't know where to shoot.

He looked back out into the clearing. Lieutenant Campbell's lifeless body lay there. "Who's in charge?" yelled Babcock. The gunfire around them continued to escalate. One of the soldiers rolled over. "The lieutenant is dead. Who is the ranking officer?" Babcock demanded.

"Lieutenant Campbell was the ranking officer. I'm Corporal Wesson. I'm the ranking NCO in the squad."

"What the hell do they have up there?" screamed Babcock.

"AK-47s. Sounds like at least a dozen of them."

"Can we take them?"

"They've got the high ground. They can see us as plain as day."

"How?"

Corporal Wesson looked at Babcock with disbelief. "Civilians can buy night vision goggles too."

"Can we attack them?"

"We're too exposed. We need to fall back down the slope to give us more cover."

Corporal Wesson signaled his men to retreat. Suddenly the ground behind them exploded.

"What the hell was that?" asked Babcock.

"Grenades. They have a grenade launcher." Corporal Wesson signaled his men to hold their position. They were pinned down and they all knew it.

"Can we move when they reload?" asked Babcock.

Corporal Wesson pointed up toward the summit. "Somewhere up there is their basecamp. They have automatic weapons and grenade launchers. We don't know what else they have up there. We can't engage them in a prolonged firefight because they're probably sitting on all their ammo. Bottom line is that we can't wait for them to provide us an opportunity."

"Then what the hell are we supposed to do?" asked Babcock.

The gunfire continued to rain down on them. Corporal Wesson pushed Babcock's head into the ground. "Keep your fucking head down!" he screamed.

The soldiers continued to sporadically return fire. Corporal Wesson signaled to Babcock. "Your intel says we're tracking two guys and a teenage girl? Whoever is up on that ridgeline is more than two guys and a girl. Your intel is wrong."

"What the hell do you want me to do about it now?"

Corporal Wesson could sense Babcock's defensiveness. "I need to know what kind of bastards are up there."

"I don't know!" screamed Babcock.

"Jesus fuck! You ran us up here on a hot pursuit. Why do you have such a hard on for these guys? Who the fuck are they?"

"They're terrorists!" said Babcock.

"They're not the airplane flying kind of terrorists, numbnuts! What are we up against? Chemical? Bio? Nuclear? What is it? You better tell me what you know you pencilneck motherfucker 'cause if I make the wrong decision, a lot more people than us are going to die!"

The gunfire continued to rain down on them. "Chemicals. He knows chemicals," said Babcock.

"That would have been a good piece of intel to have before we came up here. We're just fucking mushrooms to you. Keep us in the dark and feed us shit."

"How are you going to stop them?" asked Babcock.

"You mean how am I going to clean up your fucking mess?" Corporal Wesson turned to his men. "Walker! Get on the squawk box!" Corporal Wesson turned to Babcock. "When this is over, you have a lot to explain, poindexter."

Private Walker rolled over to them and handed Corporal Wesson a satellite phone. "Alpha dog actual, this is Wesson, over." The pause seemed to last forever as the gunfire continued. "Alpha dog, we are under fire. L.T. is down. Request an airstrike." After another pause he resumed. "Roger, over and out."

Corporal Wesson handed the satellite phone back to Private Walker. "Davis! I need you for a mission!"

Babcock intervened. "If there's something that needs to be done, I can do it."

"This isn't a time for heroes. This is what we're trained to do."

"I got you into this, let me get you out," begged Babcock.

Corporal Wesson handed Babcock two devices. "This is a GPS receiver. This is the display. Once you've found the center of their basecamp, push this button and take a reading. This is a walkie talkie. Once you have their position, radio it back to us."

"You don't have to talk to me like I'm a twelve year old," replied Babcock.

"Don't know what you civvies know," said Corporal Wesson. "Once you radio us, ankle bone express it as fast as you can out of there. You'll have about two minutes. Understand?"

Babcock nodded.

"We'll lay down some suppressive fire for you. Stay on the far side of the ridgeline, that way their infrared won't pick you up. We'll hold out until we hear from you."

"What if I get killed?" asked Babcock.

"Then we all die," said Corporal Wesson.

Another grenade exploded, this time even closer than the one before.

"You don't have much time. They'll zero our position soon enough." Corporal Wesson turned to his men. "I need suppressive fire now!"

The soldiers opened up a temporary barrage toward the summit as Babcock began running toward the south. He had a long way to go to get to that basecamp. This is what he felt like he was born to do.

#

"It's suicide!" screamed Clyde.

"I'll kill them all!" yelled back Henry. Henry reached for Clyde's M-16 but Clyde pulled it away. Henry lunged at Clyde and managed to get both hands on the M-16.

"What are you going to do?" pressed Clyde. "You hear all that gunfire out there? We can't engage in a firefight with that!"

Clyde tugged hard at the M-16 but Henry held his grip firm.

"This is our chance to leave. By the time they're done with their firefight, we could have a day's headstart. We engage, we're dead where we stand."

"I want them to pay!"

"Survival first. Revenge later," implored Clyde. "Elizabeth needs your help now."

Henry exhaled as he let go of the M-16. They both turned to Elizabeth. Henry had covered her with a plastic tarp.

"Honey, sweetheart, can you stand?"

Elizabeth drew in a shallow breath but her eyes remained closed. "Sweetheart, I need you to stand up now." Clyde ran to the tent opening, threw on the backpack and the other M-16.

"I can lead us out if Elizabeth can walk," yelled Clyde. Henry lifted Elizabeth to her feet as she gave him her weight.

As they stepped out of the tent, they could hear the gunfire from the west. Henry had lost track of how long the firefight had been going on. Even though they were armed to the teeth, Henry wanted all of them dead. But he knew Clyde was right. He knew Clyde's strategy would get them out safe and alive. That didn't stop Henry from wanting to stay and inflict a slow painful death to these scumbags.

They had cleared the campsite when Elizabeth began to show signs of coherence. "Stop... stop..."

"Elizabeth, are you okay?" Her grip around Henry tightened. She pulled herself into him and began sobbing. "Elizabeth, it's okay, it's okay. You're safe now." She held her father tightly, as if for dear life. Henry pulled her arms from around his neck and kneeled down before her. "It's okay... it's okay... can you walk?"

Elizabeth began to compose herself. "Yes, I think I can."

"Good."

"Dad, he called Mom a whore," she stated flatly. Something snapped inside Henry.

"Clyde, take her. I'll catch up. Give me the backpack."

Clyde knew there was no way to argue with Henry now.

"Head north, I'll find you." Henry grabbed the M-16 and the backpack. Just before Henry headed back down to the campsite, Clyde grabbed his arm.

"We need you alive."

Henry grabbed Clyde by the arm to make sure he had his complete attention. "If you have to choose between saving me or saving Elizabeth, save her."

"I got it," replied Clyde.

And Henry took off.

Henry descended back down into the campsite. He crouched low as he approached the western trench. About a dozen men were dug in, spread out like wide receivers on a Hail Mary pass. Whatever they were shooting at, they had no sense of conserving ammo. Henry could hear the return fire impotently hit the treetops overhead. These yokels had the advantage but didn't know what to do with it.

Clyde's words echoed in his head. He didn't have a clear shot at everyone on the line. He didn't want to take the chance that they could get a lucky shot on him. Under fire, he didn't have time to do an adequate recon.

Henry laid down on the ground in the prone firing position. He raised his M-16 at them. His finger deftly flipped off the safety.

Killing half of them would have felt really good but wouldn't get the job done. Henry wanted to do a complete job. He wanted to kill them. He wanted to kill them all.

Henry tried to squeeze the trigger but found that he couldn't. His heart was hot with revenge but he couldn't shoot these men in the back. No amount of justification in his mind would let him pull the trigger. Some of it was his training. Most of it was fear. Fear that he would die here and no longer be able to protect his daughter.

I've failed Elizabeth so far, thought Henry. These were bad men. They deserved to die. Tactically, at this moment, it didn't make sense for him to be their executioner. He had to ensure all of their deaths while making sure he'd be able to make his own escape.

Plan B.

Henry knew that the tent they had put him and Elizabeth in was where they cooked meth. He had tasted the pseudoephedrine residue on the table. He knew they had hastily moved their meth lab out of sight. There were two things he knew they must have: propane tanks and alcohol.

Moving quickly and quietly, Henry found what he was looking for behind the mess tent under a green tarp. He found three full propane tanks and duct taped them together into a triangle.

Then he took a hand grenade and duct taped the spoon in place so it would remain unarmed even with the pin pulled out. He found some cheesecloth and doused it with rubbing alcohol and wrapped it around the grenade. Then he taped the grenade to the center of the propane tank triangle.

The gunfire had not abated. Henry loaded his backpack on and threw his M-16 over his shoulder. He reached down and pulled out the grenade pin. The duct tape held the spoon in place.

He took a deep breath and lit the cheesecloth.

Henry calculated he probably had about thirty seconds before the cheesecloth melted the duct tape holding the grenade's spoon. Once the spoon was free, Henry maybe had five seconds before the grenade detonated.

Henry ran as fast as he could toward the eastern edge of the camp, away from the gunfire. He looked back over his shoulder. A giant flare shot up into the air. Too much alcohol, Henry realized. That was going to burn hot and quick. Hopefully, the militia wouldn't be able to put out the fire before it burned through the duct tape holding the spoon.

He could hear the men yelling at each other about the fire. Would it be too late for them to do anything about it? They ran over to the propane tanks and threw tarps over it to smother it.

C'mon, blow! willed Henry. But the men were able to extinguish the fire before it burned through the duct tape.

Henry switched his M-16 to full automatic and opened fire on the propane tanks. The bullets ricocheted wildly. It was a futile gesture. Armor piercing bullets might have penetrated but they would also have to be tracers to ignite the gas.

Bullets danced on the ground near Henry's feet. Lynch ran up to Henry with his AK-47 drawn. Henry realized that he wasn't running up to subdue him, he was getting a better angle to shoot him.

Henry dove to the ground as Lynch opened fire. Henry landed on his M-16 and couldn't swing it around fast enough as Lynch stood over him. "Nice try." Lynch was point blank when pulled the trigger but his AK-47 jammed. Henry had no time to react. He slipped the backpack off and dove at Lynch. His first punch landed on Lynch's throat. His next punch landed on Lynch's ribcage.

Henry was sure he had snapped a few of Lynch's ribs. He pulled Lynch's AK-47 out of his hands and aimed it at him.

"It's out of ammo!" sputtered Lynch.

"This is a stovepipe jam," began Henry. He pulled back on the bolt ejecting the spent shell. "That was how you clear it."

Lynch threw his hands up in surrender as he looked away from Henry. "Don't shoot!"

Henry gritted his teeth and blew Lynch's head off. Then he quickly turned and fired at the approaching militiamen. The fire was nearly out but Henry couldn't count on it to detonate the grenade.

Henry sensed something was not right. He slowed his breathing down and tried to listen over the sound of his heartbeat. He felt a rumble in his chest before he heard the sound: an all too familiar combination for Henry. Then Henry recognized it as the afterburners of an approaching F-18 Hornet flying just above the tops of the trees.

Henry covered his ears to protect them from the deafening roar as the F-18 Hornet passed overhead. Henry's body pumped adrenaline into his blood. Henry grabbed his M-16 and ran.

It was one of the few times Clyde didn't listen to Henry. Elizabeth was badly shaken up. She was in shock and she was in physical pain. Clyde held her but she was cold to the touch. He felt they could afford a little bit of time here as long as they stayed low and out of sight.

Clyde was worried for his old friend. He had seen that look in other men's eyes but never in Henry's. Once a man had that cold stare of revenge in his eyes, there was no way to turn him back. Clyde hoped that Henry was sensible enough not to turn his quest for vengeance into a suicide mission.

Elizabeth's eyes were still closed. He would let her rest for as long as he could. Then Clyde saw it. A giant flare in the center of the campsite.

What the hell did Henry do? wondered Clyde. Knowing Henry as well as he did, something was supposed to go boom! But nothing did. Clyde could hear the sound of men screaming at each other below.

Clyde's eyes needed some time to adjust to the glare. He strained and squinted to see what was going on below but couldn't see anything. Clyde was so distracted by trying to see what was going on in the campsite that he didn't notice his chest was vibrating. It began as a low rumble but then suddenly, Clyde realized it was a familiar feeling. The low rumble soon turned into a deafening roar as an F-18 Hornet flew overhead.

"Wake up Elizabeth. We have to run. We have to run now!" Elizabeth could barely open her eyes. "I'm so sorry," Clyde said as he tossed Elizabeth over his shoulder.

Corporal Wesson covered his head as dirt rained down on him. By his count that was the sixth grenade they fired down here. So far, Lieutenant Campbell was the only fatality but his men were taking bullets. He held the walkie talkie close by waiting for Babcock's signal. If he didn't call in the coordinates soon, there wouldn't be any men left to save. His men were sporadically returning fire to conserve ammo. The barrage of bullets and grenades coming down on them was relentless.

Maybe it was a mistake to trust a pencilneck bureaucrat with the task but if he were going to send someone out on what amounted to a suicide mission, he would send the least valuable team member. No matter what he decided to do, Babcock was going to slow them down.

The approval had come down from command for the airstrike. He had radioed their position but couldn't give them the exact coordinates of the hidden base up there. It was night so any smoke he'd pop wouldn't be visible. Corporal Wesson didn't know how much longer he could wait for Babcock.

Then he saw something.

Just beneath the summit, he saw a bright flare. Something happened up there and something caught fire. Corporal Wesson had to act quickly. He got on the squawk. "Alpha dog actual, this is Wesson, over... Alpha dog, target is the flare just below the summit, over." Babcock would be unfortunate collateral damage. Corporal Wesson made a mental note to say something nice at the pencilneck's memorial.

Two F-18 Hornets were scrambled out of Naval Air Station Point Mugu. They wouldn't have time to break Mach One but the distance they had to travel from Ventura County to the Angeles National Forest was barely seventy miles and would take less than ten minutes to traverse.

The Weapons System Operator in the lead F-18 Hornet checked his HUD as they flew past the Santa Susanna Mountains and over the San Fernando Valley. The flare they were told about would only be visible for a few more moments but if they were lucky, it would still give off a heat signature for minutes after that.

At the speed they were coming in, they would have a fraction of a second to lock one AGM-65 Maverick on the target. The way the mission was designed, they would have only one shot. The lead F-18 Hornet was solely to function as eyes and ears for the second plane.

They zoomed over La Cañada Flintridge and ascended over the Angeles National Forest. Within seconds the first pilot spotted the heat signature. The second pilot locked target on it and fired.

Babcock saw the flare. He was very close to the camp. He had circled wide around it and was beginning to double back. He didn't know what caused that flare. He didn't think he was close enough and now with all that light, he was positive he wouldn't be able to get the coordinates from the middle of the campsite. Babcock reasoned that the readings from the rear of the camp would have to do.

He pushed away branches as he ran the circumference of the campsite. He looked down to make sure the GPS receiver was turned on. He could feel the walkie talkie wedged firmly in his back pocket. Babcock was certain that his hands and face were cut up and bleeding from all the low branches he ran into. At full speed, Babcock pivoted and ran into the rear section of the camp...

But collided with someone.

He had collided with Henry Chin. "Don't move!" Babcock commanded.

Before he knew it, Babcock felt Henry's thumb gouge out his left eye. He tried to pull back but the pain knocked him to the ground. He felt his own blood run down his cheek. Then, as quickly as the thumb had gone into his eye, it was gone. Babcock swung wildly but couldn't connect any of his punches. He tried to open his eye but couldn't see anything. He hoped that it was because the blood obscured his sight until he felt his eyeball smack against his cheek before it broke off and hit the ground.

He could hear Henry's footsteps run off. With his good eye, he was able to see Henry. Instinct took over and Babcock ran. He ran in the same direction as Henry. He didn't question himself or wonder why. Henry was fleeing at top speed and Babcock's instincts told him to do the same thing.

The missile found its target. The explosion incinerated the surrounding trees and sent more than a ton of dirt and debris into the air. The blast could be seen miles away in Pasadena, Sylmar, Hollywood and Chatsworth. If you were unlucky enough to live in La Cañada Flintridge or Sun Valley, your car windows would have shattered if you didn't park it in your garage. The dirt rained back down and collected in a deep loose layer of debris.

The Army soldiers kept their heads down. They expected this. They trained for this. The militiamen were not as fortunate. They never knew what hit them. In one instant, their rebellion came to an end.

The sound of the blast echoed across the valley three or four times before giving away to silence. Even the crickets were quiet now.

Even though his cell phone was set to vibrate, Don could hear it buzzing on his nightstand. No call between midnight and 4 a.m. is ever good news. Don reached over. He was surprised to find the other half of his bed empty. He was a little disappointed. He had planned to call in late and spend the morning having a leisurely breakfast.

Don grabbed his cell phone and flipped it open. He waited for the operator to connect him with the duty officer before he was relayed the news. Don couldn't believe what he was hearing.

"Jesus Christ."

§

CHAPTER FIFTEEN

Floodlights illuminated the former campsite which was now little more than a crater. Fresh dirt covered everything. Smoke drifted off the charred trees but there was no more fire. Soldiers sank ankle deep in the loose dirt as they searched the area for survivors.

A temporary command post was set up under a canopy. Medics treated Corporal Wesson for minor burns, bruises and dehydration. Nearby, Lieutenant Campbell's body was being prepared for transportation.

The sound of an arriving helicopter filled the air.

"Incoming!" screamed Corporal Wesson. He turned to the medic and smiled, "I always wanted to say that."

The helicopter set itself down a good distance away from the crater. Despite that, the vortex kicked up all the loose dirt into the air creating a nearly impenetrable haze. Injured soldiers and Lieutenant Campbell's body were loaded onto the helicopter as Don alit.

"Who is senior on site?" called out Don.

Corporal Wesson stood up and walked over to him. "I'm Corporal Wesson. I inherited Lieutenant Campbell's squad."

"Where's Lieutenant Campbell?"

"I believe he took your seat on the chopper."

"I'm sorry for your loss."

"Thank you."

Don and Corporal Wesson walked around the fresh crater as Corporal Wesson briefed him on the events of the last few hours. Corporal Wesson brought Don over to a table where they were collecting artifacts and fragments. On it were burnt pieces of rifles, part of a propane stove, and ammo cases.

"These guys were heavily armed. They kept firing at us like there was no tomorrow. We've found remnants of what amounts to a warehouse of ammo and weapons they had up here. We're lucky to be alive," reported Corporal Wesson.

"Any idea who these guys were?" asked Don.

"Just what the SAIC told us."

"Which is?"

"Domestic terrorists who were in the process of creating a chemical weapon. That's why I requested the airstrike. Figured it was safer to incinerate whatever they had up here before they could release it on the valley below."

"Where is your SAIC?" asked Don.

Corporal Wesson hesitated before giving his answer. "He's still MIA. He came up here to infiltrate the campsite. We couldn't gauge their position while under fire. We believe he started a fire and that's what we were able to zero."

Don was good at reading people and he knew Corporal Wesson wasn't telling him everything. He found it hard to believe that Babcock could have earned their respect but if that's the story Corporal Wesson wanted to tell, he wasn't going to press him any harder unless he had to. If Babcock was killed, Don was content to let him be remembered as a hero.

Don stood as soldiers brought more pieces and artifacts. One private held a burnt branch in his hand and complained about how that was all he could find. Before Corporal Wesson could say anything, Don spoke up. "Son, take a closer look. That's not a burnt branch you're holding in your hand."

It was more than the private could handle. What he held was actually a charred ulna bone with some fingers still attached.

Don looked over the soldiers that were scouring the mountainside. They were all so young. He would've bet that they were barely out of basic training. This is probably the closest they've ever come to actual combat. I'll bet they didn't plan to get shot at in Los Angeles's backyard, Don thought.

Don paced around the area for the better part of an hour wondering how he was going to write up this incident. Babcock had misappropriated Don's authorization to bring this military task force up here in hot pursuit of a so called domestic terrorist. Sonuvabitch found something up here, but what? If Babcock was right, and he did stumble upon an organized Chinese fifth column up here, Don was inclined not to hang him out to dry. But he needed more information. Where the hell was Babcock?

Soldiers continued to catalogue the debris they were finding in the dirt. One piece caught Don's eye. It was a piece of fabric, charred around the edges. It looked like an American flag but some of the colors were wrong. Once Don saw it, he instantly knew what had happened up here.

"Corporal! We found him!" Corporal Wesson signaled Don to follow him.

They turned on their flashlights and circled the perimeter of the crater to the far side. Several soldiers were digging out Babcock. He was almost unrecognizable under all the dirt. He coughed several times before he realized Don was standing before him.

"Medic!" screamed Corporal Wesson. Mud had caked on the left side of Babcock's face where his eye had bled.

"They were here," began Babcock. "All of them. Chin, his daughter and Wilson. They had their own terrorist cell stationed up here. Well armed, well organized. This was the base of operations for their terrorist cell. If there's one, there's got to be more."

"Did you see the other members of this terrorist cell?" asked Don.

"You can see the results of what they did."

Don continued to press Babcock. "Did you actually see anyone else other than Chin, Elizabeth or Wilson?"

"They were here. I'm certain of it."

"Why so certain? Did you see him?"

"I saw Chin. We followed Wilson's trail right to him so Wilson had to be here. Chin was on the run with his daughter so she had to be here too."

"Did you see them?" reiterated Don.

"It's the only explanation."

"Okay." Don turned to Corporal Wesson. "Get this man some medical treatment. Once he's back on his feet, place him under arrest."

"What?" screamed Babcock.

Don turned to Babcock and stared him down. "You didn't see a Chinese American terrorist cell up here."

"Director Morgan, the threat is real," pleaded Babcock.

"Yes, the threat is real but not from Chinese Americans."

"They had weapons up here! They fired on us! They killed American soldiers! What more proof do you need?"

"Sir, he's right. We were fired upon," concurred Corporal Wesson.

"Corporal Wesson, I'm going to use this as a teachable moment. Everything this man has told you is true. You were fired upon and you did sustain casualties. But you do not know who it was that fired upon you."

"Who else could it be?" asked Corporal Wesson.

Don showed him the flag. "This is the flag of the California Native Son Vipers. They're distant cousins of the Arizona Viper Militia. You stumbled across a bunch of White guys who like to shoot guns and not pay taxes."

"You don't know that for sure," defended Babcock. "You're not FBI or ATF. I saw them! Henry Chin took my fucking eye!"

"I don't know what you saw, but it wasn't a Chinese Fifth Column."

"You're turning your back on a domestic terrorist. Don't you know how to protect your country?"

Don turned to Corporal Wesson. "Corporal Wesson, could your men give us a moment?" Corporal Wesson signaled his men to follow him away. As soon as they were clear, Don socked Babcock in the mouth.

"Don't ever question my loyalty to my country again," warned Don.

Babcock faced Don. "Then stop defending traitors."

Don called Corporal Wesson back over. "Yeah, what I said before... Place him under arrest once he's had medical treatment."

"Yes sir." Corporal Wesson saluted Don.

"Yes, thank you. I have a very difficult phone call to make."

# # #

This was the three a.m. phone call that every President dreads. While he was getting briefed in the Situation Room, the crisis came to a sudden end with a spectacular explosion deep in the Angeles National Forest that was seen for miles. Very quickly, local news in Los Angeles had begun reporting about the mysterious explosion but the story wouldn't gain much traction until the east coast wakes up within the next few hours. They had to assess the situation as quickly as possible.

The Chairman of the Joint Chiefs turned off the video monitor. The video conference call with the Southwestern District Director of Immigration and Customs Enforcement wasn't satisfactory. Don Morgan came across as sincere in his explanation but the President couldn't believe that an airstrike was ordered on our American soil because of a misunderstanding.

There were facts but connecting the dots was proving to be difficult.

Parts of fifteen bodies were found up there, but were all male with no other identifying characteristics. If Henry's daughter Elizabeth was up there, where was she?

Clyde's house was filled with M-16 rifles. The campsite was littered with pieces of AK-47s. Why would they stockpile two very different weapons that didn't have interchangeable ammo or parts?

The flag of a known White militia group was found. It seemed unlikely they would ally themselves with newly illegal Chinese Americans. What was their connection?

A part of a Joint Commendation Service Medal was found yet no such honor appeared on the service record of either Henry Chin or Clyde Wilson. Were these men ex-military as well?

Director Morgan's explanation seemed to cover all the bases. To avoid repatriation, Henry Chin and his daughter Elizabeth, with the help of Clyde Wilson, an old Army buddy, escaped into the Angeles National Forest where they led their Army pursuers to a hidden White militia campsite, whereupon the militia engaged the Army squad in a firefight. Pinned down and unable to return fire, the squad radioed for assistance and an airstrike was authorized per the military's rules of engagement: authorized without the President's knowledge due to the immediacy of the situation. Director Morgan considered the incident isolated and anomalous.

As soon as the video feed ended, the President spoke up. "Who ordered the airstrike?"

The Chairman of the Joint Chiefs of Staff spoke up. "An Army squad was engaged in apprehending two repatriots when our men were fired upon with no provocation. We defended ourselves per our rules of engagement. It was not our job to determine who was firing on us. My men did exactly the right thing. Who were they and why did they fire us? That's someone else's job."

"You've told me what happened," interrupted the President. What I need to know is, are American lives still in danger?"

The President stood up. "It's going to be dawn soon. Most Americans still remember what it was like to wake up to see a plume of smoke on the morning news. While our country was trying to piece together what had happened, we all witnessed the second attack live. I ask you again, is the threat over or is it still ongoing?"

Blank looks came on everyone's face.

"I thought so. Who was the ICE agent in charge?"

The Department of Homeland Security Secretary leafed through some papers. "Agent Nicholas P. Babcock."

"I wish to speak with him," said the President.

"Our men have placed him under arrest," countered the Chairman.

"I want him up on that monitor now," he ordered.

The glare of the floodlights nearly washed out all of Babcock's facial features except the dirt and mud that was still caked on his face under his eye socket. His hair was disheveled and he was still handcuffed. He had a white bandage wrapped around his head covering his left eye.

"Can someone get the light out of his face? This isn't an interrogation," asked the President.

The floodlight was angled off his face. Babcock was still up in the Angeles National Forest. Now you could see where his perspiration had streaked the dirt on his face. Babcock blinked a few times but still squinted at the camera.

"Agent Babcock, this is DHS Secretary Halloran, I'm here in Washington, D.C. with the heads of FBI and CIA, the National Security Advisor, the Chairman of the Joint Chiefs and the President's Chief of Staff. Tell us what happened."

Despite the dedicated and encrypted video feed, there was still a slight transmission delay before Babcock answered.

"Henry Chin is a domestic terrorist specializing in chemical weapons. He was responsible for an improvised bomb at a supermarket and at the repatriation assembly center in Los Angeles. He is heavily armed through the assistance of one of his old squadron buddies."

"Buddies? You mean more than one?" asked the FBI Director.

"This was a Chinese encampment up here," reported Babcock. "This was where the repatriots were going to launch some terrorist attack against the U.S."

"The flag we found belonged to a known White militia group," responded Secretary Halloran.

"These men were Chinese, all of them," reiterated Babcock. "They were well supplied and must have had help. This is only the tip of the iceberg of a much larger conspiracy."

"Who is supplying them?" asked the President.

Babcock was startled at the sound of his voice. "Son, this is the President of the United States. Who do you believe was supplying them?"

Babcock didn't hesitate to answer this time. "China."

The Situation Room fell silent.

"I believe they had Chinese made AK-47s up here," clarified Babcock.

The Chairman spoke up. "Thank you. Corporal, are you still there?"

Corporal Wesson stepped into the picture. "Make sure this man gets medical attention," ordered the Chairman.

"Yes sir," snapped Corporal Wesson.

"Over and out." The video screen went dark.

The FBI Director spoke right up. "Why would the Chinese set up secret camps inside the United States?"

"Camp, singular. This is the only one we know of," corrected the Chairman.

"I would debate even that point. There's no evidence of newly formed Chinese American militias. The flag found up there clearly belonged to an established White militia group," said the FBI Director.

"Unless the Chinese Militia adopted the flag as their own. Snakes are popular iconography in Chinese culture," offered the Chief of Staff.

"But not as popular as the dragon," countered the FBI Director.

"Very simply put, the Chinese could have adopted the White militia flag to point blame at Americans if they were caught," amended the Chief of Staff.

"Hold on a second," interrupted the President. "I'm losing the distinction between Chinese Americans who are citizens and foreign Chinese nationals who are part of the Beijing government."

The Chief of Staff spoke what was in everyone else's mind. "Mr. President, that may not be a distinction worth noting anymore."

"Stop. Draw me a straight line. Something that I can explain to the American people in less than twenty five words," demanded the President.

The FBI Director took a deep breath and began to speak. "Chinese American militants have established a network of basecamps in the United States from which to launch terrorist attacks. Last night, we took one out."

"That's twenty six words."

"Mr. President, all joking aside..." began the FBI Director.

"The only way that would even be plausible is if the Chinese Americans knew about our secret pact with Beijing," shouted the President.

"Then the Chinese Americans must know," said the National Security Advisor. "Someone in this administration must have leaked information about your secret pact with Beijing to them. Someone in this administration is a traitor. And I think we all know who that person is."

"Would you like me to take care of it, sir?" asked Secretary Halloran.

"No. I've known Don Morgan a long time. He should hear it from me." The President allowed himself a moment to compose himself. "I ask again, are American lives still in imminent danger?"

"Yes," said Secretary Halloran.

"Yes," said the Chairman of the Joint Chiefs.

"Yes," said the FBI Director.

"Yes," said the CIA Director.

"Yes," said the National Security Advisor.

"Yes," said his Chief of Staff.

The President searched his soul for any reason to stop what he felt would soon be inevitable.

"Mr. President," said the Chief of Staff. "You have to be decisive. You can't afford a repeat of the seven minutes fiasco.

"What if it happened exactly as Director Morgan laid it out?"

The Chief of Staff chose his next words very carefully. "The American people will find it impossible to believe that the search for two innocent Chinese Americans could escalate into a missile strike on American soil. It has to be part of a larger conspiracy."

"And exactly what is that conspiracy?" asked the President.

Without a quaver in his voice the Chief of Staff said, "Invasion."

The President took a moment to exhale before he spoke.

"Set force protection condition at charlie. General, place our troops on DEFCON 4. We'll also need to accelerate the timetable of the Repatriation Act to stage two."

"You're going to keep your word on the pact?" asked the Chief of Staff.

"Just in case this is all one giant misunderstanding, I want to make sure we meet our obligation to China to the letter," said the President.

"Is that really necessary? Their intentions have never been clearer."

"We don't know what their plans are. I want us to be prepared, but not provocative. I think you have to allow for the fact that the world is not as black and white as you think it is."

The Chief of Staff stood his ground. "If I'm wrong, an apology can fix it. If you're wrong, no one will be around to apologize."

"Repatriation Act, stage two is the order."

"Mr. President," began the Chief of Staff.

"Yes, I know. Have White House counsel draft an Executive Order suspending the Posse Comitatus Act."

"No. Do this instead: have the order declare all Chinese Americans as enemy combatants."

"What?" The President was stunned at the suggestion.

"If Chinese Americans are designated as enemy combatants, then by definition the Posse Comitatus Act does not apply to them under the Patriot Act. It's much easier to redesignate someone's citizenship status than to nullify a law that's been on the books since 1878."

The President felt he had to look decisive in front of this group.

"Very well. Change their citizenship status."

The sun hadn't yet risen when Don arrived at his office. It would be dawn soon on the east coast. Whatever the President would decide to do, he'd be on TV soon and start steering public perception about the incident. He figured his old protégé would give him a courtesy call so he could get his men in place for what would happen next.

The phone rang. It caught him off guard. He picked it up. "Yes sir? Yes, Mr. President... I find your decision unexpected. You know I disagree with that interpretation... With all due respect, what we're doing to our own citizens is wrong... I understand. I take full responsibility. You'll have my resignation in a few minutes. It's been a privilege serving at your pleasure."

Don hung up the phone. He took out his badge and dropped it on his desk.

§

Chapter Sixteen

Private Chin's M-16 discharge sprayed blood, brains and bone all over his men. Though no one said it out loud, the men knew better than to confront Private Chin about shooting a dead man. No one had ever been through this before. All the live round training exercises the Army put them through could never prepare anyone for the moment when he would have to squeeze the trigger and end someone's life. They all were dealing with it. Private Chin just happened to be dealing with it in the most visible way.

The guerilla was already dead. There were no degrees of death. You were dead. What did it matter to shoot a man who was already dead?

The squad cleared the area to make sure there were no survivors. There were none. They did their job, of course with a little help from the U.S. Navy. Private Chin suppressed the urge to feel sympathy for the dead guerillas. He knew what it meant to pick up a gun. These men must have known too. If they didn't, they were stupid motherfuckers.

It was one of those few moments in life when you had total clarity. No one in this area was innocent. If you were here, you were here to kill someone. Or die. Private Chin wasn't here to die and with all his might and power, he wasn't about to let any of his men die either. It was that clear to him. 'Death from above.' They were America's whupass. Gray areas were for politicians and diplomats.

They radioed in their position and situation. Basecamp acknowledged their message and signed off. The problem was, they were still on their LRRP. Despite their actions, they were still not called back to basecamp. They had to finish their LRRP, which meant they had to find that water buffalo.

A water buffalo was, essentially, a giant tank of fresh water with legs that was airdropped at designated coordinates. Their positions were supposed to be secret but they were so large, they were impossible to miss. The closest one was still a few hours away but now, the men were tired and were coming down off an adrenaline rush from the firefight. They needed to find that water buffalo and find it quickly. Private Chin rounded up his men and gave them the order to move out.

They kept up a steady pace. The airstrike was probably seen for miles and echoed for miles beyond that. Chances were that the guerillas would huddle back at their camps to assess the damage. It was a safe bet, but Private Chin wasn't taking any chances.

Private Chin's squad was moving quickly but not carelessly. The lack of sleep for the last three days was taking its toll, not only on Private Chin, but on the entire squad. This is what they were trained for. There was no time to celebrate the deaths of the guerillas or to take a moment to rest. They had their mission to complete and they desperately needed water to do that. They were starving but a grown man could last a week without eating. In this tropical heat and humidity, they had to drink water every day.

Private Chin pushed those thoughts out of his head. Focus and discipline. That was a big difference between Private Chin's squad and the guerillas. That's why the guerillas didn't stand a chance.

One last push through the thick underbrush and the squad finally reached their target. Private Chin dispersed his men to make sure the area was secure. Private Wilson finally gave the all clear.

Because water buffaloes were so exposed, they were potential targets of sabotage. Guerillas would use them and afterwards, shoot holes to drain them or defecate in them to poison them. There were no holes in the exterior and the hatch looked untampered.

Private Wilson ordered the squad to spread out and circle the water buffalo with their weapons trained outward. Private Chin was up on top of the water buffalo opening the valve. Up here, he was the most vulnerable. He opened the valve, lifted the hatch and smelled the water. His nose was a much quicker judge of contamination than any chemical kit a scientist could dream up.

There was no odor. The water wasn't foul. Private Chin splashed some of the water so he could feel for any oiliness on his fingers. There was none. The only drawback was that the water was lukewarm, bordering on hot, but it was potable. Private Chin gave his men the okay sign and then unscrewed his canteen and began to fill it.

What Private Chin saw in the water buffalo shocked him. He was frozen in place. He couldn't move a muscle. Private Wilson immediately sensed something was wrong. "Chin, what do you see?" Private Chin couldn't answer. Private Wilson signaled the men to hold their positions while he climbed up to join Private Chin.

Despite having his friend next to him, Private Chin couldn't take his eyes off what he saw. Just beneath the surface of the water was his daughter Elizabeth as she looked today. A grown teenager except she was pale, bloated and lifeless.

Henry's arms reached out to grab his M-16 but it wasn't there. He lost his balance and collapsed onto the ground. Still not quite fully conscious, Henry could feel the dirt against his face and between his fingers. He had fallen asleep sitting up, but Henry didn't remember falling asleep. Henry searched his memory… he couldn't remember what he was doing just before he fell asleep.

His muscles ached with exhaustion. Henry couldn't remember the last time he was this tired. And then the pieces of his memory came together.

"Elizabeth!"

Henry opened his eyes. He wasn't sure where he was. It was still night and he was outdoors. He was lying on the ground beneath a large sandstone overhang. The air had a dewy scent and the sky was still dark and moonless.

"You have to remember to tuck your chin when you fall."

Henry nearly hyperventilated at the sound of Clyde's voice. Henry looked over at his old friend.

"How soon we forget our basic training," Clyde continued. "You're alive Henry."

Without allowing himself a moment of relief, Henry asked, "Where's Elizabeth?"

Clyde pointed to the small campfire behind Henry. Elizabeth lay sleeping, covered with the plastic tarp. "She's asleep. Let her rest. She's badly bruised but her pulse is strong and regular."

"He's dead. What's his name? Lynch. The one that I think…"

"The blast probably got him," offered Clyde.

"No, I mean, he's dead. I killed him. I shot him."

Henry kept searching his memory to piece out what happened. "I rigged three propane tanks to explode. They didn't. They got to them before…" Henry sat back down on the ground as he searched his memory. "There was an airstrike."

"Yeah," concurred Clyde.

"They were firing on the U.S. Army?"

"And had them pinned. Otherwise, they wouldn't have called in an airstrike."

Henry tried to analyze this new piece of data. "That's really bad luck, us stumbling across a White militia group just as the Army was about to engage them."

"I don't think the Army was after them."

"Then who…? You think the Army was after us?"

"A SWAT team raided my house. I barely got away. Once they saw my stockpile I thinking someone made a phone call," explained Clyde.

"There was a guy... when I realized the propane tanks weren't going to explode. He didn't belong up there. He wasn't one of them. He was at the Rose Bowl. Not Army. Suit and tie. He was watching me then." Henry closed his eyes. "Six foot tall, blonde hair cut short, but not as short as a buzz or a crew. About a buck ninety."

"Kind of looks like Mickey Mantle?"

"Yeah," said Henry.

"He was at my house. He was the point man on the raid. He must have figured out who you were and then found me."

With his eyes still closed, Henry continued to rattle off characteristics. "Dark suit. Ear piece. Smartphone. This guy was part of Immigration and Customs Enforcement. He was in my way. I took his eye out."

Henry showed Clyde his right thumb, which was stained with Babcock's blood and caked with mud.

"It makes sense up to a point. But the airstrike..." asked Clyde.

"No, it's not about the airstrike. Someone must have dispatched an Army squad after us long before the airstrike," began Henry.

"We're on someone's radar big time," finished Clyde.

Henry chuckled. "For the past ten years, I lived such a bland life, I couldn't get arrested. Now we're wanted men being hunted down by the highest levels of our government. At least it's over now."

"Over?" asked Clyde.

"There's no way he could have survived that airstrike," concluded Henry.

"You survived it," pointed out Clyde. "I survived it. Elizabeth survived it. It's not that big a stretch of the imagination to believe he survived it. If he did, then we can't stay here."

Their conversation was interrupted by the crinkling of the plastic tarp.

"Elizabeth?"

"Daddy?"

"I'm here, sweetheart." Henry held out his hand for her. Almost as soon as she took his hand, she pulled herself up and wrapped her arms around her father and began crying.

"It's okay sweetheart, I'm here. You're safe now," consoled Henry. Soon, Elizabeth pulled away from her father, grabbing her left side in pain.

"What's wrong?" asked Henry.

Still holding onto her left side, Elizabeth rolled over and curled into a ball. Henry tried to soothe her pain by gently rubbing his hand on her back.

"There, there," continued Henry.

"Henry." Clyde pointed down at her waist. Her shirt had ridden up on her and exposed part of her abdomen. It was swollen and discolored. "I think her spleen ruptured."

"Okay, well, that answers the question of where we should go next." Elizabeth dry heaved a few more times before she rolled back over onto her side and curled into the fetal position.

"Daddy, what happened to those men..."

"Those men won't be able to hurt you anymore."

"Are they dead?" she asked.

"Yes."

"Good," she responded with a sense of grave finality. Henry didn't quite know how to react to this. There was a weight to her voice that was never there before. There wasn't a trace left of the frivolous, scatterbrained teenage girl whose biggest worry was getting a zit on her face the night before senior photos. Henry had mixed feelings. He had wanted to protect his daughter's innocence, not destroy it.

Elizabeth gripped her left side trying as hard as she could to ignore the pain.

"We don't have much time," said Clyde.

Henry pulled out his hunting knife. "I have this."

"Put that away, MacGyver. You're not going to operate on her. She needs a real doctor." Clyde pointed to the M-16 leaning against the rocks. "I found that near you. You've got about ten rounds left in the magazine."

Clyde pulled a grenade out of his back pocket. "I have one of these left."

"One M-16 with ten rounds, a hunting knife and one grenade. That should be enough to take on the U.S. Army," said Henry.

"You two always have such happy conversations," interjected Elizabeth.

Henry knew it was well after midnight. Henry had hypothesized that the Eldridge's men had used a fire road to get their equipment up there. Knowing the Chilao and Colby Canyon areas as well as they did, Henry speculated that there must have been a fire road to the north and after about a mile of hiking in the dark they found it. In actuality, they didn't have a choice but to go in that direction. Any other direction would have led them straight into one of the search parties combing the area.

They made an improvised stretcher for Elizabeth using the tarp and several large branches. They followed the fire road westward until they cleared the valley and then cut south. Their goal was to detour off this fire road and scale down one particular steep incline to get to the Monte Cristo campground.

Henry and Clyde had methodically carried Elizabeth for nearly two hours while she slept. Clyde could almost hear Henry's thoughts grind through his mind. He knew his friend well enough to let him work out his conflicted feelings on his own for a while. Even when they stopped for their brief rests, Henry didn't say anything. It was like an unspoken agreement. When Henry had something to say, Clyde would be there to listen, but until then he would let Henry search for those words alone.

Lynch was dead. There was no doubt in Henry's mind that he raped Elizabeth. And if he didn't, he allowed it to happen. He had learned in Panama that dead was dead; that as a soldier, killing was part of his job. Despite his revenge, Henry found no satisfaction in killing Lynch. Even if he had killed him and all his men with his bare hands, that wouldn't have avenged what they did to Elizabeth.

The rage that Henry felt was like no other rage he'd ever felt before in his life. Lynch's death did nothing to abate his fury. Lynch was the bottom of the barrel, the symptom of the disease. As a grunt, Henry followed someone else's orders. Now, Henry wanted to dictate the mission. Henry felt in his gut that the blame for Elizabeth's rape went far beyond Lynch. Henry's decision to bring her into the Angeles National Forest made them vulnerable but Henry was mad that he had to make that decision in the first place.

Getting medical help for Elizabeth's injury consumed his attention for now. What would happen when his mind finally had a chance to sit idle? Henry didn't know if he'd be strong enough to control himself when that time came.

The last stretch of this hike required them to slide down a gravel incline for nearly a quarter of a mile into the Monte Cristo campground.

This campsite was a shithole. It was at a lower elevation and was susceptible to the camping equivalent of squatters: people who would come up after the park rangers had finished collecting the campsite fees and leave early in the morning before the rangers did their vehicle checks. The people who practiced this tended to smash glass bottles on rocks and litter the area with crushed beer cans.

If you had paid for your campsite, you had to leave a receipt on your dashboard for easy verification by the rangers. Henry and Clyde were looking for some karmic payback against those who abused their mountains.

It didn't take them long to find their mark: an old model Toyota Corolla. The owner of the car was in a nearby sleeping bag with no tent or canopy to protect him from the night sky.

There was no need to jimmy the lock. The driver had left his window cracked slightly. There was just enough room for Clyde to grab the top of the driver's side window and force it open. Clyde was diligent about keeping the noise down but their intrusion was enough to wake up the driver. As soon as Henry heard the sleeping driver stir, he slammed his elbow into the side of his head. The sound of crunching bone was unmistakable despite being muffled by the sleeping bag.

Clyde didn't say anything. That guy didn't deserve to die, but he deserved something. In this case, a broken jaw and really bad headache. Henry and Clyde gently put Elizabeth in the backseat before they hotwired the car and quietly drove out of the campsite.

Normally, they would have slipped down the Angeles Forest Highway but that would have taken at least an hour to get to Route 210 and Sun Valley. Taking Big Tujunga Canyon Road to the Angeles Crest Highway to get to La Cañada Flintridge would save them at least half an hour.

Henry had ten bullets. In his heart and in his mind, he was ready to wage war with anyone who got in their way. Clyde knew that it was his job to make sure that didn't happen.

Their travel along Big Tujunga Canyon Road was without incident. They turned south onto the Angeles Crest Highway and began their descent to La Cañada Flintridge.

Henry sat in silence, while Elizabeth slept in the backseat. Henry turned around every few minutes to make sure she was still breathing. After nearly twenty minutes, absent mindedly, Clyde clicked on the radio. Loud Mexican music blared over the speakers for a second before Clyde knocked down the volume. Clyde searched the FM dial for a rock and roll station when they heard the President's voice. "Leave it," said Henry.

"Good morning. Several days ago the FBI, in cooperation with Immigration and Customs Enforcement, began investigating suspicious activity in the Angeles National Forest near Los Angeles. Agents discovered a clandestine guerilla training camp with a large cache of weapons and precursors related to chemical weapons. I immediately authorized military action to take control of this secret encampment. When the guerillas resisted, a naval airstrike was ordered to prevent their use of any potential chemical weapons of mass destruction.

"Going forward, our government's emergency response plan has been implemented and new investigations have been initiated to determine if more facilities such as this exist on American soil. We recognize our responsibility requires every possible protection against espionage and against sabotage to our nation and way of life.

"As President, I hereby authorize and direct the Secretary of Homeland Security and all Military Commanders with the assistance of state and local agencies to take appropriate measures to investigate any extremist activity that may aid and abet any foreign intrusion within our borders and to prescribe the necessary remedies to restrict and curtail such activity.

"It is our duty to purge ourselves of the dark forces who would threaten our borders from within. Our way of life almost always seems to be under attack. With your diligence, the United States will forever remain a beacon of hope and freedom for the rest of the world.

"Thank you. May God bless you and may God bless the United States of America."

Henry clicked off the radio and stared at the road ahead. Clyde drove for nearly half an hour with the headlights off before he decided to break the silence. "Do you buy what the President said?" asked Clyde.

"It's what he didn't say," said Henry. "He didn't identify who the guerrillas were. There's only one country the President is afraid to accuse of anything."

"The President thinks we're in league with Beijing?" asked Clyde.

"Why else would he order a naval airstrike?"

The sun was rising as Henry leaned forward looking out across the San Fernando Valley. Military helicopters, dozens of them, were flying in low circles. Plumes of black smoke rose up from the valley floor. But most disturbing to Henry and Clyde was the roadblock about a quarter mile up ahead.

§

CHAPTER SEVENTEEN

Though no one used the words martial law, the government's activity during the past few hours had all the earmarks of a police state. That morning, the Department of Homeland Security installed barricades in front of every government building, from downtown L.A. to West Hollywood to Van Nuys. Roadblocks were set up at entrances of all the city and county parks denying access. Checkpoints were set up along Mulholland Drive and Wilshire Boulevard.

Police helicopters flew overhead while all the news and traffic choppers were grounded. Every media commentator and blogger floated their own conspiracy theory about the fireball that had lit up the night sky over Los Angeles.

Anonymous sources say that in the predawn hours at a secret military facility in the Angeles National Forest, the test of a new stealth weapon went tragically awry.

Or:

A scientist, speaking on the condition of anonymity, says instruments registered radiation fallout from a nuclear device detonated overnight in the Angeles National Forest.

Or:

NTSB officials won't confirm that an airplane was hijacked out of LAX by terrorists and crashed in the Angeles National Forest when passengers tried to take back control of the plane.

Or:

It was reported on another news outlet that a Chinese jet fighter was shot down over Los Angeles during the night and crash landed in the Angeles National Forest.

Or:

Speaking off the record, a highly placed senior government official said that shortly after midnight, U.S. troops repelled an invasion force in the Angeles National Forest.

There was a strange recklessness in the search for any sliver of information. Anyone with even a hint of special access to government secrets was more than happy to feed speculation and rumor as fact to reporters hungry for an exclusive and a public searching for answers. In a strange reversal of logic, the more sensational the supposition the more plausibility it was given by news outlets. It was the natural culmination of an era where people were ready to believe the worst about one another.

By sunrise, the conspiracy theory that had gained the most traction, that Americans most wanted to believe, was that the United States was hit by a surprise attack from China. When that rumor broke, all the simmering anti-Chinese resentment exploded.

With the rise of China's global economic dominance, many Americans believed that a war between the United States and China was inevitable. Today, they believed that fear had come to fruition.

Blame came swiftly. The President was already polling very low in his job approval ratings. Many Americans believed his weakness allowed China to gain economic dominance over the United States. He had very little credibility with the American people to begin with. Now, his national address fell upon deaf ears.

The explanations the President gave in his speech did nothing to quell the panic. With the sight of the billow of smoke over the Angeles National Forest against the morning sun, many Angelinos felt their government had failed them and now had to take their own safety and security into their own hands.

Believing that war with China had already begun, many Angelinos tried to flee the city, taking with them whatever belongings they could pack into their cars. Many planned to head east along I-10 into Arizona. Those with bigger cars tried to go north along I-5 into California's Central Valley. Nobody got very far. The mass exodus jammed all the major exit routes out of the city to a standstill.

Los Angeles erupted into a riot zone. Angelinos were either willing or wanting to believe that their city was under attack. Supermarkets were looted. Fistfights broke out at gas stations. A woman was shot for a case of bottled water. Angelinos did more damage to themselves in the immediate wake of the missile strike than the missile strike itself.

Hardest hit were the areas where Chinese Americans used to live. The U.S. Army saw no strategic advantage in protecting empty houses in Alhambra, Monterey Park, Rosemead, San Gabriel and Chinatown and redeployed their men to protect the larger shopping meccas such as Culver City and the Grove. Half the city was consumed with fear, the other half with anger. Without significant reinforcements, these troops would not be able to keep order.

Panic was not restricted to the Los Angeles area. Rioting occurred all along the west coast in every city that had a significant Chinese population: San Francisco, Sacramento, Fresno and San Jose.

In the southern California area, the Chinese Americans being held under the Repatriation Act at the Rose Bowl came under attack by a lynch mob and were repelled by the Army soldiers safeguarding the Chinese Americans.

The façade of the Rose Bowl sustained damage from gunfire. The iconic sign that hung over Gate A was destroyed. Twenty five members of the lynch mob were killed before order was restored. There was outrage that "real" Americans were killed to protect the "traitorous Chinese."

Clyde pulled the Toyota over to the side of the road so that Henry could climb up onto the embankment to do a quick recon of the roadblock below. There were no side streets up here to detour to, no alternative routes to the Verdugo Hills Hospital, about two miles past the roadblock. A roadblock and two miles separated Elizabeth from medical attention.

From Henry's vantage point, something struck him as very odd about the roadblock. It wasn't a military roadblock set up to check vehicles coming down the mountain. They were stopping people from driving up into the mountains. Henry deduced that these Angelinos were planning to use the Angeles Crest Highway as an alternate route to I-15 and Las Vegas beyond.

Henry returned to the car and pulled out his M-16 and flipped off the safety.

"What you're thinking of doing is a suicide mission," protested Clyde.

"It's the only way," said Henry.

"No it's not. Assaulting the enemy at their strongest point is a tactical mistake," said Clyde.

"We can't waste any time. Elizabeth needs a medic now!"

"You mean a doctor. Right Henry? You meant Elizabeth needs a doctor. We're not in Panama anymore."

"Elizabeth could die! We have to get her help!"

"Yeah, I agree," began Clyde. "But you always pick the hardest way to do things."

Henry gave Clyde a puzzled look before Clyde pulled their last grenade out of his pocket.

"Give me a hand with the spare tire," said Clyde.

They propped the spare tire up against the backseat behind Clyde. In between was wedged Henry. On the floor of the backseat lay Elizabeth. She was still asleep but her breathing was shallow and her complexion pallid. Henry kept his head low, below the level of the rear windshield. Clyde scrunched himself as far down into the drivers seat as he could.

Henry rolled down the rear passenger window and gingerly propped his M-16 on the door with the muzzle pointed outward. Henry gripped the grenade, holding the spoon in place with his left hand as he yanked out the pin. Tossing aside the pin, he took hold of the M-16 with his right hand and flipped off the safety. "Ready," said Henry.

Clyde started the Toyota and threw it into reverse. He put the car in neutral and rode the brake as it coasted downhill slowly toward the checkpoint backwards.

Henry had angled the passenger rear view mirror so he could see where they were going. He had already determined that the roadblock was not military. Army soldiers or marines would have been in BDU's and would have been wearing a military cap with a visor. They weren't wearing the dark blue uniforms of the LAPD. His best guess was that the roadblock was being manned by the Los Angeles County Sheriff.

What gave Henry relief was that the Sheriff's deputies were not in SWAT or riot gear. Henry's guess was that they didn't want to deploy their SWAT guys up into the mountains but keep them close to protect more urban vulnerabilities. He was trying to read their body language. There was no urgency or purpose to the way they moved. They were probably rookies who felt like they had drawn a bullshit assignment.

As much as Henry wanted to believe that, he couldn't underestimate his adversaries. He couldn't count on someone else screwing up, he had to count on him getting everything right. Depending on your adversary to fail is a sure recipe for getting people killed. Unfortunately, that was the position that Henry was in right now. Henry and Clyde needed to confuse them for about five seconds: if the deputies lived up their training, they won't be fooled.

They crept closer to the roadblock. The deputies' attention were trained on the cars heading up into the mountain. They weren't letting anyone through, forcing the cars to turn around and head back down.

The sheriff's deputies heard the Toyota before they spotted it. One rookie raised his rifle. Henry couldn't tell exactly what it was he had: he was pretty sure it looked like a Heckler & Koch MP5. Whatever it was, it looked squatter and fatter than Henry's M-16. It had what looked like a thirty round clip attached.

Each deputy would have his own personal sidearm in addition to the MP5. Three deputies and one ranking officer. That was easily seventy rounds they had immediate access to against the ten rounds Henry had. Their ruse had to work.

The ranking officer put his hand on the deputy's muzzle and lowered it. By backing down the road in reverse at a slow speed, Henry and Clyde didn't present themselves as an immediate threat. The rules of engagement for police were to ascertain the threat level before taking action: unless the threat was imminent.

Clyde had explained the strategy to Henry. When he was a child, Clyde's father would drive the family into New York City. Living in the suburbs of New Jersey, there were certain foods that weren't available there that mandated a weekly trip into Harlem. Many of the streets in New York City were narrow and ran in only one direction. Finding parking was a nightmare. The worst situation was if Clyde's dad spotted a parking spot on a one way street but had to loop around the block to get to that spot. By the time his Dad got there, the spot was usually gone.

Clyde's father came up with an ingenious solution: if he saw a parking spot that required him to go the wrong way down a one way street to get there, he threw his car into reverse and backed into the street. Clyde observed that the cars coming in the correct direction would get out of his dad's way. Routinely his dad was able to get the parking spot. Even the time he was almost ticketed for going down the street in the wrong direction, he managed to talk the traffic cop out of issuing the ticket because he was, in fact, backing up.

Clyde was fairly sure that driving downhill in reverse was not a tactical maneuver taught to law enforcement officers. He hoped that by appearing confused and lost, he would appeal to that desire in human nature that made us want to help one another.

Henry watched the deputies' body language. They were curious and cautious, not aggressive or defensive.

What Clyde was looking for was the distance between his car and the wooden barricade they had erected. There was an invisible line that told the deputies that they had to act no matter how slow the car was coming. It wasn't written as data in a book but an instinctive measurement, like how close you'd let someone invade your personal space before you push back. Henry and Clyde were hoping that because the sheriff had to deal with irate civilians all the time, they might have a higher threshold for threats than say, a SWAT team or a military squad expecting to come under fire.

As they came closer, Henry and Clyde confirmed what they were up against. Two patrol cars, three deputies and one ranking officer, maybe a sergeant. The two patrol cars were parked above the barricade along the side of the road, not blocking it. Another fortunate happenstance for Henry.

Henry counted off the distance until the barricade, about thirty feet now. They had to come up parallel with one of the patrol cars before anyone hit the panic button. The senior deputy put up his hand to tell them to stop. Clyde delicately applied a slight bit of pressure to the brake, enough to flash the brake lights and make the deputy think they were complying without discernibly slowing down.

Fifteen feet. The deputy was still standing there with his hand up. He didn't have his free hand on his sidearm. He must have been the ranking officer. The rest were waiting for orders.

Ten feet. The lead car has its windows shut. The rear car has its windows open. Henry couldn't remember if patrol cars had bullet proof glass on the side windows. He couldn't take a chance that he was wrong. If this plan were to succeed, they had to instantly incapacitate at least one of the patrol cars.

"We'll need ten more feet," whispered Henry.

"But we're almost there," said Clyde.

"Ten more feet."

The ranking deputy started walking over to their car.

"On my mark," said Henry. Henry could tell the officer was squinting into their Toyota. At that moment, one of the cars on the other side of the roadblock must have felt he wasn't getting enough attention from the Sheriff deputies and honked his horn. The ranking officer looked away. That distraction was enough to allow Clyde to come side by side with the rear patrol car.

Henry tossed the grenade into the rear patrol car.

"Hit it!"

Clyde threw the Toyota from neutral into reverse and slammed on the gas as Henry leaned out of the backseat with his M-16 raised. He fired one round over the deputies heads sending them into the ground for cover.

The rear of the Toyota smashed through the wood barricades. Clyde floored the gas to gain speed. He cocked the steering wheel slightly sending the Toyota into the beginning of a skid as he shifted into neutral.

As the front of the car came around, Clyde shifted the Toyota into drive, controlling and completing the 180 degree skid. Now the Toyota was pointing in the correct direction for the rest of its trip down the mountain.

Bullets began to shatter the rear windshield of the Toyota. He could hear the bullets hitting the trunk and rear bumper. Henry kept his head down low covering as much of Elizabeth with his body as he could. His adrenaline was pumping through his blood so much now, he had lost track of the time. The grenade should have detonated by now. It seemed like minutes had passed when in actuality, it was barely three seconds.

Boom!

The grenade sent the roof of the patrol car into the air. The cars that were backed up, suddenly turned around and began going back down the way they came up en masse.

The gunfire stopped. Clyde slowed the Toyota down enough that the cars coming down could pass them. Tactically, it wasn't a good strategy to lead this caravan down the mountain but it was also counter-productive to let the deputies catch up to them.

Clyde pulled out back onto the road to continue their descent. Henry swung his M-16 out the window and aimed it at the car following them. At the sight of the machine gun, the driver behind them panicked and lost control of his car, crashing into the queue of backed up cars in the next lane, sending him into a roll and blocking the road.

Henry pulled the M-16 back into the car. He could see Clyde's eyes staring at him through the rear view mirror.

"What? I didn't fire a shot."

Clyde drove through La Cañada Flintridge as nonchalantly as possible, but it's hard not to draw attention when your car is missing its rear windshield and has bullet holes on the side. Eventually, they reached the Verdugo Hills Hospital.

It was a sprawling complex with the main building set in the middle of a giant parking lot. To the west, you could see the new multi-story parking garage under construction. Clyde drove up to the emergency room and stopped short of the entrance.

"Take her inside," said Henry.

"What?" asked Clyde.

"I'll ditch the car and come back and look for you but you have to take Elizabeth inside."

One of the rules of improv comedy is never say no. Don't reject the premise your partner proposes but rather, run with it. Clyde didn't have time to consider Henry's analysis but he knew he also didn't have time to argue with him.

Clyde jumped out of the car and gently lifted Elizabeth out of the backseat. He gave Henry a look.

"I'll find you," said Henry.

Clyde gave Henry a quick nod. One of these days, that look was going to be the last time he'd ever put his eyes on his old friend. Today wasn't going to be that day.

Clyde burst into the E.R. holding Elizabeth. "She needs help!" Clyde yelled. The nurses froze at the sight of them but Clyde reassured them. "She's Mexican."

Henry drove the Toyota into the partially constructed parking structure. He was taking a risk ditching the car so close to his actual location. If authorities found the car here, they would logically search the hospital. Henry hoped that Elizabeth would be in and out before they found it. He drove the Toyota up as many levels as he could before he parked and covered it with a plastic tarp.

Just before Henry abandoned the Toyota, his curiosity got the better of him. He looked at the spare tire they had used as a shield. He pulled the tire forward and saw where about half a dozen bullets had pierced through the backseat but were stopped by the metal rim and thick rubber of the spare tire.

Henry was lucky again. He knew that luck would eventually run out. He knew that every decision he still had to make had no margin for error.

Don arrived back at his house. On the kitchen table was a note wrapped around a candy bar. The note read, "Saw the news. Food in fridge. Call if you want to talk." Don crumpled the note and tossed it in the garbage. He opened the refrigerator and saw a hero sandwich wrapped in white butcher paper. He wondered if the gesture was a pun on "hero." Don certainly didn't feel like one.

He grabbed a beer and popped the top off. He sat down at the kitchen table and took a swig. He exhaled deeply before he put his feet up on the table and finished the bottle. He closed his eyes and leaned back his head to let what little alcohol there was in a lager seep into his bloodstream.

Don knew that he had grown complacent in his job. He searched his mind to see if he had had any opportunity to stop all this military action before it escalated into a national crisis.

Don kicked off his shoes and went into the bedroom. He looked in his closet. He owned about a dozen suits but hadn't bought a new one in almost a decade. He had put in his time but was more concerned about beating traffic home on Friday afternoons than connecting the dots in front of him.

It was the job that made him numb. Back when he first managed this district, the illegals they took into custody usually had at least a felony on their jacket. He had no problem deporting illegals with criminal records. However, nothing was ever that simple.

Today, deporting an illegal almost always meant breaking up a family. The hard core criminals had gotten better at hiding themselves leaving the day laborers and fruit pickers vulnerable. Don had sympathy for the day laborers. He knew that if he were in their shoes he would probably do the same thing. Hell, he moved his wife and sons here to Los Angeles from New Orleans to accept the promotion. He only went through a divorce once the stress of his job caught up with him. He didn't lose his sons until they graduated high school and moved back to Louisiana to be closer to their cousins.

After losing them, the job was the only thing he had left. In some twisted way, he felt that he had to stick to his job to justify the sacrifice of his marriage and his relationship with his two sons.

Because the truly criminal illegals were getting harder to find, the new administration implemented a new policy that emphasized quantity. Poor, urban illegals were easy targets. For nearly all of them, their crime was being in the country illegally. For a lot of Americans, especially this administration, that crime was worthy of the death penalty.

That argument had always bothered Don. Sure, we took an economic hit for having a lot of cheap, unskilled labor flooding the market but no one ever complained about the profits big business reaped from their exploitation. As long as tomatoes were cheap for struggling middle class families, no one paid much attention to the fat bonuses in a CEO's wallet.

For Don, it was the merging of two philosophies. One from our government to ensure a fair opportunity for all to succeed. One from his religion that says Christ is embodied in everyone, especially the poor. Don always felt that his role as a government employee was to protect those who were powerless to protect themselves. One particular Bible verse had stuck with him all these years. And he will answer, *'I tell you the truth, when you refused to help the least of these my brothers and sisters, you were refusing to help me.* His moral conviction to treat everyone as a child of God had finally collided with his sworn duty to uphold the law.

Over the years, he had turned a blind eye to his own moral convictions. He excused his behavior by convincing himself that being in America without proper papers was empirically a crime.

However, this new action against the Chinese Americans he couldn't stomach. They had committed no crime. Many were native born Americans but with the stroke of the President's pen, they were suddenly stateless. Not because of a war, or an uprising or a rebellion but because of fear.

Being an American, Don knew The Repatriation Act was a repeat of a dark chapter during World War II. Being an African American, Don understood prejudice on a deeply personal level.

He knew that if he didn't do something to help the Chinese Americans, he would punish himself for the rest of his life.

§

CHAPTER EIGHTEEN

Elizabeth had no sense about how long she had been asleep. The last thing she remembered was that her father had found her. It was then she let go of all her fear, knowing that he wouldn't let anything happen to her.

But she knew something bad had happened to her. She remembered getting hit and punched in her face a few times.

What are you doing here? echoed the baritone voice in her head.

She remembered feeling hands grab her and nearly yank her arms out of her shoulder. She couldn't open her eyes. Bad breath and body odor and the stench of stale beer. And hands all over her, pulling at her, tearing at her clothes.

You don't belong here, you're not one of us! the baritone voice continued to bellow at her.

Elizabeth kept her eyes closed. She was powerless. These men could pick her up and toss her around at will. She felt her shirt and bra getting torn off.

This was what she tried to block out of her mind. This was what she desperately tried not to remember. She tried to push those feelings out of her mind. She was thankful that she wasn't going to lose her virginity to these men. She had taken care of that rite of passage already.

He was a high school boy and, at the time, he was a senior and she was a sophomore. Taking her virginity was such a big deal to him. He thought it meant that they were forever tied together because he was her first. Strange, she couldn't remember his name now.

She never understood why those boys had such an unrealistic, overly romantic view of sex. She liked him and chose him because she wanted it to be memorable, not because she was looking for true love forever.

What she didn't like was the way he treated her in school once they went back to their classes on Monday. No matter how progressive women believe they've become, one on one, men like to treat women like property.

Elizabeth didn't like how he always seemed to be waiting for her when her classes were done. She didn't like how he talked to her friends trying to get any inside information. She didn't like how his buddies seemed to know everything about her (even though they didn't). Before she was with this boy, no one paid her much attention. Once the gossip started that she was 'in practice,' the euphemism of the day for sexually active teens, the boys gave her a lot of attention hoping they would be next in line should her relationship with the senior sour.

Those were the polite boys. What she really learned was that men generally will try to take what they want and it was up to her to push back. Right now, she was powerless to push back.

You don't exist! You don't belong! the baritone voice continued inside Elizabeth's head.

She kept her eyes closed as she swung her arms wildly but they easily pushed her down onto the ground and held her in place. She was outnumbered. There was nothing she could do. She couldn't punch, she couldn't kick. She could bite and spit but that wouldn't be enough but in her mind, she wouldn't give up. She would fight for as long as she could.

"Quit it. You're just making things harder for yourself," said Lynch. When she refused to hold still, Lynch punched her across the face again.

"Your mother had no respect for her own kind. Your mother was a whore and you're the bastard child of a bastard race," she heard him say. That was the last thing she remembered clearly. She wasn't unconscious. She didn't remember blacking out. In her mind's eye, everything she saw, she saw through a curtained haze.

Elizabeth knew she was outside. She was standing in an open field nestled at the foot of a mountain range. In the distance, she saw a man digging a deep hole. Her father was nowhere to be seen. Elizabeth approached the digging man. It was her grandfather, Sebastian Colville. He was a great bull of a man, lifting enormous amounts of dirt with each shovelful.

As she walked up to her grandfather, she realized that she wasn't standing in a field but in the middle of a large cemetery. At one end of the deep hole was a gravestone with Veronique Chin inscribed on it.

"Grandfather?" Elizabeth prompted.

Without a word, he climbed up out of the hole and threw down the shovel. She ran up to him but he turned and shoved her to the ground before he walked away. With great effort, she stood up. For some reason, she didn't give any chase after her grandfather. Her curiosity led her back to the open grave. Before she looked down, she glanced over at the gravestone. This time her name, Elizabeth Chin, was inscribed on it. She looked down into grave. She saw a mirror image of herself partially buried in the dirt.

She would be alive if it weren't for you, echoed the baritone voice inside her head.

Blood gushed into the open grave. It sprayed up and washed over her. Her clothes were soaked in red. Elizabeth tried to scream for her mother but no sound would come out.

Babcock opened his eye. The doctor had done a thorough job cleaning out the empty socket. Babcock was ambivalent about losing his left eye. When he was a kid and had aspirations of becoming a professional baseball player. He had heard that a lot of left handed power hitters were right eye dominant. He thought that if he could teach himself to bat left handed, that would help him make the varsity team in high school. Unfortunately, he never quite got the mechanics of batting lefty correct. It was being right handed with a weak left eye that gave him such a low batting average.

Babcock took comfort in the Bible. *And if thine eye offend thee, pluck it out, and cast it from thee: it is better for thee to enter into life with one eye, rather than having two eyes to be cast into hell fire.* He believed that Chinese Americans represented a clear and present threat to our way of life. Better to cast them out than to allow our country to descend into the hell fire of anarchy.

The doctor gave him a prescription for antibiotics as a precaution against infection. He would have to drain his eye socket daily until the wound healed. Once the swelling went down, he would have to make an appointment with a specialist so he could be fitted with a prosthetic eye. For now, he'd have to settle for looking like a pirate.

It had been a long day for him. He was glad that his choices were vindicated by the President. So few men were willing to do what was necessary to protect this country. He wanted to believe that if he were on duty that September morning...

The only hope for the country's survival was to give more power and control to men like him. Old men become complacent. Young men are never satisfied.

Babcock was sore as he stood up. The doctor had also prescribed some pain killers. Babcock had no intention of filling that prescription unless it was absolutely necessary. His car was still up in the Colby Canyon parking lot. The soldier who drove him down had left to rejoin his unit. He thought about calling one of the junior ICE agents to give him a ride home but he figured he'd probably catch hell from Director Morgan for that.

He took out his smartphone. The display was cracked and the keyboard was caked with mud. He wouldn't be able to call anyone anyway.

Babcock slid off the examination table and walked out into the emergency room waiting area. He spotted a payphone opposite the nurse's station. He still had his wallet with his credit cards and some cash but no change. He tried to make change at the nurse's station but his cash was also caked with mud. He finally got some quarters from a janitor once he flashed his badge.

Taped to the wall around the payphone were ads for taxicabs. Most of them had toll free numbers. Babcock dialed the only phone number he'd memorized as an adult.

"Hey Natasha, sorry about last night. Things suddenly got really busy and I'm sorry we didn't have time to talk more. I was wondering if you could do me a favor? I'm at the Verdugo Hills Hospital. We had an incident last night and my car is still at the scene. If you could give me a ride to my car, you'd have my undying appreciation."

Babcock hung up the phone and exhaled. He realized he forgot to leave her the phone number of the payphone to call him back. The quarters slipped out of his hand and hit the floor. As he stood up, he saw a familiar face in the reflection of the candy bar vending machine.

Clyde peered into the operating room. It pained him to see Elizabeth with a breathing tube. Clyde never had kids but he always knew in the back of his mind that if anything ever happened to Henry, he would treat Elizabeth as his own. As soon as the triage nurse saw Elizabeth she was immediately rushed into surgery.

Clyde could tell from the beeps that her heart rate was fluctuating. Sometimes it was normal but every now and then he could hear it leap into a race. He felt bad for what she was going through. He could only imagine how Henry felt.

His self-preservation instincts still functioned. Clyde was aware of the security cameras and did his best to avoid them as much as possible. He was lost in his thoughts when an admissions nurse came up to him to get Elizabeth's vital information.

"What's her name?" asked the admissions nurse.

It wasn't a trick question but sometimes when you're put on the spot, you have trouble pulling even the most basic information out of your head. When he brought her in, he declared Elizabeth was Mexican but for the life of him, at this very moment, he couldn't think of a single Mexican surname. The only Mexican name he could think of was Cheech Marin but Marin didn't sound particularly Mexican.

"Elizabeth Cheech," said Clyde. As soon as the words came out of his mouth, he wanted to kick himself.

"Date of birth?" asked the nurse without missing a beat. Clyde knew Elizabeth was eighteen... or was she nineteen? He couldn't remember what year it was. Clyde deduced that if he couldn't pull the year out of his mind, he wouldn't be able to sub tract Elizabeth's age correctly either. He gently reached out his hand toward the nurse's clipboard.

"Maybe it would be easier if you let me have that so I can fill it out once I'm not so distracted," offered Clyde.

"Of course. Are you her father?" asked the nurse.

"Um... er... uncle," blustered Clyde. "I'm just worried about my niece."

"I can come back and ask you these questions later when you're more settled," offered the nurse.

"Thank you," said Clyde. He was ready to breathe a sigh of relief, thinking he was off the hook for now.

"You can't stay here. You'll have to wait in the waiting area." Her voice was much more stern and she wasn't going to take no for an answer. Clyde nodded his head and retreated to the waiting area.

As Clyde sat down he realized what had happened. He saw this tactic used at airports to supplement the full body security scans. Guards would approach passengers queued up and ask them innocuous questions and gauge their reactions. You'd be surprised how many would-be terrorists were incapable of answering the question, "How do you feel today?"

It was a matter of time now before someone higher up would take a closer look at him either in person or on video. Now, he would have to keep an eye on that nurse without tipping her off that he was keeping an eye on her. Elizabeth Cheech. Sheesh, thought Clyde.

There were no magazines out for patients to read. Other patients read articles off their smartphones. Clyde didn't even have a cell phone. Clyde knew he was going to have a very difficult time blending in here.

He suddenly realized how hungry he was. He walked over to the vending machine. A chocolate bar would taste really good right now if Clyde had any money on him.

Clyde looked at the clock on the wall. Whatever Henry was going to do with the car, he would have done it by now. Clyde looked around and spotted a stairwell door. As hard as he tried to look natural walking over to the door, Clyde couldn't help but feel like he was moseying. Being unselfconscious was something he never had to master, not like Henry who turned blending in into an art form.

Clyde briefly stood by the door. He checked out the stairwells for video cameras. There was one. He wouldn't be able to do anything about that. Clyde rapped three times gently on the emergency exit door at the foot of the stairwell. Two quiet knocks came the reply. Clyde used his body to block the line of sight of the security camera and opened the door.

Clyde feigned smoking a cigarette for the benefit of the security camera while he let Henry in and gestured for him to sit under the staircase.

"How is she?" asked Henry.

"She's in surgery. No word yet. Where's Bessie?"

"Bessie?" asked Henry.

"Your M-16. What did you do with it?"

"I hid it in the bushes just outside the fire exit."

Henry sat down on the staircase and leaned back against the wall. Clyde sensed that he wanted to say something. If he did, he would. If he didn't, Clyde wouldn't press him.

"You know, when we left Panama, all I wanted was a dull, boring life," Henry began. "After the shit we saw down there, I never wanted to harm another person. I never wanted to look at another gun."

"I put Panama behind me a long time ago. How come you can't let go?" asked Clyde.

"When you and I came back from our three day LRRP, which ended up being a fourteen day survival ordeal, I was dehydrated and running a fever from that tainted water buffalo."

"I remember," said Clyde.

"At triage, the medics were working on the Panamanian kid we shot and a newbie told me to wait. You grabbed his face and told him, 'Treat him now. He's one of ours.' That was the first time in my life I didn't feel like an outsider in my own country. My family has been in this country for eight generations and I'm still treated like a foreigner."

"Worse," began Clyde. "Now we're treated like terrorists in our own country."

"I can always count on you to look on the bright side of things," chuckled Henry.

"Better that than letting you feel sorry for yourself."

"You better get back inside if there's any change," said Henry.

"You want me to bring you anything from the vending machine?"

"Yeah, whatever."

"You have any money?"

Henry reached into his pockets. They were empty.

"Sometimes you do fit the stereotype," Clyde said dryly.

"Is that why you won't let me drive?" quipped Henry.

"I'll try and sweet talk one of the nurses," said Clyde as he slipped back into the waiting room.

As Clyde emerged from the stairwell, he heard the sound of some coins clink on the floor. For a moment, he thought he might have a free pass at some overloaded carbohydrates. In his mind, a chocolate bar was a poor substitute for steak. Clyde let his mind fantasize about his next steak... if he was ever going to have one again.

He scanned the waiting area, trying to spot the source of the fallen coins. That's when he saw Babcock stand up by the payphone. Instinctively, Clyde turned his back and faced the vending machine. In the reflection, he tried to get a better view of Babcock. It couldn't be a coincidence that another man of his size and build would be wearing an eye patch.

As Clyde tried to study Babcock in the reflection of the vending machine, he suddenly noticed that Babcock was staring back at him.

Babcock began to move slowly toward Clyde.

Dr. Srinivasamurthy removed the laparoscope from Elizabeth's abdomen and stitched her closed. The removal of her spleen went without a hitch. Today had been an exceedingly busy day in the emergency room. He hadn't had a chance to watch the news but something must have happened. An unusually high number of fender benders resulting in fistfights but nothing like the violence he saw left on this poor girl's body.

When Dr. Srinivasamurthy first saw her, he suspected abuse and ordered a rape kit performed. He was obligated to report any potential rapes to the police but he wanted to talk with the man who brought her in first. Now that he had a chance to perform a cursory examination, there was no doubt in his mind she had been raped multiple times and with considerable violence.

Once he stitched Elizabeth up, Dr. Srinivasamurthy removed his mask revealing his thick, black beard and mustache. Dr. Srinivasamurthy was chronically bad with names and faces but there was one thing he was certain of: this girl was not Mexican.

The admissions nurse had told him that Elizabeth had come into the hospital with a middle aged African American male. He stepped out into the waiting area and easily spotted Clyde. As he walked over to him, Dr. Srinivasamurthy considered what he would say next. If that man was involved in Elizabeth's rape, he didn't want to alarm him.

Whatever it was that was about to transpire, it would have to happen quickly. The emergency room looked twice as crowded as it was barely half an hour earlier.

"Are you the man that brought in Elizabeth Cheech?" Clyde nearly jumped out of skin. He spun around to see the surgeon who had operated on Elizabeth.

"Yes, that's me. I'm her uncle," said Clyde. Dr. Srinivasamurthy sensed that this man was a little tweaked. His eyes darted quickly around the room and he could feel his stress level rise.

"How is she doctor...?" began Clyde.

"Dr. Srinivasamurthy," he answered.

"How is she doc?" asked Clyde.

"She's out of danger. We were able to successfully perform a laparoscopic splenectomy but I'm more concerned about her other injuries."

Clyde knew where the doctor was going with this. "Can we talk about this somewhere with a little more privacy?" asked Clyde. Before Dr. Srinivasamurthy a chance to reply, Clyde took him by the shoulder and led him away from the waiting area while making small talk.

Before Babcock could reach the African American, a doctor was taking him away, or maybe it was the other way around; it seemed like the African American was escorting the doctor away. Babcock was convinced that the man he was looking at was Clyde Wilson. If he was alive, then Henry Chin couldn't be that far behind. Babcock drew his sidearm and chambered a round as he followed Clyde and the doctor to the stairwell door.

Babcock ran up to the door as it slowly swung shut. He put his hand on the doorknob and threw it open as he stepped into the stairwell with his sidearm drawn. Sitting on the floor was Dr. Srinivasamurthy.

As the stairwell door closed behind him, Babcock felt a rifle muzzle press against his temple.

"Why the hell are you after me?" asked Henry.

§

Chapter Nineteen

Clyde took Babcock's sidearm while Henry held him at bay with his M-16. As soon as Babcock was disarmed, Clyde twisted his arm forcing Babcock to kneel. Henry kept his M-16 aimed at Babcock's head.

"I asked you a question. Why are you after me?"

Babcock remained silent. "Who the hell are you?" Babcock turned to Henry and tried to stare him down. Henry gestured to Clyde who pushed Babcock all the way prone before he searched his pockets and pulled out his wallet. "He's a Fed. Immigration," began Clyde. "This is the guy that was at my house."

"And I saw you at the assembly center," continued Henry. "And at the campsite. The hell?" Henry pushed the muzzle of his M-16 into Babcock's cheek.

"We know who you are," shouted Babcock. "The best thing you can do is surrender. I've spoken personally with the President of the United States. Your Commander in Chief has ordered you to surrender."

"Bullshit," retorted Henry. "You packed fifty thousand Chinese into the Rose Bowl. Wasn't that enough? You couldn't leave us alone?"

"By holding a gun to my head, you're simply proving we made the right decision," taunted Babcock.

Henry couldn't contain his rage. He swung the butt of his M-16 around and slammed Babcock in the face with it, knocking him unconscious.

"You knew you weren't going to get any answers from him, right?" consoled Clyde.

"Well, I know one way to end this." Henry stood over Babcock's unconscious body and put the muzzle of his M-16 right at the base of his head. Immediately, Clyde reached out and grabbed Henry's arm.

"Are you kidding me? We don't kill people in cold blood."

"I have a right to execute my enemies," exclaimed Henry.

"What he said is right! You kill him and you'll prove to every redneck cracker that the repatriation camps were too good for you."

"The war begins today and he gets to be the first casualty," said Henry.

"That's today. What about tomorrow?" Clyde tightened his grip around Henry's arm. "You kill him and tomorrow we're a bona fide high value target. Our government will send guys after us. Younger, stronger and better trained than us. How long do you think we would survive against them? One rifle and nine bullets. How long?"

Clyde could see he was making a difference. Henry began to exhale. Clyde didn't loosen his grip. He remembered vividly what happened when Henry lost his temper in Panama.

Clyde continued, "Right from the word 'go' all you wanted to do was escape. You can do that. You don't need to kill him to do that. Just put him out of pocket for a day or two. It'll mean something if they know we could have killed him but we didn't."

Henry lowered his weapon and sat down next to Babcock's unconscious body. "Treat a friend like an enemy long enough and they will eventually be your enemy. You've created a self fulfilling prophecy." Clyde wasn't sure to whom Henry was speaking but decided it was best not to interrupt him.

Henry finally looked up at Clyde. "So, keep him under wraps for a few days so we can get away?"

Dr. Srinivasamurthy spoke up. "I can help you with that."

Henry and Clyde had all but forgotten the doctor they had shoved against the wall. "I can give him something that will keep him out for a few days."

"Why would you do that for us?" asked Henry.

Dr. Srinivasamurthy replied, "My skin color doesn't make me immune to being a scapegoat."

Henry nodded, "Thank you, Doctor..."

"Doctor S is fine." Dr. Srinivasamurthy stood up. "My guess is you are the father of Elizabeth Cheech?"

Henry threw a puzzled glance at Clyde. "Elizabeth Cheech?"

"Don't ask," deflected Clyde.

"How is my daughter?" asked Henry.

"We removed her spleen. She'll need a day or two to rest..."

"We don't have a day or two," said Henry.

"We've just given her a pint of blood. It'll be about fifteen more minutes before she's done infusing it. You can take her then."

"Thanks Doc."

Dr. Srinivasamurthy turned to leave the stairwell when Henry took him by the arm.

"Doc, my daughter was raped..."

"Yes," concurred Dr. Srinivasamurthy. Henry didn't know how to say what he wanted to say. Lucky for him, he didn't have to. "When?" asked Dr. Srinivasamurthy.

"A few hours ago? Less than twenty four hours."

"I'll put together a kit for you. We'll also need some time to perform a rape kit to preserve any DNA evidence the rapist left behind."

"They're all dead."

Dr. Srinivasamurthy was at a loss for words as he left the stairwell.

Clyde lifted Babcock's eye patch and examined his empty socket. He patted Henry on the back. "You did a good job on his eye."

"Muscle memory," said Henry flatly.

Even though the chart said the patient was a teenage girl, Babcock lay in the hospital bed with his face all bandaged up and a catheter inserted. Regular doses of phenobarbital guaranteed unconsciousness for at least a few days. As a bonus, Dr. Srinivasamurthy added diazepam to his IV so when they'd have to eventually wake Babcock up, at least he'll be in a good mood.

Henry and Clyde took advantage of their brief down time to clean up in the staff restroom. They raided a custodian's closet and procured two janitor uniforms. As they got dressed, Clyde tossed Henry a chocolate bar.

"I thought you didn't have any money," said Henry.

"I don't. But the immigration guy does." Clyde held up Babcock's wallet. "And this might come in handy." He flashed Babcock's ICE badge.

Henry chuckled. "Yeah, we'll need to change the photo."

Dr. Srinivasamurthy left Elizabeth unattended in the emergency room on a gurney. She had been disconnected from the electronic monitors and her IV. Tucked under her sheet was a white paper bag prepared and left behind by Dr. Srinivasamurthy. Henry and Clyde wheeled her out the emergency room entrance and onto a waiting ambulance. The regular EMTs were on their lunch break and would provide them at least an hour head start before they would discover their ambulance was stolen.

The chaos in the San Fernando Valley had not quieted down. Traffic remained at a standstill on the major arteries. Clyde stayed on surface streets as long as possible, driving the ambulance along Foothill Boulevard, cutting over to Glenoaks Boulevard before hopping onto I-210, merging onto I-5 and finally turning onto Route 14. He had thought about cutting through the lower elevations of the Angeles National Forest but felt the ambulance would be less conspicuous in plain sight.

Once they got onto Route 14, they breathed a sigh of relief. By far, the most popular route out of Los Angeles was the I-10 heading east through Palm Springs, Coachella to Phoenix. The closest major city along Route 14 was Barstow in the middle of the Mojave Desert if you took Route 38 to Route 18 to I-15. At Barstow, they cut over onto I-40 which took them away from Las Vegas.

"Where are we going?" asked Henry.

"Some old timers at the V.A. talked about a gathering area in the Mojave Desert somewhere in the Mojave National Preserve. It's where you go when you want to completely fall off the grid.

"How do you know?" asked Henry.

"I thought about moving there. Someone there must have an idea about how to get to Canada. Why don't you rest up? We got about a hundred and eighty miles of nothing before we get there."

Henry sat in the back of the ambulance with Elizabeth. She was still asleep. Henry took the paper bag kit that Dr. Srinivasamurthy had left for him. The first thing Henry took out was a vial of penicillin and a syringe. He found some cotton balls and alcohol and sterilized a small area on her thigh before he gave her the injection.

Elizabeth began to stir. She was still groggy from the anesthesia. Henry found a bottle of water and helped Elizabeth sit up.

"Have some water," he offered. She was able to take a swig from the bottle. "Hold on. You need to take an antibiotic," Henry lied. Henry reached into the kit and pulled out a single dose of levonorgestrel. He held it close to her mouth.

"C'mon, you need to take this pill." Elizabeth cleared her throat and took the pill into her mouth. She took a swig of water and washed it down. Henry laid her down and she was back asleep in an instant. Her eyes remained closed the entire time.

Inside the kit Dr. Srinivasamurthy had also left him a dose of mifepristone and misoprostol just in case the levonorgestrel didn't work.

"You're doing the right thing, Henry," consoled Clyde.

"She shouldn't have to make this decision," said Henry.

"She doesn't have to know," said Clyde.

Henry sat down and tried to fall asleep without crying.

At Barstow, Clyde used the last of Babcock's cash to refill the gas tank. He had turned off the air conditioning inside the ambulance and just ran the fan to help their gas mileage. Ambulances really weren't designed for long distance traveling and Clyde's best guess was that this beast got less than ten miles per gallon on a good day.

He bought some cold sodas. He figured this might be the last cold soda they'd have for a while. He got three. Elizabeth was still asleep.

It was mid afternoon by the time the ambulance reached the edge of the Mojave National Preserve. Henry was sitting up front with Clyde.

"Mojave is kind of big. Do you know where the vets would be?"

"Before the homeless vets were kicked out of skid row, they used to refer to their SROs as their own personal hole in the wall." Henry looked out the window as they drove through the Hole in the Wall campsite and turned off the road.

All that remained of this ancient volcano was an enormous caldera. There was hardly any difference between the campsite and the desert beyond. Yucca plants provided the only color in this desolate dirt beige pallet of dead chaparral and sagebrush.

The ambulance easily made its way over the gentle rolling lowlands following what looked like an old hiking trail. If there were an encampment here, it would be on the shade side of the giant pluton. Clyde glanced down at the gas gauge. There wasn't enough gas to make it back to Barstow. If his information about the veterans encampment was wrong, this desert campground would be the end of their journey.

He wasn't wrong.

The encampment had about fifty makeshift tents. Tarps hung off the Joshua trees, small campfires dotted the terain. As Clyde drove closer, he realized the inhabitants were not grizzled old war veterans suffering from PTSD. The population was mainly Chinese American families.

As the ambulance came to a stop, the Chinese Americans slowly approached. Henry rolled down his window and leaned out. "We're Chinese!" he shouted.

The Chinese Americans continued to approach at a slow pace, like zombies. As they continued to encroach upon the ambulance, Henry brandished his M-16.

"That's close enough!" Henry threatened. The crowd of Chinese Americans stopped. Some women retreated with their children. The men held their position for the moment. Henry wondered how long he could maintain this standoff.

Finally, one woman stepped forward and gestured to the men to stay put. She approached the ambulance. She wore a large, wide brimmed straw hat, sunglasses, khaki shorts and a tank top. As she came closer, Henry could recognize she was Chinese American and in her mid forties.

"My name is Judy Liu. Are you here to help us?" she asked. Henry didn't know how to answer her. "We have some diabetics. We've run out of insulin. Can you help us?"

"We can help," said Henry as he lowered his M-16.

"Thank God," she said. "Are you a doctor?"

"No," replied Henry. "I'm a pharmacist."

Henry raided the medical supplies onboard the ambulance to provide some very general health care. Besides a few insulin shots, he administered albuterol for the asthma sufferers, nitroglycerine for some of the older Chinese Americans with heart problems and laxatives for the children suffering from constipation.

As night came, they detached a portable generator off the ambulance and used it to power floodlights as Henry continued to help the Chinese Americans. Most of the complaints were the result of dehydration, sun exposure and boredom.

As he treated them, Judy performed crowd control, wrangling the Chinese Americans into orderly lines. Henry found out that Judy Liu was, in fact, California State Assemblywoman Judy Liu. She wasn't the first Chinese American woman to serve in the California legislature but she was the youngest. Once the lines had died down she brought some food over for Henry and Clyde.

"It's jackrabbit stew," she said. She took off her hat and sunglasses and sat on the bumper next to them. Henry couldn't help but notice her salt and pepper roots were beginning to supplant her long brown hair. He deduced they had been away from civilization for at least two months.

"Just before the Chinese neighborhoods were placed under martial law, we grabbed whatever we could and I led them out here. There's a water supply inside the campgrounds and we've been able to hunt for everything else." She paused as she heard a noise from inside the ambulance.

"That's my daughter, Elizabeth. She's recovering from a splenectomy." Elizabeth poked her head out of the ambulance.

"Dad? Where are we?" she asked.

"You're safe for now," said Judy. "You're in the Mojave Desert. I'm Judy Liu. I'm kind of the welcoming committee."

"You feel like eating something?" Henry offered her his bowl of rabbit stew. She took it and began eating it without hesitation.

"It's..." began Judy.

"No, don't tell me. With my father, I've learned sometimes it's better to not know what I'm eating."

Judy looked over at Henry. "You are a sight for sore eyes. All of you. Once we got here, a few Chinese from the outlying areas trickled in but after the Repatriation Act was signed, we haven't seen anyone. You're the first Chinese we've seen since the roundup."

"Why are you so surprised about that?" asked Clyde.

"You don't know?" Judy took a folded piece of paper out of her back pocket and handed it to Henry. He unfolded it. It was a fax of a photocopy of a proclamation with both the Chinese National Emblem and the U.S. Presidential Seal watermarked with the word CLASSIFIED.

Henry glanced down at the document. "I don't know what it says. I can't read Chinese," he said as he handed the document to Clyde.

"Uncle Clyde, you can read Chinese?" asked Elizabeth.

"I had some free time after my divorce." Clyde held up the document and squinted as he translated the Chinese on the fly.

"Historically, China has forbid its sojourners from renouncing their allegiance to the land of their ancestors. All persons of Chinese descent living in the United States, irrespective of their place of birth, are not now, nor have they ever been, legal citizens of the United States and therefore must immediately return to China for repatriation."

Henry couldn't believe what he heard.

"What does it mean?" asked Elizabeth.

"It means the U.S. and China are pretending you and your father were never U.S. citizens," interpreted Clyde. "It means all Chinese Americans were on loan from China and now they want you back."

"Why?" asked Elizabeth.

Clyde scanned the document. "It doesn't say."

"Where did you get this?" Henry asked Judy. "No disrespect intended but how does a California Assemblywoman rate getting a classified White House document?"

"We have some help," said Judy. "An old family friend worked for the government. He gave me that document. He used to work for the Department of Homeland Security."

Clyde and Henry exchanged worried glances. Clyde asked, "Would your old friend happen to be about six foot tall, White and about a hundred and ninety pounds?"

"He's Black and in his sixties," she answered with a puzzled look. Clyde and Henry both breathed a sigh of relief.

"What?" asked Elizabeth.

"I'll explain later," said Henry.

"He's in Barstow now picking up supplies for us. I'll introduce you to him when he gets back." Judy stood up. "It's story time for the children. Come join us if you'd like."

"Maybe..." said Henry. Judy gave him a little wave goodbye as she headed back to the camp.

Clyde gave Henry a little nudge. "I think she likes you."

"Shut up."

In the awkward silence, they could hear Elizabeth giggle to herself.

Henry found a secluded swell a distance away from the main campsite. Tonight there was just the beginning of a sliver of a crescent moon. He could see the shadows of the scrubland out before him. The air had cooled down and Henry could feel the residual heat from the sun radiating up from the ground. He stared out into the distance lost in his own thoughts.

He wondered how many people had sat here over the years and contemplated their place in the universe. Geologically, this place once used to be inside a volcano millions of years ago, long before the first human ever laid eyes on this landscape. That was a good thing. If there were humans here then, they would have been obliterated by the eruption.

The Egyptians and the Chinese built monuments to withstand the test of time. But even if the pyramids and the Great Wall survived another thousand years, they would be a mere blink of an eye compared to how long the dinosaurs reigned the planet.

What difference does any of this make? All human strife is manmade, Henry thought to himself. *In the sweat of thy face shalt thou eat bread, till thou return unto the ground; for out of it wast thou taken: for dust thou art, and unto dust shalt thou return.* Within a few generations, his ashes would indistinguishable from the ash that once covered this landscape. Nearly every person who ever lived died poor, starving and anonymous. It was hubris to believe that his fate would be any different.

"Dad?" Henry was startled at the sound of his daughter's voice.

"Yes sweetheart?"

Elizabeth sat beside him and handed him a mug.

"What's this?"

"Judy made a pot of tea. I thought I should bring you some."

"You're on a first name basis with Ms. Liu already?"

"I'm a people person Dad."

Henry took a sip from the steaming hot mug. It was Chinese black tea.

"I told Judy that we could try to rescue some of the Chinese being held at the Rose Bowl," Elizabeth said.

Henry nearly spilled his tea. "What did you tell her?"

"I told Judy you and Uncle Clyde used to be in the Army. That if anyone could free the Chinese, it was you two."

"Why on earth would you tell her that?"

"We were lied to. We weren't being put away for our own protection. They were going to deport us. Can you picture me living in China? I don't speak Chinese, I don't understand Chinese. How would I fit in?"

"Elizabeth, you're talking about the U.S. Army. We might get lucky at first if we catch them by surprise but after that we wouldn't stand a chance. The best thing for us to do is just get the hell out of here."

"How do you know we'll be treated better somewhere else? I grew up here. This is my home."

"Elizabeth, staying and fighting would be suicide."

Elizabeth looked out over the desert.

"Eight and one third pounds."

Henry turned to look at her. "What are you talking about?"

"The weight of one gallon of water. Eight and one third pounds. I've had some time to think. I want to stay and fight. I want you to teach me how to shoot."

§

CHAPTER TWENTY

Now that he was a good distance away from the highway, Don turned back on his headlights. In the backseat and trunk of his car were canned vegetables, canned stew, canned meat and canned fruit. He also had economy sizes of Gatorade and water as well as two cases of propane cylinders. And just for good measure, he also bought four can openers.

He had heard some troubling information on the radio and ended up filling his car with as many supplies as he could. The President was moving much faster than anyone had anticipated and he felt he needed to be prepared for anything.

As he drove around the pluton, he could see the light cast by the floodlights and the ambulance parked nearby. He killed the headlights on his car. Something had changed since he left the campsite hours earlier. He couldn't take the chance that their hideout had been compromised. He pulled his sidearm out of the glove box.

He parked his car just shy of the campsite and crept up alongside the perimeter of the campsite. Judy came trotting up to him.

"I thought I saw you drive up. We have visitors."

"The ambulance?" asked Don.

"Yes. They spent the afternoon giving health checkups to everyone. Let me take you over to meet them."

Judy walked Don over to the central campfire. As they approached, they could hear Elizabeth's animated voice.

"Dad, we have to do something! You knew this was going to happen. Why did you want to run away? Why didn't you want to stay and fight?"

"That's not the decision you would have made three days ago," implored Henry.

Judy thought it best at that moment to interrupt the Henry and Elizabeth's fight. "Henry, Clyde, Elizabeth, this is my friend Don Morgan. He's the one who knew what the government was planning."

Don extended his hand. "Henry? Clyde? Elizabeth?" As Don shook their hands, he smiled at them with a sense of familiarity. "Corporal Henry Chin. Private Clyde Wilson. It's my pleasure to meet you."

Henry gave Don a puzzled look. "How do you know who we are?"

"Your files were on my desk before I left the department."

"Department of Homeland Security?" asked Clyde.

"Yes. We had a junior agent who was pushing hard for the complete roundup of all Chinese Americans. You slipped through the cracks and became his personal mission."

Henry held out Babcock's ICE badge for Don to inspect.

"Yep. That's him. Nicholas Babcock. He's one of those guys who believes the U.S. Constitution is the sacred word of God, second only to the Bible. Don't get me wrong. He's dedicated and ambitious but green. That's why I assigned him to bring you in. I'm sorry. I had no idea it would have escalated into this."

"What do you mean?" asked Judy.

"The missile strike in the Angeles National Forest? That was for you. He forged my credentials on the order. Because it was an aggressive, proactive move to safeguard our nation's security, he got away with it. It made him look tough against the Chinese in the eyes of the President. He took initiative where I didn't and it cost me my job. America goes through these bouts of nativism every generation or two. Usually, it happens when the economy is bad or when we have a Democrat in the White House. Unfortunately, both happened at the same time. I'm sorry that Chinese Americans were the scapegoats this time."

"We have to do something. We have to fight back somehow, don't we?" said Elizabeth.

Judy spoke up. "We've generally fought restrictions like these in the legislature and in the courts. Especially since World War Two, we put in place safeguards that stopped the roundup of Arab Americans after 9/11."

"What went wrong this time?" asked Clyde.

"The roundup was planned in secret. It was treated as a covert operation at the highest levels of national security," said Don. "There was no way any of this would have stood up to judicial scrutiny. What the administration was counting on was that by the time a habeas corpus motion was filed and got to the Supreme Court, it would have been too late. Even if the action was reversed, it would have been too late to do anything about it."

"And it worked," said Judy. "We were locked up so quickly, no one had time to hoard any weapons, arms or supplies."

"Then we have to act now," demanded Elizabeth. "There are thousands of Chinese Americans being held at the Rose Bowl. We should try to set them free."

Don sighed. "You haven't heard the news have you? The first shipload of Chinese American repatriots left for China today. The entire Chinese American population will be gone within a month."

"That's almost four million people," added Judy.

"It's amazing what this country can do when it puts its mind to it," Don said sarcastically.

"Why?" asked Elizabeth. "Why would they allow China to take us like that? Don't they have enough people?"

Everyone looked at Don. "The United States dominated the twentieth century mostly due to our ability to invent and innovate. China's not good at that. Out of four million Chinese American repatriots, if they can find one Albert Einstein, one Henry Ford or one Steve Jobs, it'll be worth it."

"What about everyone else?" asked Elizabeth.

"Chances are, they'll do everything to prevent finding one Martin Luther King, one Susan B. Anthony or one Bob Dylan," said Don. "China doesn't need more people. It needs more creative people and they are willing to search high and low for a few diamonds in the rough. That's China's long term plan. They can afford to think this way. Our government is stuck making self destructive short term decisions to accommodate our two year election cycle. Eventually, we're going to implode."

"We have to do something," insisted Elizabeth.

"There's nothing we can do now but survive," said Henry flatly.

"No there isn't. We have to do something," demanded Elizabeth. "Dad, you know how to blow things up. Blow things up!"

Henry was shocked by his daughter's suggestion. He shook his head. "It's wrong... it's wrong." He had no words for Elizabeth as he turned and walked out beyond the campsite.

"What's wrong? What did I say?" asked Elizabeth.

"What you suggested," began Clyde. "It's a violation of our training and our oaths."

"But they broke the law first," said Elizabeth.

"That doesn't mean we can break it now," said Clyde.

"Why not?" asked Elizabeth.

Don cleared his throat. "These men are soldiers. They're not terrorists."

Clyde found Henry sitting by himself staring off into the distance. "You have to talk to Elizabeth. She's all fired up about doing something. I can't say she's completely wrong."

"You were the one who said we couldn't kill one agent. The one agent who was trying to kill us. It was too dangerous you said. It would instantly make us high value targets. Imagine how popular we would be if we go all Timothy McVeigh on their ass," said Henry.

"I'm not saying we go all Timothy McVeigh. That man was misguided. He broke his oath. Too much collateral damage. Children died," said Clyde.

"So if we don't kill any children, we're okay?" asked Henry. "Good strategy."

"We kill the people who are behind this. We kill only the people who are responsible," said Clyde.

"Look at us!" pushed back Henry. "When was the last time you weighed one hundred and eighty five pounds? When was the last time you did two hundred push ups or ran ten miles with ninety pounds strapped to your back? When was the last time you pointed a gun at someone fully intending to kill them?"

Don walked up behind Clyde. "May I join you two gentlemen?"

"You have to talk some sense into my daughter," said Henry.

"Your daughter makes pretty good sense right now," said Don.

"This conversation is obscene," Henry declared.

"I can train her. I served in Vietnam. Two hundred twenty fourth Military Police Company," said Don.

"No offense, but there's a big difference between the 82nd Airborne and the military police," said Henry.

"Yes, there is," said Don. "That's why you're the best person to train her."

"Train her? I could barely raise her," cried Henry.

"That's not what your daughter said. Apparently you've saved her life several times since escaping the repatriation assembly center," said Don.

"In more ways than one," said Clyde.

"Shut up," shot Henry.

"She wants to survive. She wants to fight. And she trusts you," said Don. "We all have to fight back. What our government did to the Chinese Americans is a stain on all Americans. It only takes only one man to start a revolution."

"You lose a lot of credibility when you start quoting Captain Kirk," said Henry.

Henry took a deep breath. He looked at Clyde and thought about all the hell they had gone through. And then he thought about Elizabeth and the hell he was about to put her through. Finally he looked up at Don.

"Very specific targets. The people who are responsible and only the people responsible." Henry was never more serious about anything in his life. "That's the only chance we have of being remembered as freedom fighters instead of traitors."

"That's going to take a lot of planning and a lot of money," said Don. "I have access to some resources."

Henry took a deep breath. "Who do we go after first?"

Don nodded his head. "There's one man in the administration who engineered this entire betrayal. He'll be hard to get to. He'll have Secret Service protection."

Elizabeth emptied out her pockets. She had found the box of levonorgestrel on the floor of the ambulance. Back in high school, her friends had one box that they rotated through the lockers. For her classmates, the morning after pill was their aspiration and contradiction. Everyone wanted to use it but at the same time, no one did. The pill pack was empty. She had a vague recollection that she had taken it. She knew her father had given it to her because she found the unopened mifepristone and would use that if the rapists had left her any... the only word Elizabeth could think of was souvenirs. She heard Judy approaching and quickly hid the mifepristone as she tossed the empty boxes and blister packs into the campfire.

Judy poured Elizabeth another cup of tea. Elizabeth listened to her tell her story about how she got into politics. She was amazed that anyone could have that kind of clarity at such a young age. Judy wasn't much older than Elizabeth when she first became a staffer for a city councilman.

Elizabeth was ashamed that she never knew Judy was her state assemblywoman and that she could have voted for her in the very near future if she hadn't been expelled with all the other Chinese members of the state assembly.

But despite Judy's inner strength and fortitude, she had failed in Elizabeth's mind. Diplomacy and negotiations didn't work this time. In her mind, she had replaced all the girls who had pushed her around with a demonized monolithic government that didn't care about individuals. As with the bullies in school, this monolith had to be wiped off the face of the earth and she wanted the strength and power to do it.

What happened to her... she couldn't even bring herself to hear the word 'rape' in her head... she would never let herself be so weak to allow that to happen to her ever again.

Elizabeth didn't confide in Judy about her rape. She didn't know how. She just knew she had to do something or else she was going to lose her mind. She heard her father's footsteps as he returned to the campfire with Uncle Clyde and the government man.

"Ms. Liu, would you mind giving us a moment?" asked Henry. She gave Henry a quick nod and squeezed Elizabeth's hand before she retreated back to the main campsite.

Henry took out his hunting knife and handed it to Elizabeth. "I want you to have this. You should always have some kind of weapon on you."

"Okay..." said Elizabeth.

"This is one of those decisions that will forever change your life. There's no turning back. You're going to do some things that might be difficult to live with. I won't ask you to do more than you're capable of but you have to do everything to the best of your ability otherwise, innocent people will die. Do you understand me?"

Elizabeth nodded her head.

"I need you to say it out loud."

"I understand."

"Say out loud what you understand," pressed Henry.

"I understand that what I'm going to do may give me nightmares for the rest of my life," said Elizabeth.

Henry looked at his daughter. No trace of the spoiled princess was apparent anywhere. She had a dark, seething focus she never had before. Just like the guys in basic training, jonesin' for their first taste of combat.

"Okay," said Henry. "This is how it will happen..."

SANTA BARBARA, CALIFORNIA — ONE YEAR LATER

Henry didn't realize what a difference a new pair of eyeglasses could make. He hadn't changed his old prescription in almost ten years. Don had also managed to procure a single bolt action rifle for him. Henry didn't recognize the make but it looked like it has some kind of Eastern European language engraved on it though it used the standard 7.62×51mm NATO cartridge.

Henry had several months to train with this weapon. It had a good weight and a low center of gravity when steadied with the tripod. He had practiced on targets as far away as five hundred yards. That was about all Henry was good for. His accuracy dramatically fell off at greater distances.

After nearly six months of quiet digging, Don was finally able to identify their target's vacation retreat. It was a cottage that belonged to his brother's son. Cottage was a euphemism. It was a sprawling, walled estate in the heart of wine country.

Henry and Clyde designed the mission (with intel provided by Don) to put Henry about three hundred yards from the target, well within his capacity to execute. They were actually in a town just north of Santa Barbara called Los Alamos, which was a few miles from Vandenberg Air Force Base.

For the past three months, Henry, Elizabeth and Clyde had been living in the mountains overlooking the compound performing reconnaissance. He taught his daughter how to make detailed topography maps and how to record the comings and goings on the estate.

They were very diligent about leaving no trace of their presence up on the mountain because they knew there would be a security sweep of the area before their target arrived.

The vegetation was dense but the soil was rocky and crumbly. They had to move their camp every night to conceal their presence. It wasn't very hard to do. They were living out of rucksacks and sleeping in bivvy bags and protected from the sun by plastic tarps. The equipment Henry had up in the Angeles National Forest was luxurious compared to the bare bones survival and recon they were performing now.

At night they practiced land navigation and light and heat discipline. Henry was astonished how quickly Elizabeth mastered these skills. She had an exceptional memory when it came to remembering terrain and spotting disturbances. She was quiet and stealthful in her movements. She didn't complain anymore.

Their target rarely took vacations so the odds were good that his security detail wouldn't have as much experience in this area as they did. Henry, Clyde and Elizabeth had become experts.

The target's security detail dispatched one sniper up onto the mountainside the day before the target arrived. Henry, Elizabeth and Clyde stayed in hiding while the sniper did his own recon unaware he was under observation. There were three good vantage points to watch the compound. Elizabeth had guessed correctly which of the vantage points the sniper would pick.

Based on their knowledge of tactics, this sniper would remain up here for the duration of the target's visit. Looking at his equipment, Henry deduced that the target's length of stay would be no more than three days. The compound, and in fact, most of the town, had no exterior lights. On a moonless night, it would be so dark outside you would not be able to see your own hand in front of your face. Their target had a reliable history of early morning jogs. The morning of the second day would be when they would strike.

The one piece of intel they needed to ascertain was the sniper's communication protocol. What was his call sign if any? How often did he have to check in? What kind of communication equipment did he have? Whoever it was would have top notch training and hi tech gear. Under the cover of the dark and stillness of the moonless night would be their best chance to acquire this information. That was Clyde's job. He would be their ears so they had scheduled Clyde for the overnight shift while Elizabeth kept guard over Henry.

During the past year, Henry had gotten to know Assemblywoman Liu. Despite her insistence that Henry call her Judy, he never did. Some of the reasons were practical, some were stupid. Henry had watched more than his fair share of action movies in his life. Every time the hero fell in love, his object of affection is either taken hostage or killed. It was a part of American mythology he was most superstitious. That was the stupid reason.

For practicality, he had assumed the role of protector of her small band of refugees. He didn't want to cloud his judgment or be accused of favoritism in case he ever had to make a tough call.

He admired Assemblywoman Liu. She was a natural leader and might have been a serious candidate for California governor had it not been for this mess. During their time in the Mojave Desert, Elizabeth had gotten close to her. After Veronique died, Henry thought about remarrying but he never met a woman who was able to get along with Elizabeth. At first she wanted her father all to herself but as she grew older and more rebellious, she wanted nothing to do with him.

Elizabeth respected Judy like no other adult Henry knew. Maybe if he had met her five years earlier...

Henry pushed that thought out of his head. He could not allow himself to indulge in that kind of emotional wallowing. They had a job to do and he needed to stay sharp and focused.

In the hour before dawn, they regrouped. Clyde reported that the sniper checked in roughly every six hours. His last check in was about three a.m. They could take him out at anytime and not worry about their communication protocol, but just in case, the sniper was Condor Three and basecamp was Padre One.

Their plan was to knock out the sniper, take out the target and then use improvised explosives controlled by a disposable cell phone they had preset several hundred feet below in the foothills. The explosion was meant as a diversion so they wouldn't be able to triangulate where Henry's shot came from. It was also meant to provide cover so they could escape backwards into the Los Padres National Forest. By the time the sniper regained consciousness, they would be long gone, on their way to rejoin Assemblywoman Liu and her band of refugees.

Surprisingly, Elizabeth turned out to be the most stealthful of the three of them. Chances were that the sniper would have a helmet so any kind of blow to the head would be unproductive. A sharp blow to the side of the neck would be more than enough to disable the sniper, possibly even render him unsconscious.

Elizabeth had been gone for barely ten minutes before she signaled her task was done. Henry took the sniper's position while Elizabeth and Clyde flanked out to keep an eye for any unexpected incoming bogies. It was half an hour before dawn. They would all have to wait at least that long for Henry to take the shot.

Henry set up his tripod exactly where the sniper had set up his. Elevation, air density, wind speed, humidity were all taken into account. Henry had his rifle set up exactly the same way he had practiced several hundred times in the past few months.

Henry settled into place and began to breathe slowly. Elizabeth wanted to be the triggerman but Henry wouldn't allow it. He had never killed anyone in cold blood before and he wasn't going to permit Elizabeth to go down that dark road. She was a pretty good shot but didn't have enough training yet to be a sharpshooter. Henry and Clyde had taken basic sharpshooting in the Army but it was nothing compared to how the Navy Seals could shoot from a moving boat or the Army Ranger's record setting one and a half mile kill shot. Even at this distance, halfway up the side of the mountain would test all of Henry's skills. Elizabeth didn't have the skills yet.

Henry could hear his own heart beating, the blood going through his veins and the air coming in and out of his lungs. But there was something missing. It took him another moment to realize that the immobilized sniper next to him was making no sound at all. Henry checked him for a pulse. The sniper was dead. The blood on Henry's fingers told him that Elizabeth had slit his throat.

Henry was shaken by this realization. This is exactly what he didn't want for Elizabeth. This was the innocence he was trying to protect. And now, he had to mourn the death of his daughter's innocence: She had killed a man in cold blood.

Henry did his best to slow his heart rate down. The government's plan was to remove all the Chinese Americans from American soil as quickly as possible so that they wouldn't have an opportunity to become radicalized. Unfortunately, history has proved with the Japanese Americans and the Arab Americans that when you treat your friends as enemies, radicalization becomes a self-fulfilling prophecy. And now it's claimed Elizabeth.

The pre-dawn sunlight had begun to fill the sky. The temperature and humidity would change rapidly in the next hour. Henry had begun to calculate the adjustments in his head when the target stepped out of the central cottage.

Dressed in gray sweats, the Chief of Staff began stretching out his legs and swinging his arms. He reached into his pocket and pulled out a pack of cigarettes and a lighter. He lit one and took a few drags before crushing it out. He handed the pack and the lighter to his security detail before he finished his stretching. This was the man who backed the President into a corner by secretly engineering the Repatriation Treaty with China. This was the man who forfeited the rights of Chinese Americans for money.

Enter ye in at the strait gate: for wide is the gate, and broad is the way, that leadeth to destruction, and many there be which go in thereat: Because strait is the gate, and narrow is the way, which leadeth unto life, and few there be that find it.

Henry took a deep breath and then slowly exhaled through his nose as he gently squeezed the trigger.

Goodbye.

§

EPILOGUE

T he President briskly entered the East Room of the White House and took his place at the podium as all the gathered reporters stood. He cleared his throat before he spoke.

"Good morning everyone. Please, sit down.

"Today, we are reminded that, as a nation, when we face dark times, it is the perseverance of the American spirit that leads us back into the light.

"Our country has the brightest and most talented people in the world. There is nothing we can't do when we want to do it.

"Our mission today is to preserve the security and safety of American citizens in a world filled with global strife. The Department of Homeland Security has become a vital piece of that puzzle.

"After an exhaustive search, we discovered that the right man for the job of heading this department has been under our nose the entire time.

"The problems we face today are complex and the solutions are difficult to find.

"As we prepare for war with China, the protection of our nation's soil remains our top priority. This job requires someone who is tough, resilient and dedicated to the service and protection of our great nation. But above all that, this is a man who has proven time and time again that he will get the job done.

"Would you please come up here to the podium and allow the Vice President to administer the oath?"

Nicholas Babcock stood up and walked up to the podium. The Vice President held out a Bible as he raised his right hand. Babcock no longer needed an eye patch. He had been fitted with a prosthetic eye that was nearly indistinguishable from the real thing.

Babcock placed his hand on the Bible, raised his right hand, looked the Vice President in the eye and recited the oath from memory.

"I do solemnly swear that I will support and defend the Constitution of the United States against all enemies, foreign and domestic; that I will bear true faith and allegiance to the same; that I take this obligation freely, without any mental reservation or purpose of evasion; and that I will well and faithfully discharge the duties of the office on which I am about to enter. So help me God."

After he shook everyone's hand, Babcock turned to the press and offered the only public statement he would give during his tenure as Secretary of the Department of Homeland Security.

"It's time to get to work."

§

About the Author

Isaac Ho earned his MFA in Screenwriting from UCLA and was a semi-finalist for the ABC/Disney Writing Fellowship and a finalist for the CAPE USA New Writers Award for Television. He is a recipient of the Stephen N. Gershenson Award for Screenwriting and the SF Weekly Black Box Award for Best Play.

He is the writer of the indie film "1,001 Ways to Enjoy the Missionary Position," an Orwellian sci-fi drama starring Amanda Plummer.

§

DIGITAL fabulists

visit us online at
www.digitalfabulists.com

and check out
our great titles, including:

Berns with an "E"
Rug Berns
a rocking detective series by Paul Chitlik

Scripts from
The Twilight Zone
with rare photos and new introductions
by the original authors

Brand-New Original Works
from Established and First-Time Authors!
Deviant Numbers
The Latter History and Subsequent Burning
of Little Red Riding Hood

**new titles being added
every month!**

digital fabulists...
e-publishing for the future.

60327573R00115

Made in the USA
Lexington, KY
03 February 2017